UNANIMOUS DECISION

The men in the room included some of the most brilliant, wealthy, powerful figures in America. Their interests ranged from Texas oil to Chicago organized crime. Among them were top politicians, high-level CIA operatives, leading "think tank" experts, Harvard-trained "crisis managers." Now they had made their decision:

John F. Kennedy, President of the United States, had to be killed.

And this is how they did it....

EXECUTIVE ACTION means Assassination of a Head of State

EXECUTIVE ACTION

*ASSASSINATION OF A
HEAD OF STATE*

**Donald Freed
and Mark Lane**

Introduction by Richard H. Popkin

A DELL BOOK

Published by
Dell Publishing Co., Inc.
1 Dag Hammarskjold Plaza
New York, New York 10017

Copyright © 1973 by Donald Freed and Mark Lane

Introduction Copyright © 1973 by Richard H. Popkin
All rights reserved. No part of this book may be
reproduced in any form or by any means without the
prior written permission of the Publisher, excepting brief quotes used in connection with reviews
written specifically for inclusion in a magazine
or newspaper.

Dell ® TM 681510, Dell Publishing Co., Inc.

Printed in Canada

First printing—May 1973

Although some of the events depicted in this book are matters of historical fact, this is a work of fiction, and none of the principal characters are intended to resemble real persons, either living or dead. Any such resemblance is purely coincidental.

This book is dedicated to Herb and Shirley Magidson. And to the others who have made the film that is based on this work possible, when the consensus was that "it could not be done": Donald Sutherland, Shirley Douglas, Dalton Trumbo, Stephen Jaffe, Edward Lewis, Monica McCall, and Jo Stewart.

In the three-year period that followed the murders of President Kennedy and Lee Harvey Oswald, seventeen witnesses interviewed by the Dallas police, the FBI, or the Warren Commission died: six by gunfire, three in motor accidents, two by suicide, one from a cut throat, one from a karate chop to the neck, three from heart attacks, and two from "natural" causes.

An actuary, asked by the London Sunday Times *to compute the life expectancy of only fifteen of the deceased witnesses, concluded that on November 22, 1963, the odds against all fifteen witnesses being dead by February 1967, were one hundred thousand trillion to one:*
100,000,000,000,000,000 to 1.

This novel is an anti-mystery. The recital of the facts—and the reconstruction that must be deduced from those facts—of the assassination of John F. Kennedy aims not at suspense but at purgation.

When strange intelligence-espionage terms are used, they will be "translated" at the bottom of the page. For instance:

ONI—Office of Naval Intelligence.

False sponsors—fronts, or false leads.

Triangulation—three sources of coordinated gunfire for one target.

Running—directing an agent.

Triple-hatting—several intelligence assignments for one agent.

Deep cover—elaborate false identity.

Over the last decade, dedicated researchers into the conspiracy to assassinate John Fitzgerald Kennedy—and to cover up the deed—have made their findings available to the people of America, including the grateful authors of this book.

Stephen Welles, in charge of special research, was indispensable to the work, as was Barboura Morris Freed's encouragement and criticism.

Stephen Jaffe, Caroline Mugar, Jack Kimbrough, Mae Brussell, and professors Franz Schurmann, Peter Dale Scott, and Richard Popkin provided important research, manuscript, and critical contributions. Delmarie Fieldhammer worked with the film and book project from its inception. Louise Lengel provided the difficult manuscript preparation; and professors Dwain Houser, Jim Hill, Mike Zaslow, Robert Niemann, Robert C. Cohen, and William W. Turner, criticism and discussion, as did New Orleans district attorney Jim Garrison and Vincent J. Salandria.

Sincere thanks are due, for information provided, to the committee to investigate political assassinations, Washington, D.C., and to those members of the French, American, and Canadian intelligence services, who must remain nameless, who believe as we do in the *people's right to know*.

INTRODUCTION

They conspired against him to slay him. Gen. 37:18

On December 7, 1972, *The New York Times* published the following letter by Augustin F. Fortuno under the title "Who's in Command?":

> Statehood for Puerto Rico was defeated in the recent election. For the second time it was an issue and was turned down. No other United States territory, colony, dominion or possession, given the choice, had ever rejected statehood. Why then our decision?
>
> Political theorists may speculate for years about the multiplicity and complexity of our reasoning, but one reason that comes to my mind when I think of unbreakable union with the people of the United States is this: Who is in command in the United States?
>
> The last three elections in this country have been decided by a bullet. John F. Kennedy's assassination brought Lyndon B. Johnson as the standard bearer. Robert F. Kennedy's assassination made possible Richard Nixon's narrow victory in 1968. And George Wallace's maiming paved the way for the recent landslide.
>
> Yet no law has been or apparently will be passed in the near future regarding effective wea-

pons or arms control. Why? Who or what are the United States legislators afraid of?

Before the 1.2 million voters in Puerto Rico decide on statehood we are honestly interested in knowing: Who is really in command in the United States?

Mr. Fortuno was willing to put bluntly what a lot of us have been wondering about since November 22, 1963. A sequence of violent events has played an enormous role in the political process of this country during the last nine years. No other Western country has had its recent history so affected by bullets rather than ballots. One of the original purposes of the Warren Commission was to answer Mr. Fortuno's queries, by showing that the United States is not a "banana republic" whose policies can be transformed by political murders. The Warren Commission attempted to show this by isolating the responsibility for the assassination of John F. Kennedy to one lonely, alienated individual, so that though the event might have had significance in Lee Harvey Oswald's disturbed world, it had no significance in terms of the forces that control American life. The "one-lone-nut" theory made Kennedy's death incidental to the *real* processes of America's political life. But, nine years later, after the murders of Martin Luther King, Jr. and Robert Kennedy, and the attempted murder of George Wallace, and after the wild changes of basic policy during the Johnson and Nixon Administrations, we may all ask Mr. Fortuno's questions, "Who is really in command in the United States?"

George Orwell had once described what he and others—historians, social scientists, novelists—were trying to accomplish in their exposés of the evils of modern political developments, in these words: "Some of these are imaginative writers, some not, but they are all alike in that they are trying to write contemporary history, but *unofficial* history, the kind that is ignored in the textbooks and lied about in the newspapers." (From his essay, "Arthur Koestler," 1944)

The novel of fact, *Executive Action,* that follows is an attempt to do precisely this. Its authors, Donald Freed, a playwright, and Mark Lane, lawyer, historian, and one of the first important voices to raise doubts about the official explanations of how and why John F. Kennedy died, are trying through fictional reconstruction from fact to show how a vast conspiracy might have occurred, and to show how the "real" forces that are in command in the United States might have been able to destroy a President and, thus, radically alter American policy.

THE ONE-LONE-NUT THEORY

The Establishment has held that each political bullet fired in recent years was shot by one-lone-nut—Lee Harvey Oswald, James Earl Ray, Sirhan Sirhan, or Arthur Bremer—none of whom has any connection with actual political forces. Since these four individuals have had so much influence in American history, one would presumably have to conclude, from the Establishment view, that the United States is a super banana republic whose political destiny is buffeted about by the chance encounters of the lone nuts and leading political actors. This seems to have become popular folklore as, for example, the constant speculation about why Senator Kennedy cannot or will not run for the Presidency (namely, he would be killed if he did), or why Nixon chose Agnew as his running mate (for life insurance, since supposedly not even a nut would want Agnew as President over Nixon).

In a recent television interview, former Chief Justice Earl Warren reiterated the one-lone-nut theory, and insisted that he "had never seen any convincing evidence to disprove the Warren Commission's finding that Lee Harvey Oswald was solely responsible for assassinating Mr. Kennedy." (*Los Angeles Times,* December 9,

12 EXECUTIVE ACTION

1972). By now most of the American and world public has come to the opposite conclusion, as poll after poll shows. My own experience from lecturing all over the country and in many parts of the world on the matter is that one rarely meets anyone who *does* believe the Warren Commission, and who does not believe that some sort of conspiracy resulted in Kennedy's death.

The weaknesses of the Warren Commission's case have been pointed out and argued over for the last eight years. Many of us who have gone over the available evidence have come to the conclusion that it is not possible to construct a consistent Warren Commission case in view of the medical evidence, the ballistics evidence and data about Oswald's gun, and the information about Oswald's activities up to about 12:32 P.M. on November 22, 1963. This turns out to have also been the conclusion of J. Wesley Liebeler, a Warren Commission attorney, back at the time the report was being published. Liebeler wrote a memo on September 6, 1964, about the flaws in the Warren Commission case, going over many of the points the critics were to raise about the rifle: whether Oswald fired it; whether he brought it into the Book Depository in the brown paper bag; whether Oswald could be connected to the events by credible witnesses; whether the fingerprint and palm print evidence proved anything; whether Oswald's rifle was adequate for the assassination; whether he was capable of such remarkable shooting ability; and many other points. Liebeler concluded:

> It seems to me that the most honest and most sensible thing to do given the present state of the record on Oswald's rifle capability would be to write a very short section indicating that there is testimony on both sides of several issues. The Commission could then conclude that the best evidence that Oswald could fire his rifle as fast as he did and hit the target is the fact that he did so [shades of the old scholastic maxim—it happened,

therefore it must be possible]. It may have been pure luck. It probably was to a very great extent. But it happened. He would have had to have been lucky to hit as he did if he had only 4.8 seconds to fire the shots. Why don't we admit that instead of reaching and using only part of the record to support the propositions presently set forth in the galleys. These conclusions will never be accepted by critical persons anyway. (Cf. Introduction by David S. Lifton, *Documents Addendum to the Warren Report* [El Segundo, California: 1968], p. 360).

Liebeler was ignored by his superiors, and he, of course, turned out to be right. The critics have had a field day over the points raised, and the public has tended to accept the view that Oswald just could not have done it himself. The Establishment has persistently tried to prevent settling the argument by refusing to allow interested parties to see still classified materials, or to allow tests (such as those proposed by Dr. John Nichols of Kansas) to be made which might decisively settle the question of whether the Oswald/Lone Assassin theory is even possible.

Instead, the one-lone-nut theory is still adhered to as the official explanation, with its corollary that political assassinations by conspiracy just do not occur in the United States. In one of the first critical works—Thomas G. Buchanan's *Who Killed Kennedy?*, written in 1964—the author surveyed the history of American political assassinations, and showed that they have continuously been explained as the work of a lone mad assassin.

The one-lone-nut theory seems to have a strange status in American political thinking. It is offered by important figures almost as an unchallengeable axiom, and has been offered in the last nine years almost immediately after each violent event, before any facts to support it were known. When Bremer shot Wallace it took half an hour before the theory was being stated over the radio, but days and weeks for investigators to know enough about Bremer's background and activities to have a basis for any serious opinion as to why he did it. The theory was being offered by leading law enforcement authorities about Oswald prior to Johnson's decision to create the Warren Commission.

Why does this explanatory theory have such a strong hold, independent of the evidence? Politicians in America, we are told, and taught, can only be killed by solitary psychopaths, while anybody else can be killed by conspirators. Labor leaders, like Yablonsky, can be killed by more than one person. The Mafia, we know, or are constantly told, conspired to kill all sorts of people (but not politicians). We have recently been treated to the government's seriously presenting the news that priests and nuns could conspire to kidnap (not kill) Henry Kissinger. A jury would not believe it, but apparently the government did to the extent of being willing to waste inordinate amounts of the taxpayer's money to "prove" its case. The rash of political conspiracy trials indicates the government thinks that all sorts of dissidents are busy conspiring to create riots, bomb public buildings, give away government secrets, but *not* to commit political assassinations. Our ideology allows for any bizarre form of subversive political conspiracy short of murder, and any sort of murder short of political content.

This prevailing ideology still dominates official and Establishment thinking, and we, who think that political assassinations and attempted assassinations were, or might have been, the result of conspiratorial activities, are still being cast as cranks and crackpots. *Yet,* right now, before our very eyes, a fantastic conspiracy, run from the White House, is being unraveled in the press, and, we hope, shortly in the courts. The Watergate affair, as far as we now know, was a very high-level conspiracy to insure that Richard Nixon would be re-elected. It already has many, many elements of the Freed-Lane Scenario. Leading political figures, and some of the top intelligence operatives, financed by Texas oil millionaires, allegedly conspired to gain information about the Democratic party. They used the most modern electronic equipment to gain these ends. And they appear to have gone to extremely complicated lengths to conceal their source of funds.

The revelations of such a complex conspiracy, reaching into the highest levels of the government, the intelligence world, and the wealthy contributors to Maurice Stans' still secret account, required tremendous organization, talent, and resources. And it achieved its end, that of determining who would be elected President in 1972. The first official reaction was to insist the Watergate five were petty burglars, clowns, acting as private individuals (*five*-lone-nuts). The immediate discovery that James McCord was Director of Security for the Committee to Re-Elect the President and that E. Howard Hunt was their White House contact ended that explanation. Later we were told by Attorney-General Richard Kleindeinst that the whole matter had been investigated by the government, with the thoroughness of the Warren Commission (!), and that only seven people were involved—the Watergate five, Hunt, and Gordon Liddy—and that the conspiracy went neither higher nor lower. Just an odd, uninteresting event. Some top intelligence officers like to eavesdrop on the Democratic Party, and somebody in the White House likes to pay them for it. But it had no other significance, we were told. Finally, if we did not believe that, we were then told just before the election that such a vast conspiracy, involving such important people and receiving such opulent secret financing, was just normal politics. It was perfectly all right for America to be manipulated and controlled by a criminal conspiracy to elect a President. But it was still unthinkable that the same kind of plot might have ever existed in American history to assassinate a President. In both cases the same motives could exist, (to determine American policy), the same kind of *dramatis personae,* the same kinds of techniques, and the same results. But the Watergate conspiracy could be explained as normal American politics, and a similar conspiracy involving assassination is still claimed to be incredible, and not the sort of event that is possible in the United States.

Some people have been willing to think the unthinkable, namely that the Watergate conspiracy was connected with the attempted assassination that in fact led to the great Nixon electoral success. On election night news analysts were pointing out that Arthur Bremer had determined the result. Since then it has been said over and over again that if Wallace had not been shot, we still would not know who would be the next President. I have heard such speculation that maybe Bremer was not an isolated individual but part of a larger conspiracy. If one could entertain such an hypothesis, then the events of the last several months provide a scenario in which a large-scale conspiracy of the kind set forth in *Executive Action,* has been unfolding.

It is strange to realize that Oswald before November 22, 1963, was an interesting personality. His Marine buddy, Thornley, had written a novel about him. He had had great adventures for a high-school dropout. He had been in the Orient, in Russia, had appeared on television in New Orleans, had challenged General Walker in Dallas. He was accepted in high Russian emigré society in Dallas and Fort Worth. He went to Mexico. He was a one-man Castroite movement in hostile New Orleans and Dallas. If the Warren Commission Oswald is the real person, he was a most unusual person, and hardly a nonentity. As soon as Kennedy was shot, Oswald became a bore. For instance, the Dallas police, the FBI, and the Secret Service, instead of being impressed that they might be dealing with perhaps the most important political assassin of this century, did not bother to keep a single note on their thirteen hours of interrogation of him (if we can believe the Warren Commission). By the time Jack Ruby shot Oswald, he was not even enough of a personality to be a villain. He had changed American history, and he was just a zero. Charles Manson could have a cult, but not Oswald.

In contrast, Americans have an endless fascination with professional murderers. We have watched the Mafia killing each other from *Scarface* to *The Godfather* and *The Valachi Papers*. The people involved appear to have no deep or interesting motives. They are not Dostoeyevskian murderers. They murder as a business and terrorize society apolitically.

Thrill killers seem to be interesting. Lots of people write on their psychology, but very little is written on the political killers—who are all assumed to be spiritually empty. They are so insignificant that though newspapers occasionally mention that somebody tried to kill Nixon, the cases disappear and are never mentioned again. And, after Oswald, the government hasn't been concerned enough to have full public trials of the political assassins, or any presentation of the facts gathered by the investigative agencies. Ray's non-trial and Bremer's mini-trial are incredible if these people are seriously supposed to have shaped history.

If it really is the case that the frustrated loners are the most important menaces, why do they escape detection when they travel widely (Oswald, Ray, and Bremer) and when they exhibit their symptoms? If the country is full of these nobodies ready to commit mayhem, then why isn't the control of these people considered of the highest priority, and why do we know practically nothing about their behavior patterns? In a long feature article in the *Los Angeles Times,* December 31, 1972, on "Violence in America: Why is it Growing?" by David Shaw and Bill Hazlett, they pointed out that one reason psychiatrists are offering for the growing violence is alienation and a feeling of impotence in controlling one's fate.

> One result of this feeling of impotence and helplessness is what the psychiatrists term "magnicide"—achieving identity by killing someone

prominent (or killing so many people that your crime cannot possibly be ignored). Hence, political assassinations and mass murders.

But if this is the syndrome operating, why is there no crash program to locate the people who might commit "magnicide" before it is too late?

We live in a society where conspiracies take place on all levels, as evidenced by the endless revelations about corruption in government, in which government officials are misusing funds, or using their official power to help private business (in return for rewards, as shown in the Russian wheat deal); in the New York Police force, in which at least half the police force, according to the Knapp Commission, is taking bribes, and in which some members are stealing captured dope, money, jewels, and guns, and recycling them; in military procurement, in which government officials and large military producers are found to act to bilk the government and to gain favors for their friends; in business operations, in which price-fixing arrangements are found to have been worked out in violation of the anti-trust laws, and in which officials have looted the assets of corporations to the detriment of the stockholders, as in the case of the Penn Central Railroad; in the dope trade, in which cooperation of various law enforcement officials, organized crime groups, and foreign governmental figures all are found to be involved; in the present wave of crime, in which a whole professional level of robbers, fences, and lawyers work together; in the activities of the ITT corporation, in trying to influence government officials through financial political contributions to exempt them from laws, and in trying to influence foreign policy in Chile to help its business; and so on. We are not surprised to learn that almost anything that happens is the result of a conspiracy. But we are supposed to recoil from the possibility that political assassinations in this country (but of course not in the rest of the world) are the result of conspiracies. Some fundamental facet of our mythology is at stake, something that differentiates our national destiny from everyone else's.

The Warren Commission was designed to save this mythology. After it issued its *Report*—which was supposed to be the most exhaustive, careful investigation of all time—it was quickly shown to be slipshod, hastily done, inconsistent, incoherent in parts, and unconvincing. Instead of answering the rumors and suspicions, it created more and more. During its investigation, Mark Lane destroyed the credibility of its key witness regarding the Tippitt shooting. The critics dissected its central claims and the evidence they rested upon, and showed that the lone assassin was most implausible, if not impossible. The Commission sealed up the data that would settle the doubts, and went out of business. The medical facts to this day remain shrouded in mystery, with no plausible explanation available of how the wounds on Kennedy and Connolly could have resulted from two bullets fired from Oswald's gun. The ballistic facts are worse, since the famous mystery bullet 399 does not seem capable of having passed through two human bodies, broken a rib, smashed a wrist, and yet remained undamaged and untainted by human flesh and blood. The Zapruder pictures (still not shown publicly) have been analyzed and analyzed and clearly show that Kennedy and Connolly were hit at separate times, at an interval not possible with Oswald's rifle, and that the fatal shot exploded in the front of Kennedy's head and threw him backwards. By 1966, the critics had shown the Warren Commission just could not hold together, and the facts that became available about how they worked, how the autopsy was conducted, how unreliable some of the key witnesses were, and so on, created a monumental credibility gap. *The New York Times* then said, on July 3, 1966, as a cry of last resort, "Of course the 'single' bullet theory is porous, but no other explanation makes any sense." Murray Kempton, in the introduction to my book, *The Second Oswald,* said that prior to reading the critics "I believed that Lee Oswald was guilty alone—partly because any alternative seemed impossible and partly because any alternative was so uncomfortable." (p. 11) As the Warren Commission theory crumbled, its theoretician, Allen Dulles, was quoted in *Look* (July 12, 1966) as challenging the critics, "If they've found another assassin, let them name names and produce the evidence." (Maybe if the Warren Commission Archives were completely opened we could do so.)

THE NOVEL OF FACT

If one has to come to the conclusion, as I have, and as Donald Freed and Mark Lane have, that the Warren Commission Report is historical fiction, then the novel of fact may be a constructive way of criticizing it. The Warren Commission Report presents part of American mythology, that a political assassination is, and must be, the work of one lone individual with no interesting political motive. The novel of fact presents another possible reality, a political conspiracy that could account for what happened and make it a meaningful event, and indicate who is in command in the United States.

We have seen many instances in recent years of leading intellectuals presenting us with historical fiction to cover up the actual reality. The explanations of our involvement in Viet Nam are the prime example. So many intellectuals supported the rationales of the government, which have only recently been exposed by the publication of the Pentagon Papers. Since the Warren Commission still has so many classified papers, and no Ellsberg has appeared to show us what is in them, a novel of fact may open the door to destroying what is left of the historical fiction.

George Orwell in *1984* (a superb novel of fact) had his totalitarian state operating on the premise that whoever controls the past controls the future. Orwell's state was continuously changing its past by creating different documents. Each past was a historical fiction. His hero tried to fight back by clinging to one scrap of fact that he possessed.

Executive Action challenges the Warren Commission's scenario that a chance encounter between lonely, unhappy Lee Harvey Oswald and John F. Kennedy, plus a fantastic number of coincidences, led to the assassination of our late President. For some time, for good reason, most of the public here and abroad has believed something more dramatic and fundamental occurred, namely that an organized conspiracy succeeded in Dealey Plaza. People have offered a great variety of theories about the nature of such a conspiracy. Freed and Lane start from one extreme end of the speculations, and present a maximal conspiracy directed by very powerful interests—leaders of American intelligence, big business, and organized crime, as well as some of the right-wing military. The force of their plot is that it begins with a possible motive, the common concern of these groups to alter American policy before a real Kennedy era was established. The running commentary of Kennedy's public statements in 1963 shows that he was seeking to accomplish a pretty drastic change in America's role in the world, and a basic alteration concerning who could really exercise power. Certain strong interests were being threatened, especially with the prospect that Kennedy would gain an easy electoral victory the next year and might establish a dynasty during which the power base in America would be greatly shifted. In such circumstances it is conceivable that those most threatened, and those with the expertise, might have conspired to destroy their chief political enemy.

The strength of the plot in *Executive Action,* besides providing a meaningful motive for what happened, and portraying possible characters who might have directed

22   EXECUTIVE ACTION

the conspiracy, is that it encompasses a vast range of data, and accounts for many of the loose ends in the Warren Commission scenario. It would take an extremely lengthy analysis to separate out the strands of material being employed—those that can be documented, those that are speculative based on as yet unexplained data, and those that are purely hypothetical. The experts who have worked through the available material can separate out these levels. For the general reader I think the only brief guidance I can give is to say that a lot of the items that make up the story can be documented, such as that something happened to the Washington, D.C., phone system at the time of the assassination, such as the fact that the code book was missing on the plane the Cabinet was flying in, and such as what happened to Mary Sue Arnett. Other key items such as the messages of Bolton Andrews warning of the impending assassination are inferred from the fact that an agent who seems to have warned his superiors was put away incommunicado. The alleged FBI message-warning has been reported by an ex-FBI man, but to the best of my knowledge nobody else has seen it. The episodes about the conversations among the chief plotters are of course completely speculative.

The story meshes with enough known data to make it possible. Certain conflicting masses of data are given amazingly coherent explanations, such as the sequence of events in Dealey Plaza, and how the assassins could have escaped. (The umbrella man is real, and the Warren Commission never explained why somebody was standing at the point in the parade where the ambush occurred holding an open umbrella over his head on a balmy, sunny day, and the person in question was never located.)

Looking at the drama as the result of a high-level conspiracy allows one to construct the sequence of events if Oswald was a minor character. Oswald obviously could not influence the behavior of the Dallas police, the Secret Service, the autopsy doctors, the Warren Commission and the subsequent guardians of whatever secrets there may be. If he was a peripheral character, a minor employee of some American intelligence organization—which lots of episodes in his career from the time he left high school until he died strongly suggest—then it is not through him that one is to understand the series of strange actions by the government agents that both preceded and followed the assassination. And many who performed strange and unusual acts may have done so unwittingly and may not know to this day that they played any role in the assassination.

There are a few points which I feel need amplification. A more convincing explanation of the apparent lack of concern on the part of the Kennedy family to clear up the mystery of what happened in Dallas appeared recently in a story in *The Washington Post* on November 6, 1972. In a report by Virginia Armat of a book by Onassis' ex-butler, Christian Cafarakis, it is stated that according to Cafarakis a couple of months after the assassination, Onassis hired a team of detectives to find out what happened. After nineteen months they presented a report giving the names of the "real" murderers.

> On receipt of the study, Jackie gathered friends one evening for consultation and then decided to send it to President Johnson. The next morning, an anonymous phone call warned her to leave the report unpublished if she feared for her own and her children's safety. Now, says Cafarakis, the report is locked away in Onassis' private safe at Glyfada and protected at all times by guards and burglar alarms.

If true, this would give a more plausible motivation for the behavior of the Kennedys over the last nine years with regard to the Warren Commission Report.

A second point—one of the few, solid new points to come out at the Clay Shaw trial, was that Oswald went to Clinton, Louisiana, early in September, 1963, to register to vote. Several apparently reliable people encountered him there including a state legislator, a labor leader, and a leader of the black vote registration campaign. Oswald made himself conspicuous. But what was the point of the episode? I think neither Jim Garrison nor Freed and Lane has found a serious relationship of this event with anything else in Oswald's known career.

Regarding the scenario of the two assassination attempts, I think this is just the beginning of finding that a sequence of such attempts probably occurred. Last fall, for instance, a Latin American in Paris claimed he was offered money by American Intelligence agents to participate in an assassination plot when Kennedy visited De Gaulle in 1962. If true, this may have been the first try. Freed and Lane indicate in their plot that the November 22, 1963 attempt almost failed. Perhaps if we ever find out the true history of all of this, it may turn out to be like the attempts to kill Hitler and De Gaulle, with very ingenious people managing to bungle time after time.

THE TREASON OF THE CLERKS

I do not know whether anything like the Freed-Lane scenario took place. The Freed-Lane scenario is a possible construction that would explain many mysteries about the assassination and the subsequent events, which the Warren Commission failed to do. One question that comes to mind at once is how is it possible, if so many people were involved, that in nine years nobody has convincingly spilled the beans? I think a partial answer can be given in terms of what else we have learned in the last decade. Professional killers do not discuss their work. Valachi is famous because he is the first one to give first-hand knowledge about a large number of murders. The assassination team in *Execu-*

tive Action may be happily living in other countries, may still be in business working on other plots, or may have been silenced in various ways, including death. Those higher up in such a plot obviously could not possibly gain by revealing their roles.

The Pentagon Papers are a prime example of how well secrets are kept, even by people who disagree with the policies being protected. Until Daniel Ellsberg gave them to *The New York Times,* nobody among the hundreds of people involved who had turned against the Viet Nam policy by 1967–68 revealed that the Pentagon Papers existed, or that one could document what the most extreme critics of the war were saying.

So, I do not find it surprising that no one has talked, if Kennedy was killed by a conspiracy. I, like many others, find it more surprising and more suspicious that governmental organizations have gone—and are still going—to such lengths to prevent a satisfactory airing of the facts about the deaths of John F. Kennedy, Robert F. Kennedy, Martin Luther King, Jr., and the wounding of George Wallace. All four cases contain mysterious elements suggesting possible conspiratorial plots. Yet those interested in finding out such facts as whether Sirhan had a U.S. passport, what Oswald paid in income taxes in 1962, how Ray and Bremer financed their activities, etc., are met with a complete stone wall, and the public is told that the cases have all been solved, and in each case, one-lone-nut did it. Ray's only public statement, in his non-trial, was that he was engaged in a conspiracy. He was not allowed to explain what he meant, and those trying to get a hearing on his various appeals are, as yet, getting nowhere.

Why is this happening? Why doesn't the government try to dispel the suspicions and rumors; in fact, why doesn't it go out of its way to do so? Perhaps because there is a reality the Establishment feels that it has to hide, a reality that might change our whole conception of what is really going on in America, who controls our country, and how its history actually operates. If we cannot get the facts, then maybe the next line of attack is the novel of fact, to awaken people to what the reality may be.

The conspiracies of silence have been so all encompassing that we are faced with what Julien Benda called *"la trahison des clercs."* It is now a betrayal of the bureaucrats, the officials, and of far too many of the intellectuals. They have made lying for the "public good"—a way of life. They would rather have us living in a meaningless historical fiction than in the genuinely desperate world we should be facing and trying to overcome.

>   Richard H. Popkin
>   University of California, San Diego
>   January, 1973

I / SEPTEMBER

Red Rocks Park, Colorado—September 5, 1963

The technician looked down the naked barrel. His finger tightened on the trigger: a tight click, no explosion.

He lowered the big 7.65 Mauser, studied his stopwatch, sank to one knee to make a notation: 3 seconds. He looked down on the red rock formation that fell away from his vantage point; in the sinking sun the rocks radiated a red life force that half-hypnotized him so that for a moment he could not pick out the four men standing fifty yards down below looking up at him. His eyes blinked like a sleepwalker's as one of the two Cubans slowly waved a small white flag. He stood up and walked down into the shadows.

The technician (code name "King")—six-foot-two, forty years old, his skin almost as red as the burning rocks, towheaded, blue-eyed—descended to the dry stream bed at the base of the canyon. He faced the men. His hoarse voice snapped in the rising wind: *"Puede hacerse."* Then he said it for the two North Americans:

"It can be done."

Vienna, Virginia—September 5, 1963

The Foster estate was about to disappear into the darkening woods of the Virginia countryside. Inside, the white-haired black butler circulated through the magnificent drawing room, silhouetted in relief by the blazing eastern sun as it sank beneath the level of the long glass windows that looked out on stately Etruscan columns, the setting for a dramatic, near-perfect copy of the legendary *Nike of Brescia*. The butler served the drinks, moving noiselessly from man to man in the semicircle around the glowing eye of the television. The sinking sun set the legend inscribed on the vine-covered archway aglow: *cui servire est regnare* "To Serve Is to Rule." The television screen came into focus.

> The news continues direct from our newsrooms in Washington and New York.
>
> FBI special agents swooped down on a house in a resort section near New Orleans today and seized more than a ton of dynamite and twenty bomb casings.
>
> An informed source said the explosives were part of a Central Intelligence Agency cache to be used in an attack on Cuba.

"That son-of-a-bitching playboy," said W. L. (Billy) Smythe, General, United States Army, Retired.

Of the seven men in the classic nineteenth-century drawing room one, Van Preston (code name "White"), was thirty-nine. The others were square, old, male but somehow sexless. Some were sixty, some seventy, but they had in common a kind of armored body image of masculine protest. They sat as if in an evolutionary niche among the antique Spanish velvet hangings, the Isfahan carpet; sat, eyes fixed on the television that was cleverly set in a sixteenth-century chest.

There was no artificial light in the huge paneled room except the television screen. Outside the windows, the superb gardens had almost completely disappeared. The rolling grounds and the small *Birth of Venus* pool were gone now, and only the head of the television commentator swam back to them from the reflecting glass of the long windows.

But the FBI would say only that the materials were, quote, "seized in connection with an investigation of an effort to carry out a military operation from the United States against a country with which the United States is at peace." Unquote.

Now the men shift, one mutters. The butler reenters, followed by a hulking old hound, a former world champion. More drinks. Thomas Langston Foster gestures to his butler to stir the fire to life in the mammoth French Gothic fireplace. The walls, the frames of the glowing paintings in the style of Murillo, the Flemish tapestries, the Italian wall paneling spring out from the darkness as the fire burns. Along the windows the announcer's head speaks out of the reflected fire like an oracle in a burning penumbra.

Diplomats note that for more than a month the Cuban Premier, Fidel Castro, has been charging that the United States is behind naval and air raids staged by Cuban exiles. To support their charges these critics have been emphasizing reports published by the Washington *Post* that infiltration into Cuba by the Central Intelligence Agency has increased dramatically in recent months.

The butler and the old dog leave. A few of the men reach out to pat the failing beast as it passes. Foster leaves the group to stare out the window into the blind gardens of the Virginia night. In his mind's eye he can picture the agony of *The Wrestlers,* the Carrara marble of two striated and struggling white bodies set on the green in the darkness. In the window's reflection he sees the impeccable cut of his London suit, the high white collar with the delicate gray stripe, the dark Sulka tie, the old-fashioned vest; sees the wavy gray hair, the high forehead, the compact frame, the blur of a moustache. The other men, except for one, are dressed expensively and immaculately in dark blues and grays, but Foster wears his clothes like a costume of royalty. He turns away to drink, and the aureole of the fiery head swims back into dominance.

> In Vietnam, martial law continues, as do rumors of impending coup. After an emergency meeting called today by President Kennedy, and attended by George W. Ball, Undersecretary of State, and John A. McCone, director of the CIA, among other top officials, the State Department charged that the government of South Vietnam was guilty of violent attacks against Buddhist pagodas and leaders. The vagueness of the situation in Saigon is said to have made it impossible for the President to recommend specific policy steps in what the administration regards as a crisis of the utmost seriousness. The situation is further complicated by persistent rumors that it is CIA-financed special forces that have raided the pagodas.

The butler whispers to Foster and leaves. As he turns through the heavy oak doors, a piano sounds somewhere in the mansion. Preston, the youngest man of the group, looks away from the screen toward the faint sound of Mozart and closes his eyes for a moment; the long, sensitive face seems out of place in this drawing room of powerful profiles fixed on the square of light in front of them.

> In a moment, a direct report on troubled integration attempts at Baton Rouge, Louisiana, and Brooklyn, New York. And a report from John Wilson, on the road with the Reverend Dr. Martin Luther King, Jr., in . . .

Foster snaps the remote control, and the image spins to black. In the near-dark, he pushes another button to turn on the high-fidelity machine; softly Dvorak's *Violin-cello Concerto* makes its famous dramatic entrance.

I / SEPTEMBER

The firelight flickers on the empty glasses. Cigar and cigarette ends glow, Preston covertly wipes his hands with a handkerchief and peers at the visages, mottled by shadow, of the old men. He loves this noble room and house of his mentor, Thomas Foster, with its polished wood and gold leaf, as if the place had been carved out of the past itself. As his eyes grow accustomed to the dimness, he notes the miniature insignia and medals that most of them wear on the lapels of their dark suits. Only one strikes Preston as out of place—Henry Prince. Preston's mind is a dossier:

> Henry Prince. Syndicate money funneled into bankrupt electronics firm. Little companies swallowed up to feed new consortium, "American Synergy." Billions in armament contracts. Huge scandal looming over company for defective airplane and extensive cost overruns. Caribbean gambling and vice interests, silent partners Meyer Lansky, R. Howard Ferguson. Syndicate and oil financing for aerospace swindle of Defense Department. . . .

Prince was a big, honest-looking man, but Preston thought to himself that Prince was going to go to the penitentiary and should not be there. But he would trust Foster. Foster was his Case Officer.[1] In the clandestine service, only the most rigid chain of command stood between the operative and his equally secret enemies in a world where every man's hand was turned against every other.

Some people are disturbed by compulsive pictures in their thoughts, but Preston always had dossiers and intelligence files in his mind's eye. Even while he was talking to someone, the other person would be transformed into a set of index cards. This process sometimes frightened him, even though it was useful in the work he did. Now as he looked around, his mind began to scan like a

---

[1] Case Officer—man in charge of a secret intelligence operation.

34　EXECUTIVE ACTION

computer. Ranks of names of the military-industrial and foundation complex of which these men were interlocked directors filed into his inner eye; then another read-out and a new word-salad in his head:

> Permindex, Double-Chex, Radio Free World . . . Trade Mart . . . Yale University . . . Dir., Harlem Savings Bank, Dir., Liberty Life Assurance . . . member Real Estate Board . . . King Thomas Timber. . . . Dir., New World Aviation . . . Life Trustee, Columbia University . . . Dir., Great South West Electronics . . . Anti-Communist League of . . . United Hospital Fund . . . Foreign Service China; England 1914–1936 . . . Adams Savings and . . . Friends of Free China . . . Free World Security Council . . . Christian Liberty Foundation; World Anti-Communist . . . Animal Rescue League . . . Chairman of the Board, South-West Bank of . . . Dir., International Student. . . .

He closed his eyes again, forced himself to listen to the music to cool the feverish computation of his mind.

Preston had seen these men's names and photographs thousands of times in the dossiers of the intelligence fronts that had crossed his desk. In a sense their pictures and biographies were more real to him than their actual presence here tonight. Inexorably the tyrant of his calculating mind broke into the music like a harsh teacher who has caught a small boy daydreaming.

> The Andrew Hamilton Fund, Beacon Fund, Benjamin Rosenthal Foundation, Borden Trust, Broad-High Foundation, Catherwood Foundation, Chesapeake Foundation, David, Joseph, and Winfield Baird Foundation, Dodge Foundation, Edsel Fund, Florence Foundation, Gothan Fund, Heights Fund, Independence Foundation, J. Frederick Brown Foundation, J. M. Kaplan Foundation, Jones-O'Donnell, Kentfield Fund, Littauer

Foundation, Marshall Foundation, McGregor Fund, Michigan Fund, Monroe Fund, Norman Fund, Pappas Charitable Trust, Price Fund, Robert E. Smith Fund, San Miguel Fund, Sydney and Esther Rabb Charitable Foundation, Tower Fund, Vernon Fund, Warden Trust, Williford-Telford Fund.

Preston smiled to himself. Total recall, and yet sometimes in the last few years he would forget simple things for a moment: his own birthdate or his ex-wife's name; or the name of the Vietnamese double agent he had had to shoot in the back of the head—a man he had worked with for eighteen months and had learned to respect and admire.

When Foster speaks, in his strong New England twang, the voice sounds disembodied and somehow uncanny. The heads turn toward him. "Gentlemen, I've asked Professor Claude Paulitz to join us. He's waiting for us now in the library." Foster walks to a door and opens it, to let a thin wedge of light fall on the thick, dark carpet. As if on a beam of gold, the men single-file into the library.

In the doorway Foster stands silhouetted—half-firelit, half-dark—waiting for Preston to leave the music, to move into the next room and the next increment of the agenda.

Preston, the last in, lingered for a moment in front of the heavily carved walnut shelves of expensively bound classics, then dragged an exquisitely proportioned Dante chair to one side. The others sat at the oversized nineteenth-century table. Foster stepped slowly over the rich Tabriz rug, to stand beside a fattish man in his middle forties. "This is Professor Claude Paulitz. Claude, I think you know Van and William."

The baby-faced academic adviser from the Rand Corporation looked around owlishly. Paulitz blinked at the proud, flushed faces of the older men; his eyes sought Preston for reassurance. He had worked briefly with Preston in interrogation in Vietnam on a Rand Corporation contract. He had met only two of the others before—at the War College during the Korean intervention—but already he felt self-conscious about how his middle-European speech would measure against their southern, midwestern, and New England native accents. But he knew that once he began his lecture he would transcend the sense and aura of nonentity and alienation that he wore always like his ill-fitting though expensively tailored suits.

In his formative years as a student in Vienna, Austria, little Claude had been a slow boy, a sly boy full of resentment, but by building on his resentment and his sense of powerlessness he had made of his brain a compensatory and potent machine. Now, sitting in this library of power in Vienna, Virginia, he knew that his resentment had been finally rewarded.

Foster walked over softly and rested a surprisingly slim hand on Paulitz's thin shoulder. "Dr. Paulitz has been good enough to drop by to give us a private briefing on how he sees the next period of time. He deals in political 'futures,' as you may know, and if he's not a prophet, he is the best 'probability' and 'game-theory' man I know. I'm going to use a term that may sound alien to you, but the subject I've asked Claude to speak to tonight is 'Contradictions in the American Ruling Circle'; all off the record, of course, all very theoretical."

The eyes, except for Preston's, shifted to the pale man with the overbite, the mouth that in a moment would open to play its games for them. In the pause of silence, Preston turned slightly to listen to the violincello still playing softly from the machine in the dark drawing room. Foster continued to stand behind the speaker like a charcoal-gray eminence.

"Yes, gentlemen. Only a high abstraction overview, of course. The circle presently in power; the oldest brother is President of the United States. The second is Attorney General, head of the Department of Justice and the Federal Bureau of Investigation, and soon, I think it is obvious, of the Central Intelligence Agency as well. The third brother is a senator from Massachusetts. A brother-in-law is director of the Peace Corps. I mention only those at the highest level, for the moment."

Paulitz paused. The unwinking eyes never left his face, his mouth. In the silence, Foster left his side, rolled down a wall screen, snapped on a slide cassette, dimmed down the chandelier. Paulitz moved quickly to the cassette, already talking again.

"Never before in American history has one family held such an enormous concentration of political power. They have grasped it as a family, and they intend to hold on to it as a family. The scenario is perfectly obvious." He punched the cassette.

President John Fitzgerald Kennedy
First Term (at age 43) ....:1960-1964
Second Term 1964-1968

President Robert Francis Kennedy
First Term (at age 43) 1968-1972
Second Term 1972-1976

President Edward Moore Kennedy
First Term (at age 44) 1976-1980
Second Term 1980-1984

The Kennedy Years: 1960-1984

The family legend on the screen hung in the darkness. In the silence the Dvorak throbbed behind Preston's closed eyes. Foster turned up the soft chandelier lights. Now they could see Paulitz's mouth moving again.

"Certainly, in each administration the brothers and older male children will take over the most powerful cabinet posts. Twenty-four years of uninterrupted power!

"Our best reading indicates that he cannot be

stopped in 1964. Their new coalition is already firm: big city machines; the CIO, the Negroes, and other national minorities; the Jews; the liberal establishment *including* the media. Gentlemen, there is simply no contest."

R. Howard Ferguson blew his nose, Paulitz clamped his mouth shut. The oldest of them—and by far the richest—R. Howard Ferguson of Texas had signaled for attention. Foster studied the leathery face. He needed this man, a man who had failed him once before.

Preston studied the aging tycoon. His brain began its read-out:

> Texas Petroleum Club; Lone Star International Club; Club Empire; The Alamo Society; Radio Liberty; Liberty Lobby; Radio Fact, Inc.

As for Ferguson's domestic and international holdings, even Preston's mind, trained in the department of the Board of National Estimates, boggled.

"Now, hold on a minute, Professor." The earthy Texas accent was sobering to them after Paulitz's soliloquy. "Back up jest a damn minute. I'll never forgive him for what he done to us at the Bay of Pigs. *Never!*" Preston could see furious flushing on the big white faces. "But he appointed a Republican to the Treasury, another one to the Navy, and another one to the head of the CIA. The brother worked for Joe McCarthy years ago, and the father, the old man, is as conservative as you could want."

Foster's voice glided in, entering in counterpoint to the cello from the concerto in the drawing room. "No, Howard. We won't mention Cuba tonight either; or that he's come out for suicidal cuts in the oil depletion allowance, *280 million dollars per year!* Or that he first went along with George and Dick[2] when they explained

---

[2] George and Dick—Senator George Smathers and Richard Nixon.

to him in 1960 that Castro 'had to be destroyed,' *went along and then reneged*.

"For the first time in our history, he's sent in one intelligence agency, the FBI, to dismember another agency, the CIA; he's stopped half a dozen mergers under the antitrust act. In last year's sag the market dropped one hundred and thirty-seven *billion* dollars. Steel fell *fifty percent,* and he has the impertinence to talk about 'roll-back' of prices, or worse—a freeze. This is war, gentlemen. He campaigned on an *increased* defense budget. Now he claims we lied to him. Besides that, he has plans to close fifty-two military bases in twenty-five states, plus twenty-five overseas bases, *and* he's getting ready to quit in Southeast Asia."

"Ja." The heads rotated as Paulitz's guttural monologue overlapped Foster's distinguished eastern seaboard tones. "The administration will develop three main thrusts in the next period. First: he will make the decision to lead the Negro revolution instead of fighting it. And he will call out the Army to do it! In the climate of violence that he himself will provoke, he will be the man on the white, or, rather, the black horse." No one smiled at the little joke. Paulitz got even: "You saw with your own eyes *250,000 Negroes* and their supporters march in Washington just last week!

"Second: he will set the wheels in motion for a nuclear-test-ban treaty with the Soviet Union. He will give away Europe for peace and *votes* at home.

"Third: he *will* get out of Vietnam. And I remind you that by 1965 China will have their surface-to-air missiles in place. Ja, SAM's by 1965 at the latest; after that, China cannot be intimidated by a resource-and manpower-poor America. The East, as they say, 'will be red.' "

General Smythe, Ret., cleared his round throat. Foster frowned; he was determined to shut Smythe the hell up if the fool started any of his anti-Semitic or racist broadsides. Smythe bulled forward into the discussion. Almost everyone listened attentively.

"The current instrument of collectivism is the welfare state. The collectivists have finally realized that it is possible to institute socialism through a policy of welfare as well as by nationalization. Welfare socialism is much more difficult to combat. It takes an individual and changes him from a spiritual creature, proud, hardworking, and independent, into a dependent and animal creature.

"We must reject this notion that Communism is brought about by poverty, illness, and other similar social or economic conditions. Communism is brought about by the Communists, and by them alone. *Communism is international conspiracy!* And its goal is to reestablish slavery throughout the earth.

"The advent of a reign of freedom, justice, peace, and prosperity is impossible until Communism has been defeated. The victory over Communism must be the principal and immediate goal of American policy. All other objectives are secondary. We must take the offensive. American civilization is man's greatest achievement in the history of the world."

Foster sighed and smiled, from the nose down, at the general. Preston shaded his eyes as if searching for the lost music that the parade-ground voice had drowned out.

Foster, the spy-master, had never had any real awe or great respect for the military mind. War had taught him that. This was rich, this typical cant about JFK being a "socialist." JFK, whose father had invested bootleg millions into oil, and reaped enormous profits. "Kennedy is not dangerous because he's a 'socialist' or a 'collectivist,' for Lord's sake! The man is a menace because he is potentially a tyrant—a 'tyrant' in the Greek sense, an Alexander. 'Socialist' indeed!" Foster spoke none of this, of course; his lips merely twitched slightly with the repressed lecture. Foster gave each man a chance to talk and validate himself, and he restrained, with looks, the champing Paulitz. Then he ordered nightcaps for them.

Ferguson stared at his thin cigar. Finally, Foster nodded to Admiral James K. Reardon, Ret. "Jim, we go back to O.S.S.[3] and the China theater. I'd like to get your thinking."

"Hell, Tom, let's be blunt, then. In the last fifteen years we've lost eight hundred million people to the Communist conspiracy—and priceless resources and markets—and not a single Russian soldier has been killed in combat in Estonia, Latvia, Lithuania, Czechoslovakia, Hungary, Poland, Bulgaria, *China,* Cuba, *Vietnam!* We're being nibbled to death over there, and now in *our own hemisphere,* and this 'boy' and his 'whiz kids' talk 'love' and 'disarmament' and 'Peace Corps.' Shit! The only thing the goddamned Communists understand is *power.* If we really want peace, we have to start talking some goddamn *pragmatism.* We have to start talking about *organizing* the peace."

The violin-cello's incredible climax had begun. In the midst of it Foster spoke so quietly that they had to lean in to hear.

"Pragmatism. The end of ideology." His voice dropped even lower, below the level of the building music. "We have to organize the peace. And if the life of one man could save millions. . . . Is there any man in this room who would not give his life if it meant peace for his children and the generations to come?" They stared at him, trying to read his lips.

Foster rose slowly. The men shook hands. The butler appeared, to open another door, and they filed out slowly into the hall and seemed to merge there into the twelfth-century mural of the *Wild Horse Race* signifying the end of the world. Paulitz stood, exhausted, waiting. Foster would not look at him, turned instead to Preston. Paulitz dodged by the butler as if he had been hit on his fat rump with a paddle.

"Interesting, wasn't it, Van?" Foster shook hands with the younger man and handed him a six-by-eight

---

[3] O.S.S.—World War II U.S. foreign intelligence

card. The grip was firm, filling Preston with resolve. He knew that Foster was pleased, that he had made a judgment: of the men who were now making their exit, at least three could be counted on for material, men, and money. Personally, Preston had serious reservations about only one of them, R. Howard Ferguson of Texas.

Preston put the card in his pocket without looking at it and spoke the obligatory parting phrase, "Yes, a very interesting theoretical discussion."

The music in the farther room had played out to nothing.

SUMMARY

Executive action[4]: Terminate with extreme prejudice.[5]
Place: Chicago. Soldiers' Field.
Date: November 2, 1963.
Time: Exactly as the gun goes off at half-time. 3:00 P.M.
Method: Triangulation of fire.[6]
Escape cover: Briefed and credentialed.
                Compartmentalized.[7]
                False sponsors[8] in place.

Red Rocks Park, Colorado—September 9, 1963

The technician's Land Rover bumped over the little bridge up to the Mexican café. He got out and wiped his face. The jukebox was blaring away; through the nailed-shut dusty window he recognized Van Preston sitting uncomfortably in a corner. Preston looked only a

---

[4]Executive action—Assassination of a head of state.
[5]Terminate with extreme prejudice—Immediate assassination.
[6]Triangulation of fire—Three hidden sources of gunfire for one target.
[7]Compartmentalized—Each agent is told only what and who he needs to know.
[8]False sponsors—False leads, covers, or blind alleys.

little older to him than he had more than ten years ago when the two of them had worked together in the psy war[9] section out of Osaka and later in Korea proper. Preston was out of Harvard and the Rand Corporation and had been one of the youngest ranking officers in the entire theater. The two of them had had a professional respect for each other, and that was all.

Preston sat there in an expensive lightweight suit and tie. The technician laughed as he studied him through the window; that tie, in this fly-spattered Mexican delicatessen, was a joke.

The technician walked in through the raked and rusted screen door. The place was totally safe, but out of habit he pretended to browse through the Spanish-language scandal sheets stacked on the counter, in order to give Preston a chance to see him. He dawdled over the screaming headlines, but no sign came from Preston. Now he looked over directly at him; Preston's eyes were closed to help shut out the jukebox's ear-splitting sentiment. The technician picked up one of the rags and read loudly:

> ORGIA DE SEXO Y MUERTE:
> MUTILARON A LOS TRES
> CADAVERES!

In one corner of the *Alarma* was a picture of President Kennedy greeting the Mexican ambassador at a White House function.

"How much for this *mierda?*" The fat waitress, her thin daughter, and the two chicanos in khakis, who looked to be highway maintenance of some kind, all laughed. At the words "sex" and "death" Preston opened his eyes. They were brown, and more vulnerable than he allowed people to see.

There were only four formica-topped tables jammed in between the notions and tabloid counter and the

---

[9] Psy war—psychological warfare

cakes and dairy counter. On the wall, over the jukebox, was the sign:

> *NO BEER* OR ANY OTHER *LIQUOR* IS ALLOWED TO DRINK *HERE!!!*
>
> Mans.

The technician waved, "Hi, mind if I join you?" He walked over, tossing the tabloid on the table. They both sat there waiting for the record to end and the two chicanos to leave. When the men got up to pay, the technician pulled the plug on the jukebox. Preston could tell that the lean, bronzed man was known and liked in this place; when he had made his own entrance, pale-faced and in a suit and tie, the people had all stopped talking, and then attacked him through the jukebox with the music. In the quiet now, the flies buzzed, and Marta, the big waitress, shuffled toward them. The technician stretched his long legs. "I'm hungry. Have you eaten? Good food."

"You go ahead."

The technician began to take inventory, speaking in a strong American-accented utilitarian Spanish that he knew grated worse than the music across Preston's Castilian-accented sensibilities.

"Half a dozen tortillas, a tamale, chile relleno, an enchilada, carnitas, and rice and beans, please."

"Salad? *Quiere beber?* Anything to drink?"

"*Dos Equis.* You want a beer, too?"

"No, thanks. Uh, do you have a diet cola?"

They stared at him for a moment in silence. "No, well, nothing then, thanks." As the waitress left, Preston asked, "How are you doing?" Under the table, on the wall side, he tried to pass the technician an envelope full of money. Instead of taking it as once, he asked Preston, "Is this stuff washed[10] this time? I couldn't believe you gave me consecutive bills last time."

"It's washed. Chile to Mexico City to Miami. I'm terribly sorry about last time. The conduit[11] on this is difficult. There's more than five million dollars moving through."

The technician's blue eyes dilated slightly. The waitress staggered over with the plates, and the flies closed in for the kill. Preston watched as the technician stuffed his tortillas with the other dishes, making huge juicy, soft tacos. The technician ate deceptively like some big men, fast and quiet, with no show at all. Now he called out for extra butter and looked at Preston again, who was waiting to interrogate him.

"How is the team? How are they functioning?"

"Okay."

"Have you got a target analysis and assessment for me?"

"Yeah."

"Triangulation? Three seconds?"

The technician nodded and chewed.

"That's champion, Tom! Any personnel problems developing? Any cover problems?"

"We all love each other. No cover problems. We're supposed to be hunters, aren't we? . . . *Mas mantequilla, por favor.*"

"Equipment?"

"No mechanical problems."

"No scopes, correct? I promise you won't need them —if you get that far. You have the photographs?"

The technician fished an envelope of passport-size photos out of his bleached shirt. Preston fingered out the two Cubans. "How are they doing? Is that what's on your mind, Tom?"

The technician stacked his plates and wiped the table. He lit a cigarette and made a face. "Why did you

---

[10] Washed—washing money is disguising its source.
[11] Conduit—a system for the transfer of illegal funds.

force these *gusanos*[12] on me?" He worked a form out of his old shrunken army shirt.

AGENT	MAIN TASKS	START	REMARKS
1. TIGER (Jesús Angel Gonzales)	-long shot -backup -courier	8/15/63	
2. FOX (Esteban Fernández)	-backup -courier	8/15/63	
3. REBEL (James Ray Jordan)	-close shot -backup -electronics -courier -communications	8/21/63	
4. COWBOY (Earl Benson)	-close & last shot -training	8/25/63	

"Here. I'll make my 'remarks' in person: when I set up a SIX[13] team, I vouch for it. When you set me up with this Tiger and Fox, I do *not* vouch for it." His white teeth underscored the low, flat declaration. "A year ago I could buy using Cubans. You told me we were going in to hit the beard[14] on a straight company[15] contract, so I could buy the Cubans. Then you told me it was all off, 'scrubbed by RFK himself.' Right? I mean, these guys are nothing but Havana hoods. What for? Don't tell me it's *on* again?" He rubbed his short crop of dry hair irritably. "They're not pros, are they?" Preston adjusted his tie, waiting for the sunburned man to finish. "These guys are fanatics, and I pick my own men. What are you people sending me these insane ten/two[16] people for now?"

[12]*Gusanos*—worm: an idiom for anti-Castro exiles.
[13]SIX—S, sabotage; I, interdiction; X, experiment.
[14]The beard—Cuban Premier Fidel Castro.
[15]Company—government intelligence agency.
[16]Ten/two—assassin on contract to an intelligence agency.

"They're Batista operatives, Tom. Look, it's obvious, isn't it, that this is not a standard company operation? There's overlapping, and . . . Look, Tom, I'm being run as tight as you. That's true . . . I'm sorry, it's different. . . ."

"What's that all suppose to mean? If I don't contract for my own men, I'm *automatically* compromised—let me finish—I'm not going forward until I find out what's so 'different.' Just face it, Van."

"Clandestine op." SOP[18] vertical linkage.[19]"

"Look, Van, I know this damned thing is compartmentalized watertight." A sarcastic edge had crept into his low voice. "You're not in Virginia now, just talk."

Preston ignored a rolling bead of perspiration at his hairline. "What do you have to know?"

"Are we setting on go? The company's got to be running a couple of other terms.[20] Are we number one?"

"There's an excellent chance you'll see action."

"Okay. We're number two. How soon?"

"You know that depends on contingencies."

The technician glared at him and leaned forward. Preston sighed, "For your ears only, then, probably before Thanksgiving." The technician sat back before he continued. The flies followed the plates as Marta took them into the kitchen and closed the door. Outside, the sun was beginning to slant; it was siesta time. They sat alone now, talking softly in the silence.

"This is a daylight operation. When do I get the whole story, including the backup plan?"

"The scenario is still undergoing revision at the shop.[21] I don't know myself. . . ."

"Bullshit. You and I trained Thais and Laotians here

---

[17]Clandestine op.—clandestine or secret operation.
[18]SOP—standard operating procedure.
[19]Vertical linkage—each conspirator knows only his own job and the man above him and below him.
[20]Running a team—coordinating and directing a team of agents in the field.
[21]Shop—intelligence agency.

in this same exact place in fifty-nine. I want to know if there is *any possibility* at all that we're going outside of the country either before or . . ."

Preston was sweating now, and unhappy, his ascetic face beginning to tic. He tried to bring the meeting to a close. "The probabilities for success are virtually one hundred percent."

The technician cut in on him now, "Just like Playa Giron?"[22]

The Harvard accent surfaced as Preston raised his voice slightly. "Look, Tom, you're a high-risk man—on contract. You take your chances and get well paid for it. Your people are DCA,[23] and I personally vouch for the Cubans—they were Baptista operatives, for God's sake." He leaned forward; he knew he had to give something. "I've never seen a better cover plan. You will be personally escorted from the scene by the S.S."[24] The blue eyes were open all the way; Preston could see the sky in them. Preston felt he was in charge again, the way a Control[25] has to be with his Handler.

"The S.S.?"

"Our straight penetration agents.[26] And you'll have S.S. shoes[27] too. You go out of the country afterwards, *alone*. Passports, the lot, and twenty-five thousand dollars, which you know . . . but I can tell you this: *If* you're the first team, it's definitely going to be twenty-five thousand dollars a year for the next five years, via Switzerland."

"All of us?"

"All of you. And in five years—January 2, 1969—provided no one has broken security, you will each find

[22]Playa Giron—Bay of Pigs.
[23]DCA—Department of Covert Activity: sabotage, kidnapping, assassination.
[24]S.S.—the Secret Service.
[25]Control—the man under the Case Officer and over the Handler in the chain of command in a clandestine operation.
[26]Penetration agents—agents who infiltrate another organization for life.
[27]Shoes—false documents.

one hundred thousand dollars waiting in your Swiss accounts." Preston watched him go pale under the sunburn.

The technician sagged; he felt as if he had been doped. He talked now in order to stall for time, because an unthinkable name was beginning to press to the front of his consciousness. "Oh, I don't know. These Swiss deals are overrated. They bend under pressure of the—"

Preston was too fast for him. "Tom, we're using the E and I[28]; you know the boys." The technician squinted at him stupidly. "The *boys*: the Combo, the Outfit, the Mob, the Organization—the Mafia, the *Syndicate*, Tom." Preston waited. "The deposit will be made in the *bank's* name, so you won't even have to pay the thirty percent Swiss tax. Nothing is going to go wrong." He smiled coolly. "You will be well protected by all that teamster pension fund and gambling skim." The technician closed his blue eyes and waited.

Preston looked over at the Spanish-language tabloid. The flies were back again. They did not bother him now.

He turned the newspaper around so that the technician was forced to look at the picture of John F. Kennedy on the cover.

Washington D.C.—September 10, 1963

The two Secret Service Agents on the 7:30 A.M. White House shift entered the President's cool and sunlit Oval Chamber. They quickly checked over the beige sofas, the fireplace, the rocking chair, the corners of the pale green rug. At the high French windows they slowed down. They worked carefully over to the large mahogony desk that bears the Great Seal of the United States.

---

[28] E and I—the Exchange and Investment Bank of Switzerland, founded by U.S.-organized crime interests.

50 EXECUTIVE ACTION

They crouched down and covered every increment of space and furniture out to the perimeter of the walls; checking even the collection of whales' teeth, ship models, and naval paintings—every inch of the thirty-five-foot long, twenty-eight-foot wide nerve center of power. Both presidential telephones were dismantled and searched for miniature transistor radios that could transmit conversation before the "scramblers" (an electronic device to thwart and distort telephone surveillance) render it unintelligible.

Finally, every object in the room and later the President's watch and jewelry is tested for radioactivity with a Geiger counter. The agents are looking for a new radioactive solution, contact with even a drop of which causes a lingering cancer of leukemia-like death.

Near Denver, Colorado—September 10, 1963

Lifting off the pad, the Ferguson Petroleum Company helicopter began to clear the thinning early morning haze. The surveyor looked down below at the emerging and enlarging panorama of the city as it began its daily business. From the chopper's cruising altitude the mile-high city could be seen in its primordial context of sky and mountains. The foliage and ground covering within the populated borders showed the first clear signs of approaching winter; yellows, oranges, and reds superimposed only briefly in the surrounding mountains of green and downward-creeping whites, the growing snow-cover that shortly would provide Colorado with its annual source of fame and fortune.

With his youthful face and neat dark hair, he looked a good ten years younger than thirty-five. The surveyor was actually a surveyor, and a good one. He had been surprised that his training as an intelligence officer a decade before had so quickly taken over and preempted any casual civilian attitude he had been cultivating since Korea. He was ambivalent about taking a three-month leave of absence for this clandestine operation, but his former commanding officer, Van Preston, had assured him that he was the "only man for the job." That and the sum of money that went with the job had won him over.

Appearing to be only a few inches from city center, as they looked down, the bare-earthed corridor of a new ski run was easily identified by the passenger in the modified high-altitude craft, and he congratulated himself on the good work he had done the preceding week. Soon this brown scar would be glistening white and would almost immediately be followed by hundreds of novice skiers advancing toward their goal of personal freedom and "actualization," having replaced golden psychoanalytic couches with elongated aluminum slats and staffs and artificial friction-free surfaces.

All the tools of the surveyor's trade that had been needed for completion of that assignment now lay in the back of the southward-turning machine, including the long cap-covered tubes of plans, drawings, and blueprints. Among these was one tube not yet used. It was identified only with a plain label on its cap, "E.A., O.P. II" and was scheduled to be delivered shortly to a location nearly one-third of the way toward their destination and the helicopter's home base in Dallas.

Despite his training and indoctrination, a sense of personal accomplishment compelled the surveyor to tap for attention from his pilot. Leaning close to the ugly man's hair, more purple than red, he pointed to his handiwork and invited comment. Through the high whine-whirr of operating machinery he pointed toward the fast-disappearing slice. "Finished that Friday . . . took about a week . . . think it'll do the job, though. Hope so! You ski?"

The reply came only by way of a slow, careful back-and-forth head shake. Despite the caution, the red hair moved less than its base on the dead-white skull, and within the few seconds that this "conversation" took place, one man had blown his cover and the other had

52   EXECUTIVE ACTION

surveyed him with something more than the casual curiosity that had begun their journey. The makeup that covered the burn scars on the pilot's flabby white face made the surveyor uneasy for some reason.

All three—pilot, surveyor, and machine—settled into the routine that would constitute their next period of time. Light increased to its normal daytime intensity. Below, on the mountains, it was season's end. Greens and whites gave way to the high-plateau yellowish brown that in the southern horizon begins to project the dull red of high desert. The source of the name of their intermediate destination, Red Rocks Park.

From the small pack on the floor between his feet, the surveyor began to take out those items that, when attached to his carefully chosen plain work clothes, would quickly transform him into a Colorado state-park ranger. The badge, the cloth identification insignia with pressure-sensitive backings, the distinctive headgear, and a simple rearrangement of trouser legs into the boots that had appeared to be only black shoes would make him indistinguishable from any other park ranger.

During this activity, David Ferrie, the pilot, carefully reached up with his left hand and returned his purplish-red hair to its more natural position, while offering the silent compromise, "I won't say anything about your drag if you won't say anything about mine."

The surveyor, turning around in his seat to exchange his pack for the tube of plans to be delivered, noted the subtle shift in his pilot's appearance and, also silently, agreed to the unspoken compromise. It was as if each had been trained by the same institution and teachers. The only difference being that, had this exchange been spoken, the surveyor would not have understood that in the private vernacular of his pilot, "drag" meant disguise.

Below, rushing to meet them, was the growing barren rocky redness of the edge of the southwestern desert.

The technician, in his working enclave in Red Rocks

Park, scanned the northern sky, noting no unnatural movement, and turned to his team, the two Cubans and two North Americans. "Okay, we'll start . . . but I'm damned if I know for sure what more we can do without plans."

The language was mild and revealed only a fraction of the frustration that he carried within him from his encounter the preceding day with Preston. All five men clambered from the vintage jeep, a World War II model, with its abbreviated styling. The Cubans moved to the winch in the front bumper, disengaged those gears with the hand lever there, and began to walk away with the end of its cable.

"How far?" one called back to the technician in heavily accented English.

"I don't know, I guess all the way at first, or until you. . . ." He began to scan the ground in front of the vehicle until he saw a medium-sized pile of rocks that would serve the purpose.

"There, that pile. Wrap the end around one of those," pointing with his left hand, commanding the Cubans. His frustration edged his words, so that his team, with slightly bowed heads, trudged toward the indicated pile, dragging the cable behind.

The technician jerked his pack from the jeep, while the two North Americans opened the coffin-like burial crate strapped to the rear of the vehicle. It was a plain, rectangular wooden box, the kind used by thousands of mortuary firms as casket covers. Each extracted one cotton impact dummy and placed it in the rear seat.

The technician loosened the thumb screws and pushed the windshield flat across the hood. Again his frustration betrayed his anger. He used uncommon force, and a small crack sprang to life in the glass and ran diagonally across the right-side portion like a fissure in sunweakened ice atop a pond.

The technician opened his pack, taking the walkie-talkies out and placing them on the hood of the jeep. As he extracted their antennae, he saw the crack in the windshield and muttered something under his breath. The older North American, putting the finishing touches to his dummy in the right-rear seat, looked up sharply. "What'd ya say?"

His question was ignored, as usual, but the technician began to appreciate his situation. He had to recognize that by now he was somewhat more out of control of himself than the company tolerated. His NCO training in Korea had impressed upon him that to lose control of oneself was also to lose control of his command. He seldom spoke to his team members about anything other than the minimum essentials required to complete the assignment. Having nearly always to say twice whatever he wanted, once in English and again in Spanish, helped him to rationalize his reticence. It was a small comfort to know that his Spanish sounded as bad to his Cubans as their English did to him.

He returned to his pack for the stopwatch and ammunition that would be used. The four rifles were now being lifted from the casket crate and stood on their butt ends, with barrels leaning against the jeep. Before closing the crate, the younger North American removed his jacket, out of deference to the midmorning sun that was heating the ground and rocks. A short, old, potbellied, grizzled confederate soldier tattooed on his inside left forearm stood defiantly clutching a staff from which flew the Stars and Bars in gentle ripples above his head, while the admonition below the figure, *"FORGET HELL,"* attracted the technician as it always did, and as always, he caught himself wondering what in the hell it really meant.

He turned away, forcing a calm upon himself that he really didn't feel, and searched the northern horizon for some sign of the promised contact. A slight unevenness in the otherwise clear sky alerted his sharp eyes to a presence. Turning toward the distant end of the winch's cable, he called out, "Which of you has the flag?"

The two Cubans looked up from their measured return to the jeep, and once again the technician hated them for looking so much alike to him that he seldom remembered which name went with which body. Like his keen eyesight, he was aware that this cultured blindness was a heritage of his birth and upbringing in the high country of the American West.

As the slighter of the two, Fernández, pulled the flag from inside his jacket, he also removed the jacket and passed it on to his partner, who likewise removed his coat and proceeded on to the jeep, stuffing both garments in the casket crate. The technician pointed to a spot in the sky, and the flag-bearer moved away from the jeep. After nearly fifty yards he stopped and began slowly to wave the small white flag at the approaching dot.

In the helicopter, the surveyor, with the blueprint tube held upright between his knees, shouted above the noise at his pilot, whose fantasies had wandered to the bizarre. "We should be nearly there, shouldn't we?"

The pilot, reviewing his instruments, leaned close to his passenger to answer, "Yeah . . . nearly," disengaged one hand from his controls, and placed it atop the tube. "This the delivery?" The surveyor nodded "yes" and questioned his own uneasiness closely. It was not as if he had never done anything like this; on the contrary, he could not remember how many times. He moved his right leg, permitting the tube to fall from under the pilot's fingers and lean in to rest against the right side of the cabin. The pilot again addressed himself to the instruments and controls of the craft.

The team on the ground began to load their rifles— only two rounds each—while the technician started the jeep's engine. Each rifleman took one of the walkie-talkies from the hood of the vehicle, now vacant except for the two dummies sitting correctly on the rear seat. Fernández started to wave the flag again at the approaching helicopter. The three other riflemen moved in divergent directions from the jeep: the remaining Cuban to the right front; the older grizzled man to the right rear; and the younger man, with his constant pink-blue-and-gray

Confederate companion, directly to the rear of the jeep. Each was thoroughly involved with his weapon and walkie-talkie, attempting to achieve some working balance between their own bodies and the two pieces of equipment.

The technician got out of the jeep, and moving to its winch, noted some degree of renewed confidence at this concert of action. He lightly tested the lever that would engage the winch's gears, and turned to the northern horizon again. The helicopter was now clearly distinguishable in the thin high-mountain air. The technician moved slowly toward the flag-waver with his walkie-talkie in one hand and the stopwatch in the other. His team, or at least three-quarters of it, each now about seventy-five yards from the jeep, turned as one, as if on command, and began to examine their walkie-talkies. Looking at them, he wondered if his worry was unrealistic. Could he, as Preston had insisted, weld these men into a human weapon?

From the chopper cabin the jeep and team were now clear to both pilot and passenger. As the craft approached to within a few hundred yards of the landing spot, the technician and his Cuban started back to the jeep. Midway, the technician turned to see the chopper, hovering directly above the spot on which he had just been standing, and then turned his back to the increasing noise and swirling dust. He indicated to the Cuban by a look that he should return to the jeep.

In the nearly grounded craft the surveyor, looking for some indication of the character of the man he was about to meet, noted only the efficiency of the action. He pushed open the cabin door just as he felt the craft bump down on the hard, rocky soil. As the pilot shut down the machine's operation, the surveyor gathered his transit, tripod, tape measure, and four stakes under one arm, and clasping the long blueprint tube in his right hand, strode toward the technician.

At the jeep, Fernández placed the flag in the casket

crate and took up his Mauser. He moved to the front of the vehicle after securing the top of the box and began to fit the remaining walkie-talkie to himself, as his companions had already done.

The technician and surveyor measured each other closely as the distance between them diminished. Behind him the surveyor heard the pilot, now out of the craft and standing by the open right-hand door, yell at him, "Do you want any more of this stuff?"

The surveyor half-turned back to the craft and signaled "no" with a shake of his head, never reducing his rate of approach toward the technician. His youth and vigor seemed to compliment him less than it served to illustrate his pilot's age. The technician observed this difference and wondered at the similarity between these two and his team. Not so much in their looks as in their attitudes, where there was a kind of flatness he could not explain. The surveyor thrust the tube at the technician, who reached out for it, providing the others a view of what appeared to be a handshake. His words betrayed no emotion at all. "Starting to get cold, isn't it?"

The technician nodded agreement as both turned and marched to the jeep. The pilot, Ferrie, with something less than the military cadence of the other two, followed them. His interest in their meeting faded as he found something familiar-looking in the Cuban who remained at the jeep waiting for instructions. Ferrie licked his lips slowly, and his bright eyes made a beeline for the Cuban's crotch.

From the surveyor's position by the jeep he could see the low-lying rocks to the right front and the much higher elevations to the right rear and direct rear. Their relative sizes and distance from each other seemed to be exactly right—so much so that they precipitated a vision of the plans in the tube.

The technician placed the still-unopened tube on the jeep's hood as his counterpart began to lay out his equipment alongside the tube.

One thing out of whack that the surveyor was aware of was the angle at which the jeep would be pulled through this enclave by its winch.

"I guess the first thing to do is to reset the end of the cable. It should be moved to the left." While he spoke, the technician wig-wagged his hands, pointing to a different pile of rocks to be used as the cable terminal, about twenty yards or so to the left of the grouping now used. The technician nodded toward Gonzales, the Cuban who began to move to complete the designated shift. As he passed the front of the jeep, the surveyor handed him two of the four stakes, which he took in his left hand, balancing out the weight of the rifle in his right hand.

The pilot angled sharply to his left so that he intercepted the departing Cuban along the line of the cable a few feet in front of the jeep.

"May I help?"

The Cuban responded not at all to the offer. What had been only a vague memory was by now a clear recollection of this same man, with the fake red hair and the distinctive odor of face makeup. The prior encounter several years earlier had taken place in the Cuban's country.

The surveyor responded to the inquiry. "Yeah, you can help him with the cable and then take these stakes to the other two," pointing to the North Americans, still at the rear of the jeep. The pilot returned to take the stakes and then scurried somewhat to catch up with the Cuban along his route to the cable's end.

The surveyor removed his transit from the carrying case and mounted it on the tripod. "We can assume this to be the starting point of the run, and initiate our action about here." He moved along the cable line about sixty-five feet and planted the tripod. "In the tube is something you'll need at this spot. . . ."

The technician unscrewed the stainless cap and inside found a roll of blueprints and a polished wooden handle. He pulled and extracted a plain black umbrella. He noted the cleverly designed umbrella handle, disguising a multiple-band radio. Despite his interest, he did not try it or touch the plans, but moved directly to the surveyor with the umbrella in his hand. By now the Cuban and the pilot were pulling the cable end to its new location. The surveyor checked some numbers on a plain white three-by-five card and moved the transit correspondingly.

His transit was not a remarkably fine instrument. It was surplus government issue, but was accurate enough. Moving the transit on its base, he set up the calibrations on its scale that would position each team member at the right distance from and elevation above the anticipated target. For an older, common surveyor's transit, it worked very well. He did not bother to level the instrument more than by eyeballing, since exact locations would not be that necessary, unless this actually became the first team which he had reason to doubt, just looking at them. This is not a team, he thought.

The cable now firmly attached in its new location, the Cuban joined his partner, while the pilot began his approach to the North Americans. The surveyor signaled for the Cubans' attention, and sighting through the transit, began to move first one and then the other to their correct positions. Once located, each sat using the posture taught by military organizations the world over for rifle firing. The surveyor swung the transit to his right about ninety degrees and began waving his arm at the older North American, who had difficulty finding his spot. Finally a last shift of the transit and more conductorlike movements from the surveyor placed all four riflemen in the correct positions. Each used a rock to pound his stake in.

The technician inserted the umbrella point into the ground next to the transit and tripod and returned to the still-idling jeep. He removed the rolled blueprint sheet from its tube and was just unrolling it over the hood of the jeep as the surveyor returned.

"Yeah, that's about the right angle now. . . ." He was

responding to the new position of the cable, squinting along its length as though he were firing one of the rifles also. The pilot, returning from his delivery of the stakes, approached the two leaders with a dampened spirit. "How much longer we gonna be?" he asked. He had worked up a light sweat, and the makeup was starting to get slick.

"You can get the chopper going again. It'll only be a minute now." The surveyor handed the pilot his tripod. "Put that in the back again, will you?" The pilot trudged toward his waiting craft. The surveyor gathered up his remaining instruments, and using his free hand, helped the technician unroll the plan. The label in the lower-left-hand corner zoomed up at the technician: *"SPATIAL CHART OF NORTHERN HALF OF DEALEY PLAZA, DALLAS, TEXAS."*

A glance at the chart showed the technician instantly why he was at this location, and he quickly recognized the surrounding natural formations that stood for the manmade locations in the plans. Examining the drawings more closely now, he saw that the umbrella was in the same location as a line marked "Stemmons Freeway Sign."

"Okay." The surveyor spoke quickly, with no evidence of any emotion. "You know where. You'll be notified if and when. Good luck." He turned toward the helicopter, which was now being brought back to life by the pilot. The technician continued to study his plan: checking each significant location against the conditions of his current area reminded him with disheartening certainty of his employer's efficiency. He now spoke into his walkie-talkie. "Wait for my visual signal. I'll use the umbrella."

The surveyor returned his remaining equipment to his bag and climbed aboard. Before he had time to close the door, the gears were engaged that allowed the helicopter to begin its nearly vertical ascent. The pilot, checking his instruments to determine the bearing for

SPATIAL CHART of NORTHERN HALF of DEALEY PLAZA

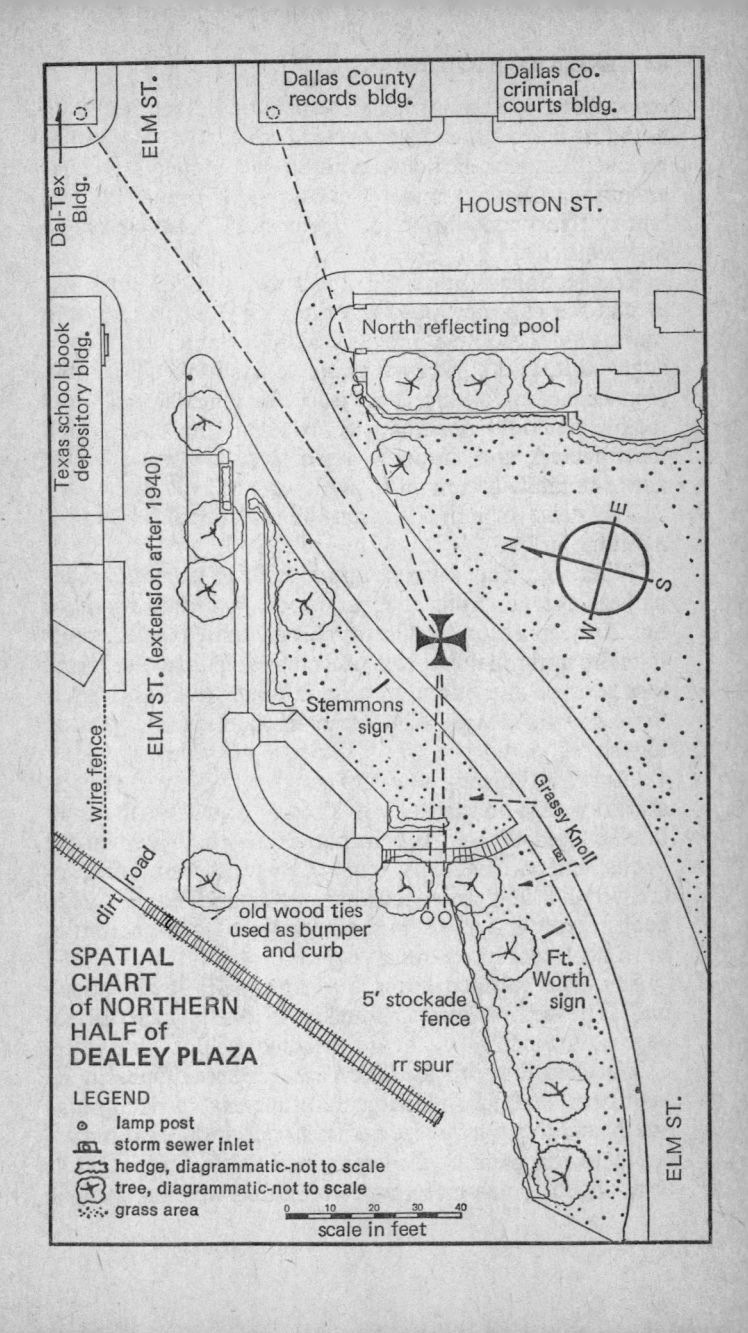

LEGEND
- lamp post
- storm sewer inlet
- hedge, diagrammatic-not to scale
- tree, diagrammatic-not to scale
- grass area

scale in feet: 0 10 20 30 40

Labels:
- Dal-Tex Bldg.
- ELM ST.
- Dallas County records bldg.
- Dallas Co. criminal courts bldg.
- HOUSTON ST.
- North reflecting pool
- Texas school book depository bldg.
- ELM ST. (extension after 1940)
- Stemmons sign
- Grassy Knoll
- wire fence
- dirt road
- old wood ties used as bumper and curb
- Ft. Worth sign
- 5' stockade fence
- rr spur
- ELM ST.

the balance of their flight, seemed to be interested in nothing more than returning home. His passenger watched the ground below with equally isolated concentration. He had to make some kind of report on this team. Everybody watching everybody else—he had never liked it.

The technician returned the drawing to its tube, replaced the cap, and put both the tube and his jacket in the casket case. He moved to the winch gear lever, engaged it, and half-ran forward to the umbrella, as the jeep began to roll along its track. Seizing the umbrella from its upright position, he turned as the cable slack disappeared, and the jeep began to follow the cable at approximately fifteen miles per hour.

The surveyor indicated that the pilot should hover for a minute or two.

When the jeep was about sixty yards from the technician, the umbrella popped open and the surveyor noted the position of his watch's second hand as puffs of white and red dust belched from a half-dozen different locations on the dummy in the left-rear seat. Only four seconds had passed. The surveyor nodded his approval, felt satisfied that he would have a positive report for Control and turning toward the pilot, indicated that he should return toward home. The pilot headed the craft in a southeasterly direction, patted his passenger on the knee, and nodded his own approval. The surveyor crossed his legs away from the pilot and put his head back, closed his eyes, and allowed the scene below to burn itself into his memory.

The jeep bumped into the pile of rocks at the cable's end. The technician ran quickly to the front to disengage the winch's gears. He climbed behind the wheel and backed the jeep to its original position. Once there, he noted that the helicopter was nearly buried in the southeastern horizon. He got out once more and moved again to the front of the jeep. Into the walkie-talkie he announced in a voice more calm than it had been all morning, "Let's try it once more—just in case. Set it up. Take a break first." He pulled out the tube and spread the plans for a proper look.

"No," he argued to himself, "I've got to keep the *gusanos* to the rear. And if we can't use scopes, then the kid, Rebel, has to shoot instead of just backing up the Cowboy." He was livid with Control for first forcing the Cubans on him and then making the unilateral decision that they could not use scopes. Then putting them so bloody far away that unless they were world champion marksmen—which he knew they were not—he really had only half a team now. At the deepest level was the fear that now he himself would somehow have to pull the trigger at the last moment—if they should be the number-one team, which he could not believe after looking at the diagram.

He fumed. He knew that a scope could bring a target four times closer but that it was not needed for a target under three hundred feet away, and also that it required too much adjustment. He debated now whether to countermand Control and get the Cubans .223 caliber 21 barrel Colt AR-15 Sporters *with* scope. That might help: the AR-15 weighed only eight pounds, with an 8,000-yard range and an initial speed of 3,000 feet per second.

"Fuck these madmen," he said out loud.

New Orleans, Louisiana—September 12, 1963

"Raise your right hand, please."

Lee Harvey Oswald took the oath and flipped a ten-dollar bill on the counter, gathered up his papers, and stepped out of the New Orleans Passport Office into the light rain.

Vienna, Virginia—September 12, 1963

The American flag fluttered atop the pole outside the Foster-estate library. The undulating reflections on the window made the faces of Foster and Preston, as they stood talking, look like sea creatures.

Foster stuffed a pipe and listened to Preston voice his field problems. He wished the younger man would go away so that he could tend to his gardens. The whirring of the big computer cut them off as the clerk entered from the private room off the library. "Ready, sir."

"This is my choice so far, and time is awfully short," Preston said, handing the older man the card as they entered the electronics communication room.

SUMMARY: WATSON, CHARLES EUGENE
Military Service: ONI.[29]
Language Skills: Italian, Spanish, Portuguese.
Intelligence Skills: Training pilot. Radio operator.
Assignments: Material transport (Guatemala, Cuba).
　　　　　　　Training (Miami, New Orleans).
Expendability: 3.6 T.D. rating.[30]
Cover: Military—Naval Intelligence (former)
　　　　Diplomatic—None
　　　　Commercial—CMV Radio Corp., Commercial Pilots Assn.
Personal: Homosexual (covert). Drinks in excess of moderation.
　　　　　Identification with Air America[31] visible.

Foster dropped the card into an electronic disposal unit, and "Watson, Charles Eugene," went up in a puff of smoke. He dumped the ashes into the accompanying receptacle and knocked out his pipe at the same time.

---

[29] ONI—Office of Naval Intelligence.
[30] T.D. rating—termination and disposal on a four-point scale.
[31] Air America—"civilian air-transport line" owned by the United States Central Intelligence Agency.

"Let me show you mine. Here is his card, and I've prepared a complete set of slides on him. We have a Fair Play for Cuba cover already started on him in New Orleans. The Chinaman's[32] been looking after him. You can take over from him, if you like the looks of this boy. He's really had a remarkably checkered career. Highly trained. Schizothymic physique, allo-plastic personality. Fits the profile we need perfectly."

Preston was stunned at the irregularity. The case officer never co-opted Control's responsibility for recruitment. He stared at the famous face; was the man losing his way at the end of all the diplomacy and intelligence and war? This was the second time; they were forcing the Cubans down everyone's throat. These were fatal errors, or was the "game plan" (Foster's words) one unknown to him? Now the clerk and Foster were both looking at him as he tried to read the print-out.

SUMMARY: OSWALD, LEE HARVEY
A.K.A. HIDELL, ALEX JAMES

Military Service:	U.S.M.C.
Language Skills:	Russian, Spanish.
Intelligence Skills:	CIA: Radar. Photography. Radio. Code.
Assignments:	U.S.S.R.
	Dallas (Eastern European Intelligence Community).
	New Orleans (FPCC).[33]
Expendability:	4.0 T.D. rating.
Cover:	Military—Marine Corps (former).
	Diplomatic contact—American Embassy, Moscow, M. Wright.
	Commercial—Raskin Photo Lab.
	M.L. Sugar Refinery.
Personal:	FBI informant, Number S-179.
	Russian wife and two children.

---

[32] Chinaman—code name for a Dallas-New Orleans operative.
[33] FPCC—pro-Castro Fair Play for Cuba Committee.

At the same time, Foster talked and the clerk switched a light on behind a glass panel, making it into a screen. "The computer threw out fourteen sponsors.[34] This young Lee Harvey Oswald strikes me as the best candidate. A very strange career. If you will just let me ramble on a bit.

"Born in New Orleans October 18, 1939, father dead, mother remarried and then divorced, the boy placed in an orphanage for a time and then shunted about with his mother from place to place until his seventeenth birthday. He was actually recruited as an informant at that tender age through the Hull Foundation. You can start now, Tim."

With the lights darkened, a photostat of a letter came up on the panel. "For example, on October 3, 1956, at the age of sixteen, he wrote this barely literate letter to the Socialist party of America."

> Dear Sirs:
> I am sixteen years of age and would like more information about your youth League. I would like to know if there is a branch in my area, how to join it, etc. I am a Marxist, and have been studying in socialist principles for well over fifteen months. I am very interested in your YPSL.[35]
>
> Sincerely,
> Lee Oswald

Foster buttoned on a seat reading light. In the thin beam he could see to read as the slides snapped on the screen.

Preston did not feel good. Since Foster was now referring to the photograph of the bright-eyed teen-ager on the screen as "subject," Preston knew that the choice had already been made. He only half-listened.

"On October 24, 1956, six days after his seventeenth birthday, subject enlisted in the United States Marine

[34]Sponsors—in this case, a decoy, diversion, or "patsy."
[35]YPSL—Young People's Socialist League.

Corps, reported for duty at Marine Corps Recruit Depot in San Diego, California."

On the screen, photostats of reports, the San Diego installation, and Oswald.

"Attended Aviation Fundamentals School at Naval Air Station in Jacksonville, Florida, studying basic radar theory, map reading, and air-traffic control procedures. Granted security clearance up to the 'confidential' level.

"Began studying Russian language and taking pro-Communist attitudes. Fellow Marines called him 'Oswaldovitch' and 'Russky.' Remember, he is in the *Marine* Corps. Obviously a cover has been prepared by—"

"Who, us?"

"No, Naval Intelligence. Arrived in Yokosuka, Japan, aboard the *Biloxi* for assignment to Marine Air Control Squadron Number 1, Marine Air Group 11, First Marine Aircraft Wing, based at Atsugi, twenty miles west of Tokyo, where we monitored the U-2's over China. That was our first contact with him.

"Court-martialed April 11, 1948, for illegal possession of a .22-caliber pistol. Sentence of six months' confinement suspended. Court-martialed a second time on June 27 for pouring a drink over an officer's head and use of insulting language. Confined seventeen days at hard labor. . . . Only seventeen *days?* We were not only giving him a cover, we were fixing him a funny.[36] And none too subtly, I think."

Didn't he know? Preston felt that Foster was selling too hard. The more he talked, the less Oswald suited him.

On the screen, slide after slide of Lee Harvey Oswald —his life and its abstractions and documents—was clicking into focus. Foster could not have seen that, in the dark, the younger man had closed his eyes against the imagery on the screen.

---

[36] Funny—creating a misleading dossier.

"Records are cloudy here. Service record says subject was transferred to another MAC-11 unit in Atsugi from October 6 to November 2, but his certified pay record shows subject left MAC-11 from September 8 until October 17. One of them's got to be wrong, but we don't know which.

"On August 17, 1959, subject requested a dependency discharge on the ground that his mother required his support. Discharge was granted on August 28."

On the panel now were photostats of affidavits from Fort Worth doctors Rex Z. Howard and Rex J. Howard.

"Otolaryngologist Rex Z. Howard's letter states that he has been treating subject's mother since September 5, 1959, although the letter is dated September 3, 1959. Other affidavits from Fort Worth, including orthopedist Rex J. Howard's, are dated September 4, which is the day *after* subject was transferred in preparation for his discharge."

(A photograph of Oswald's passport and passport application.)

"On the same day, September 4, 1959, Oswald applied for and received a passport, quote, 'in order to attend Albert Schweitzer College,' unquote. Passport granted, good for European travel, including USSR.

"Sailed from New Orleans September 20, disembarked at Le Havre, France, October 8, and flew from London to Helsinki on October 10. Applied for Russian visa and entered Soviet Union October 15. He withdrew $203 from his savings account on September 14.

(On the panel, shots of Moscow, U.S. Embassy, Hotel Berlin, Botkinskaya Hospital, and Oswald, with his ferret eyes and the twisted occlusion of his hungry mouth. Preston opened his eyes. Oswald was staring straight at him.)

"Arrived in Moscow October 16. They ordered him to leave USSR by eight P.M. October 21. Slashed wrists same day, taken to Botkinskaya Hospital, released a week later. Visited U.S. Embassy October 31, stated determination to revoke American citizenship and turn classified data over to the Russians. Can find no record that embassy tried to dissuade him from handing over classified material."

Preston spoke for the first time. "How much did he actually have?"

"Location of all bases on the West Coast, all radio frequencies for all squadrons, all tactical call signs, strength of all squadrons, number and type of aircraft in each, names of commanding officers, authentic code of entering and exiting all radio and radar ranges.

"On November 6, 1959, the embassy received written revocation of citizenship signed by Oswald. Embassy notified State Department, State notified ONI, FBI, and CIA. January 4, 1960, Oswald received permission to remain in USSR for one year. Extended for a second year in 1961. They're beginning to buy. Perhaps."

(On the panel, the photographic record is rich: Minsk, the Belorussian Radio and Television Factory, Oswald's new friends, his apartment, a girl, a dog.)

"On January 5 he is given five thousand rubles and assigned to work at the Belorussian Radio and Television Factory in Minsk.

"In 1960 he suffers a change of heart, writes a series of letters to the embassy concerning possible return to the United States."

(On the panel: first snapshots of Marina. Their wedding, her family, Lee and Marina with friends.)

"On March 17 he met Marina Nikolaevna Prusakova, a graduate pharmacist, age 19, born July 17, 1941, in Severodvinsk, Arkhangel Oblast', Russia. Six weeks later, on April 30, 1961, they were married. On February 15, 1962, a daughter was born to them in Minsk. The child was named June Lee Oswald. . . . I'll take the slides from here, Tim." Preston was confused: the material was too thick and contradictory.

Foster rubbed his eyes. This was hard work for him; he was doing his own job and Preston's, too. Preston was hurt, so he was glad, in an infantile way, that his case officer's voice and eyes were dry and strained. "Now, Marina reputedly comes from a KBG[37] family, so he was of no more use to us, except that now his wife's background is the kiss of death to him if he gives us any trouble."

At last Preston understood why Lee Harvey Oswald had been chosen: at one point in time his wife might have been a Soviet agent, at the informant level, and could be used, fatally, against Oswald now. It was Foster's guess, and Preston's too, that Oswald was ignorant of this possibility. "The Chinaman stays very close to both of them," he heard Foster's voice.

"We had him teaching Russian at the Texas Petroleum Institute for a while, and we have him in a safe house[38] there, so it's important to get him out of New Orleans and back to Dallas as soon as possible. He was recruited by the FBI in June, 1962, in New Orleans, and the entire situation is messy there. Get him to Dallas.

"As a result of Oswald's letters to the embassy in Moscow stating his desire to return to the United States, the State Department informed the embassy that for security reasons Oswald should be given a passport—and Marina, too—provided the embassy was convinced he hadn't legally abandoned his American citizenship.

"There was a long wrangle with the Russians over exit visas for his wife, but everything on our side was smooth as silk. State took Oswald's personal signature that his wife wouldn't become a public charge. The Bureau of Immigration and Naturalization waived all visa restrictions against his wife and child, after the State Department intervened in the national interest. The embassy gave him a passport good only for the U.S., lent him $435 for traveling expenses, and they passed through immigration on June 13, 1962, and were met by a 'representative' of Traveler's Aid Society

---

[37]KBG—Soviet Intelligence Agency.
[38]Safe house—a disguised intelligence residence for housing defectors and other sensitive persons.

named Spas T. Raikin, en route to Fort Worth, where they arrived two days later. To 'help them through customs,' or so he said. Is that name familiar to you, Van?

"There's a Spas T. Raikin known in Taiwan as secretary-general of the American Friends of the Anti-Bolshevik Nations, Inc." He felt better; now his head was like a computer. He touched his forehead lightly: cool, metallic, like a computer.

"Very good. Now, who would have sent *him?* Our people?"

"God knows. You get in that area, there are so many cheap little double- and triple-headers[39] you can't count them." They stretched and laughed. The presentation had been dazzling. Too much so. "The old hand hasn't lost its cunning," Preston said. Foster clapped him heartily on the shoulder and led him out.

"Let's have lunch outside; it's glorious Indian summer." He was sagging slightly from his exertions, but he hauled the spine up like a gun swinging into position. He kept talking.

"The FBI, CIA, State Department, and Office of Naval Intelligence all have files on him. The FBI interviewed him twice last year that we know of. He could be anything now. FBI, ONI, CIA—anything. Lowest possible echelon, of course. A few dollars here, a few there."

The older man was leading Preston out by the elbow, but as they hit the dazzling light and air of the green gardens and grounds, he seemed to lean on his junior officer slightly. He dropped his hand, "What do you think, Van? Would this have been your choice?" Preston's panic had evaporated; he knew he could do nothing to hurt the lean old man; with the vein throbbing in his temple and his eyes wincing against the bright sunlight, he was too vulnerable, had earned too much respect (*Ethos,* his professor of Aristotle at Harvard had called it).

---

[39] Double- and triple-headers—agents working for several employers at the same time.

Rising out of a bush, the huge old hound lumbered toward them, a lawn mower in the distance clacked, ducks could be heard but not seen in the September sky, and Preston thought to himself of Harvard days and Aristotle and how this strange new game was merely the "imitation of an action," something to be watched, as on a screen in the way that they had just now watched the rehearsal of the actor's or "subject's" life. All would be well if they did not depart from the basic unities of tragedy and allow the scenario to degenerate into a spy melodrama. No, the *Ethos* in the dark-clad gray figure reaching out to pet the hound was incapable of melodrama. All would be well.

"Would he have been your choice, Van?"

"I honestly can't say. Can he be 'Cubanized' in time to—"

"In the Soviet Union he doubled.[40]"

"But I mean, this agenda is—"

"Yes, of course. But then, you're only the backup team, aren't you? And the Chicago probabilities look very clean. But if you like, let's game some additional vignettes right now. Or should we forget about—what's his name?—Mr. Oswald, altogether, and tell him to give up his Fair Play for Cuba cover?"

"Well, but what about the FBI involvement?"

"That's precisely why I like him. We will run[41] him *through* our people in the bureau.[42] We will co-opt the fat old lady."[43] Foster chuckled dryly and turned toward the long beds of flowers, leaving Preston, like an actor without a line of dialogue, to slowly follow the retreating figure of old gray man and dog.

Birds walked about on the shining green grasses, of varying texture, that a black gardener was trimming. "The real problem is this, Van: In two decades there

---

[40] Doubled—gave or pretended to give information to two conflicting interests.
[41] Run—to direct an agent.
[42] Bureau—the Federal Bureau of Investigation.
[43] The fat old lady—The director of the FBI at that time.

will be seven *billion* human beings on this planet, most of them brown, yellow, or black—all of them hungry, and all of them determined to live. They'll swarm out of their breeding grounds into Europe and North America by the hundreds of millions, and there'll be no stopping them. No . . . stopping . . . at . . . all!" The sun hurt Preston's eyes as it danced off the white statuary: *The Wrestlers, Mercury Resting, Neptune, God of the Sea.*

Preston saw the thin eyes demanding some kind of answer. He wished the butler would arrive to break the spell. "We sound rather like gods reading the Doomsday Book, don't we?" He smiled, hoping the subject was exhausted. But Foster was deep into his reserves of nervous energy, and he rasped ahead, a little saliva forming at one corner of his red lips.

"Yet *some*one has to do something, don't they? Not only will the nations affected be better off, but the techniques developed there can be used to reduce our own excess population—blacks, Puerto Ricans, Mexican-Americans, poverty-prone whites, etc., etc., etc."

"That's one operation I'm glad I shan't have to take part in."

"I, too. New men for new times. However, it's still more humane than mass starvation or universal war. . . . These asters are doing rather well, don't you think? And the dahlias, of course—they're always marvelous. . . . It's a dirty business, isn't it?"

"Always was."

He was wound up again. The flowers had not helped. "Our greatest professional hazards are disillusionment, despair, exuberance, and madness. How many friends of yours have killed themselves?"

"Several. McIntyre was the last."

"Ah, yes. That was despair."

"I've also known one or two who went berserk and carried through an operation that wasn't in the orders. On their own—for no reason at all." Why had he said that?

"Exuberance or madness. They're much the same.

No such danger in this chap Oswald, is there? Going off on his own?" He paused at last. Someone was playing Mozart in the distance, in the house. Foster stooped a little and put his fingers to his eyes.

"Tired?"

"Didn't sleep last night."

"Plans?"

"No. Ecclesiastes."

They walked over to sit in a shaded glen. Foster talked as he moved from the brightness into the shadows. ". . . A living dog is better than a dead lion. . . . I have returned and seen that the race is not to the swift, nor the battle to the strong, nor yet riches to men of understanding; but time and chance happeneth to them all . . ." The dog came over. Foster rested his hand on the animal's head. He spoke so quietly that Preston was not sure he had heard. "I know we're doing the right thing."

Suddenly, Foster opened his eyes to study Preston's concerned look. He smiled, at last. "This is where I would like to spend the rest of my life."

"Why not quit? Who could criticize? I've thought of the same—"

The other laughed out loud this time. "Oh, no. 'I am in blood stepped in so far that to go back were as tedious as go o'er.' But you?" He stepped lightly, leaving Preston in suspense, to a concealed garden telephone, and ordered lunch. He took Preston's arm, and they began to walk slowly again. The butler passed with the wine. "No, you can't quit just yet. Not just now, when we have twenty-first-century communications and weapons systems in conflict with a primitive political system and Neanderthal politicians. In twenty years, the way time is flying, then, yes. Then our junior people—men and women who understand—will be in place on the Joint Chiefs of Staff, at the highest levels of State, Defense, Justice, and the multiversity system. Then the 'old hands' like me—and you too—and our little 'games' will all seem as remote as the Little Big Horn or the

Rough Riders, or any other glamorous American myth. Then, if you like, you can go back to the Yard[44] or take a compassionate leave."[45]

They had walked in a circle and were back at the table. Foster savored his wine, held it up to the sparkling air. "Do you know Nietzsche? . . . 'Arrows of longing for another shore.' That's what we are, Van. Arrows of longing for another shore."

Red Rocks, Colorado—September 12, 1963

The technician and his team were half-huddled around a low fire under the magnificent Colorado night sky. The technician stared up at the stars as he smoked; a plane winking by overhead intruded on the age-old symmetry of light and darkness. A cheap and sentimental pseudo-folksong about "Goin' Home" played dimly on the little portable radio. He looked over at the younger North American. "More coffee?"

"Yeah. It's cold as hell here at night. I'm glad we're gettin' out."

The Cubans smoked and listened to the music. They knew that the southerner didn't think much of them. The older cowboy type poured himself some coffee, chain-smoked, and started to talk in his usual preaching manner. "Shit, your blood's thin. Where I come from, it used to get forty below." The southerner had heard it before. "Shit."

The technician felt like an actor whose cue line had come up, "Where's that? Michigan?" Some anti-Communist radio minister was yelling just above the level of the low static on the radio.

"Minnesota."

Now the radio went dead altogether. "That's true," the technician said.

The cowboy spat; he was warming up. "Shit, I've

---
[44] The Yard—Harvard University.
[45] Compassionate leave—nervous breakdown.

seen the car stop. Frozen." He dug at his crotch. "Yeah, but that's God's country."

The technician felt obliged to go on. "Fishing?"

"Really." The southerner sat forward, hugging his legs. "That's me. God, I don't know what I'd give to be in Mississippi right now; do me some fishin' and huntin'. If there was any damn work, I believe I'd stay there for good."

The cowboy spat and nodded. "I believe I'll do me some huntin' right after Thanksgiving."

They had not been told yet that they might have to leave the country, or whether they had been chosen, or, for that matter, who they were going to kill. That information would come only five days before, too late for any carelessness or doubling. The technician refused even to think about leaving the country.

The older man continued to lecture his partner; he never even looked at the Cubans. "Hell, you can live on a lot less anywhere but New York or L.A. or like that."

The technician blew a smoke ring at the Big Dipper. "Big Dipper," he said, to no one in particular.

"Yeah, I'd rather hunt than fuck. I believe I might get me a job as a goddamned guide. Shit, yes." The southerner was interrupted by the radio suddenly starting to life again with a vicious nasal twang:

> The government of Communist Cuba has announced the execution of Benjamine Acosta Valdes. Valdes was charged with being a spy for the U.S. Central Intelligence Agency. Fidel Castro, in a bitter anti-American speech, warned that, quote, "United States leaders should not think that if they are aiding terrorist plans to eliminate Cuban leaders, they themselves will be safe"—unquote.

High above, another plane went over. Anyone looking down from that great height would not have seen the tents or the men or the fire. Would have seen nothing.

New Orleans, Louisiana—September 3, 1963

Van Preston and David Ferrie sat sipping Sazeracs at the Trade Mart bar, and commanding a spectacular view of the levee and Mississippi below. The soft light was kind to Ferrie, in his monkey hair and pancake makeup. They were discussing how to run Lee Harvey Oswald.

Preston was saying, "This is just a way to keep a most valuable man out of harm's way for a little while. You ride out there with us." They both smiled at the designation "valuable man" for Oswald. "But what am I supposed to tell Lee?" Ferrie whined. "You're not telling me *anything*."

Preston imitated Foster. "You poor boy. He has to be a registered voter first before we can get him in. Tell him it's an electrician's job at a state mental hospital for about two weeks, that he'll work with the Cubans we've got bivouacked out there. Tell him he'll have important conferences and contacts there. All right? You tell him."

"You going to give him a lie-detector test out there or something?"

"You better curb that imagination of yours. It's just a simple cover—history of mental illness. It wouldn't hurt any of us in a pinch, would it?" They laughed out loud this time and sipped their drinks cozily.

These were the few and fleeting moments of intimacy that illuminated the gloom of the clandestine life from time to time. "How about another Sazerac? Look at that—pollution pouring right into the river and the atmosphere! They're ruining the country." They both clicked their tongues and shook their heads; or, in Ferrie's case, he shook the monkey wig disapprovingly.

"Hungry?"
"Starving."
"Where shall we eat? Shall we splurge? Antoine's?"

Chicago, Illinois—September 15, 1963

A prematurely chilly Chicago Sunday.

The technician in charge of the first team stood at the bottom of the industrial dump that towered around him making a kind of natural bowl. He studied the pattern of bullet holes in the upper torso of a man drawn onto a heavy piece of cardboard. "No good," he half-shouted, against the wind, up to the thin man who looked enough like Lee Harvey Oswald to be his brother. The four men dressed in windbreakers and baseball hats began to curse and talk about the unending wind. Except for the Cuban. The Cuban cursed in Spanish about the specially tooled silencer on his Iver Johnson 22 pistol, which he was convinced was defective. The silencer was grooved out of three overlapping cylinders packed with three layers of "angel hair." He would give them an ultimatum about the thing, he decided.

The man who looked like Lee Harvey Oswald clambered down over the industrial junk and crushed automobiles to the basin of the heap. "We can't hear what you're saying in this goddamned wind. Can we please use the goddamned walkie-talkies, please."

Washington, D.C.—September 16, 1963

INTEROFFICE MEMO

> TO: JFK
> FROM: A.S.[46]
> DATE: 9-16-63
>   Maury Maverick, Jr.[47] writes that there "is a terrible fight going on down here in Texas and, to mention a highly delicate subject, this is true between Sen. Yarborough and the Vice President . . . as a private in the rear ranks of the Democratic party I deeply recommend that Yarborough be on the President's plane."
>   He also writes that Henry Gonzales[48] and some prominent Texas black be included in the group. He closed with the observation that we "should put Bobby Kennedy in the back of the plane with a whip in his hand to make everybody act nice."

(The memo was leaked to Foster within eighteen hours of the President's seeing it.)

New Orleans, Louisiana—September 16, 1963

Preston wheeled the air-conditioned, expensive black Lincoln up to the curb in front of an old white stucco house at 3330 Louisiana Avenue Parkway. As he left the air-conditioned vacuum of the interior, he was hit by the almost viscous New Orleans humidity and the

---

[46] A.S.—Arthur M. Schlesinger, Jr., presidential assistant to Mr. Kennedy.
[47] Maury Maverick, Jr.—Texas state executive committee and strong ally of Senator Ralph Yarborough, political enemy of Vice President Johnson.
[48] Henry Gonzales—Henry B. Gonzales, popular Texas Democratic Congressman.

sound of an old Dixieland jazz number. "Bucket's Got a Hole in It." He ignored the music and the weather, stepped quietly without knocking into the rooming house, climbed the stairs without losing his wind, and knocked lightly on David Ferrie's door. Silence—except for the faint sound of snoring from within, and a strange squeaking noise that he was unable to identify.

Now he opened the door slowly against the accumulated debris on the floor inside.

Inside was complete disorder, a miniature madhouse. Books on subjects from medicine and law to the occult and intelligence were thrown everywhere. Striated beams of light fighting their way through the closed and filthy window streaked off an oversize cross mounted on a homemade altar. Hand guns, rifles, and automatic weapons lay in frozen and lethal array.

David Ferrie lay sweating and asleep. He was nude. Preston stood transfixed in the doorway at the tableau before him; the stench of something unknown snapped his head back like a slap. There was no hair at all on Ferrie's body. Preston stared incredulously. Ferrie was naked even of eyebrows! A red monkey-hair wig had slipped off, to cover a corner of his face. A purplish monkey-hair eyebrow lay on the dirty pillow in its own tiny spot of light. The genitals minus the pubic protection were like a painting of a medieval saint in agony that Preston especially liked. Ferrie appeared to be dead. The exposed pink uncircumcised phallus crooked at an angle, like the worm of God, on the plump white body.

As the hellish vision washed over Preston and the stink slapped his senses, the screeching noise took on dimension and location: the floor was carpeted with squirming, racing, excreting, copulating, eating white mice.

Paralyzed, he twisted, looking for a way out. Preston was not afraid of the white mice, but the combination, the concatenation of stimuli, was an onslaught against his nervous system. To his left was another room.

Through the doorway he could see the next circle of hell: a dust-covered dining area. The first object there to catch him was a set of scarlet-and-white false teeth grinning at him from a fake-walnut sideboard. Preston's eyes limped from prop to prop: a propellerless model airplane, a piano, a chipped head of the Virgin in plaster, an American flag, a college pennant, a makeup kit, another cross, four rifles, shotgun shells and .22-rifle blanks, a radio transmitter tuning unit, signal-corps field telephones, a big practice bomb, a sword, and as many as five hundred books on cancer and other research. He did not see the whips, chains, hoods, and more exotic torture instruments that he knew David had hidden somewhere. "Discipline" and "correction" were the euphemisms used in the sexual underworld for Ferrie's habits. For a moment his mind went blank, and he felt a dizziness.

Preston turned back from the diabolical inventory. He was not frightened or disgusted by David Ferrie, nor did he think him mad. He knew him to be an accomplished pianist, a hypnotist, a chemist, a queer kind of hellish Renaissance man. He was rather fond of "fairy" (the low pun was a word of camaraderie between them), and more importantly, knew him to be a fearless and highly versatile operative. At the clandestine level, Ferrie's outrageous homosexual and religious practices were an asset for both cover and recruitment work. Ferrie was running informants, provocateurs, and penetration agents for them now as "Fairy" in the homosexual clubs; as "Father Ferette" in the Apostolic Order of the Orthodox Old Catholic Church and a dozen sectarian offshoots, including magic and witchcraft cults; as "Captain Ferrie," Civil Air Patrol and Air National Guard; and he was the prime mover in those circles of contract agents[49] working out of New Orleans, who constituted the dagger's point into Cuba and the Caribbean. A

---

[49]Contract agents—operatives, paid by a handler, but whose names will never appear anywhere in the official files of the intelligence agency.

weird but valuable man; but, not having seen his apartment before Preston had not realized how weird.

Preston now picked his way through and over the seething, squealing white mice, at one point gripping an arm of the crucifix with his fingertips. Then he stood over the fish-white creature with the scarred face; the phallus, as if sensing the presence of flesh and blood, began to twitch and then to stiffen slightly, so he was not dead. *Alopecia totalis,* that was the condition of hairlessness, Preston mused, his eyes going slightly out of focus as the worm of penis stirred. He reached down and shook the bed. "Dave, wake up, we're late."

"What?" The eye opening on the eyebrowless face was like an egg breaking.

"We're late." A chase of mice raced over his shoes. "David, what in the world *is* all of this? These *mice?*"

"Cancer research."

Clinton, Louisiana—September 16, 1963

Preston adjusted the radio dial, trying to keep the Franz Liszt concerto in focus as the black Lincoln bumped over the Parish road leading into town. Ferrie leaned forward from the back seat and patted Oswald on the back and sort of crooned the good news that "This is a sleepy old town. We'll be in and out in five minutes, and Lee will be a registered voter!" They all smiled.

Ferrie was becoming altogether too provocative, he noted; for instance, staging an anti-Castro demonstration to coincide with one of Oswald's bogus *pro*-Castro appearances. "This is always the danger with provocateurs," Foster had warned him once years ago.

Preston jammed on the brakes; the black girl with the picket sign had darted out from the curb as the car turned into the main street. Preston felt as if he were watching a television special. There were the Negroes picketing, led by the Congress of Racial Equality, and opposing their right to register and vote was a milling crowd of an ad hoc White Citizens' Council. Some local police were there joking with the whites. The poor whites and blacks all stopped to stare at the big black 1963 Lincoln and the three cool men inside who were looking out at them in the hot and dusty street of their poverty and humiliation. Inside, Preston said, "Sleepy! What in Christ's name is going on?" as if he did not know, but Ferrie chimed in, "Christ, the apes must be trying to register again; let's get out of here."

"I don't like that word," said Oswald, looking straight ahead now.

Preston cut in, "And precisely how would you suggest we escape? We'll just go ahead with our plan."

Now Ferrie cut him off, "With all these witnesses? They probably never even saw a Lincoln Continental before."

Angry black and white faces were shouting around the car. Preston turned the air-conditioning on high and turned up the volume of the music so that the passionate figures in the street—chanting and singing and cursing at the big car from time to time—looked like actors in a silent film: the teeth and tongue coming in and out of view, the eyes wide and tentative. "Birmingham." The black people seemed to keep saying something about Birmingham. A "bombing in Birmingham."

"Calm down," Preston said very low.

Oswald turned to him, "What's so top secret about registering to vote so I can get a job? I mean, it's not exactly a hot item for the press."

"Nothing. It doesn't really matter—just calm down, Mr. Ferrie—it doesn't matter." He signaled to the police to make a way for them to the courthouse.

New York, New York—September 20, 1963

John Kennedy stood at the rostrum of the United Nations.

The world has not escaped from the darkness. The long shadows of conflict and crisis envelop us still. . . . My presence here today is not a sign of crisis, but of confidence . . . we believe that all the world—in Eastern Europe as well as Western, in Southern Africa as well as Northern, in old nations as well as new—the people must be free to choose their own future, without discrimination or dictation, without coercion or subversion. . . . Why should the United States and the Soviet Union, in preparing for such . . . expeditions, become involved in immense duplications of research, construction, and expenditure? Surely we should explore whether the scientists and astronauts of our two countries—indeed of all the world—cannot work together in the conquest of space, sending someday in this decade to the moon not the representatives of a single nation, but the representatives of all our countries. . . .

The contest will continue—the contest between those who see a monolithic world and those who believe in diversity—but it should be a contest in leadership and responsibility instead of destruction, a contest in achievement instead of intimidation. Speaking for the United States of America, I welcome such a contest.

For we believe that truth is stronger than error —and that freedom is more enduring than coercion. And in the contest for a better life, all the world can be a winner. . . . Never before has man had such capacity to control his own environment, to end thirst and hunger, to conquer poverty and disease. To banish illiteracy and massive human misery. We have the power to make this the best generation of mankind in the history of the world —or to make it the last. . . . For as the world renounces the competition of weapons, competition in ideas must flourish—and that competition must be as full and as far as possible.

What the United Nations has done in the past is less important than the tasks for the future. . . .

My fellow inhabitants of this planet; let us take our stand here in this assembly of nations. And let us see if we, in our own time, can move the world to a just and lasting peace.

Red Rocks Park, Colorado, September 20, 1963

The technician slammed the jeep to a stop in the clearing, honking the horn as if he were drunk, and shouting as the team came running out of their tents: "Orders from God! Get packed! We're going to Montana, for Christ's sake! Billings, Montana!"

Vienna, Virginia—September 21, 1963

Foster and Preston settled down with coffee in the communications room. The sixteen-millimeter film of Oswald in New Orleans began as Preston narrated woodenly.

"The 'Cubanization process.' Here our candidate distributes Fair Play for Cuba leaflets on Canal Street."

"I recognize that little oyster bar." Foster smiled. "Who is the other man with him?"

"We got him from the unemployment office for two dollars an hour."

"Well within the budget." Foster beamed. He felt good. An old hand back in harness was the way he thought of himself these bracing and active autumn days.

But Preston was cold, the hot coffee did no good, Foster's glowing ambience only intensified his feeling of being like a cold machine. He went on mechanically. "No problem, they only passed them out for twenty minutes, until the media left. He's working out of Guy Bannister's building. You remember him?" In the film the camera panned the building. The address on Camp Street was 544, but the building abutted two streets, Camp and Lafayette, and the address on the other side of the same building was 531 Lafayette. So that it was obvious that the same place had two addresses: 544 Camp Street and 531 Lafayette Street. Preston's voice underscored the visuals as if it were prerecorded.

"It works out. Bannister's organizations—the Anti-Communist League of the Caribbean and Friends of Democratic Cuba are at 531 Lafayette, and Oswald's address is listed as 544 Camp. Keeps him under our wing, saves money, and no one puts them together. But we can change it."

"No, it's already done. Doesn't matter anyway. What are Bannister's details, again? Militant ultra-right-wing, isn't he?"

"Very much so. FBI special agent in charge of Chicago office. We used him in sixty-one as a cutoff man[50] and equipment purchaser for Cuba and Guatemala. Now he's a licensed private investigator. He staged a highly publicized disassociation tableau,[51] a really nasty brawl in a French Quarter restaurant, you may recall?"

Foster studied him. "Exactly what are you telling the subject, Van?"

Preston swallowed. This was key. "We're letting him 'find out'—through another man, David Ferrie actually—that he is part of an executive action aimed at Castro." Foster scrutinized him. "Telling him that it's government all the way—with the A.G.[52] himself running the show. Just as if the original action against Castro—which RFK *was* running—had been revived. If he doesn't go for it, we're prepared to let him discover that it's domestic, and merely a spectacular right-wing simu-

---
[50]Cutoff man—an intelligence network area contact for funds and communications.
[51]Disassociation tableau—a scene staged to make an intelligence agent appear available for new employment.
[52]A.G.—The U.S. Attorney General, Robert F. Kennedy

lation to, as they will put it, 'scare the shit' out of the country and alert the public to the 'Communist menace'; and that he and the others will be using blanks."

"Blanks?"

"Yes. Why do you—"

"No. No. That's very interesting. Are you satisfied that it will work?"

"I would stake my career on it."

"Yes. Indeed."

Foster finally smiled, and Preston began to breathe regularly. "All right, Van, play the Funkspiel[53] but don't ever underestimate your man; remember, he's informing for two other agencies: the FBI and the Dallas Red Squad."[54]

"Of course," interjected Preston, "the odds are still against this subject or any of my teams even seeing action . . . aren't they?"

On the screen a very unconvincing exchange of blows between Oswald and a heavyset Cuban were being acted out. The police arrived and Oswald was arrested, but not the Cuban. In the dark, Foster lifted an eyebrow as if he were watching a B movie. "This is the arrest tableau, I take it? Good. A lot of credibility; high profile[55] and deep cover[56]. The film ran out jerkily, and the operator turned up the room lights. Preston nursed his coffee, and looking at Foster, saw the eyes of the other men gleaming with a cheerful and wicked luster, as if narcotized.

"Here is the contingency list you requested." Foster read aloud: "His 'nonpolitical' touring plans include appearances in Pennsylvania, Wisconsin, Minnesota, North Dakota, Montana, Wyoming, Utah, Washington,

---

[53] Funkspiel—literally, the radio game. A World War II term referring to the feeding of false information via double agents.

[54] Red Squad—police intelligence unit in charge of surveillance of political radicals.

[55] High profile—drawing attention to an impostor.

[56] Deep cover—an agent in impenetrable disguise.

Oregon, Nevada, Florida, Illinois, California, and Texas. I think you'll agree that the choice narrows down to Chicago, Miami, Dallas—not necessarily in that order."

Preston put down the cold coffee. "What about Chicago law enforcement?"

"Did you ever see a thin Chicago policeman?" Now, what exactly did that mean, wondered Preston. "Political situation—"

" 'Hogs and damned skulking wolves,' I think the phrase is. Classic big-city machine. Concerned exclusively with covering up its own mess. Slow to react, 'clumsy.' " Foster was clearly excited by the younger man's interrogation. Preston knew this after all these years, and he kept feeding the cues to the old spy-master that made his eyes sparkle, his voice resonate.

"What about the mayor? He's a very emotional man, *and* he supported him *before* Los Angeles."

"Yes, he'll weep all night, and then support his successor—just as strongly. He's a political animal. He's typical. A sheer opportunist." He stood and spoke in a louder tone, as if he were lecturing at the War College or holding forth before some full committee meeting. Preston feigned rapt attention. He had a feeling of sadness, because once the reverence—a lifetime ago, it seemed now—had been real.

"Of course. These powerbroker 'men of the people,' they're all like the Vicar of Bray—quite prepared to 'adjust' to any scenario: communistic, fasc:stic. or even, thank God, a constitutional republic. If only these 'popular' leaders would *lead,* we could all retire quite happily.

"No, they've managed to *lead* their beloved 'masses,' happily, to the brink of hell." He was no longer talking to Preston. He seemed to be trying to convince some unseen presence.

"But if we intend to survive, then there must be a change, mustn't there? Progress, adaptation. We've gone over it again and again. We're in the midst of a triple revolution[57] *and* a cold war, and swift change from the bottom is, unfortunately, no longer possible, is it? The big bombs are 'ticking,' aren't they? So what choice have we but to press on with these extraordinary 'games' of ours, where there are no winners—only losers. And we keep the 'game' going because the alternative is World War III. Not some utopian ideology of revolution, but permanent disorder, anarchy, and the final war."

Billings, Montana—September 25, 1963

By midmorning most of the rim-rock city's downtown occupants had drifted out to line the sidewalks on either side of the street. The President had already landed at the municipal airport, delivered a few introductory remarks, placed himself in the limousine, and now moved with the motorcade through the outskirts of town. He had enjoyed seeing the Crow Indians in full regalia do a short ceremonial dance for him, and the schoolchildren and their teachers. The thirty-mile-an-hour wind had them all shivering slightly and made the "Welcome, Mr. President" banners flap erratically.

Several hours earlier, the technician had also been in the same airport. He had rented a car and followed this same route all the way through the downtown area. Passing out of the commercial section, he had parked in a nearby residential street and walked slowly back downtown. Billings residents began to fill up the downtown area, many men wearing the same style Levi's, open shirts, and western hats as the technician. He walked slowly along the several blocks to his destination, noting the provincialism that still clung to this largest Montana city. It seemed to him that such a location would be ideal, unless the leaden clouds gave way to snow.

[57]Triple revolution—the exponential growth in (1) population; (2) technology; (3) human-rights expectations.

The Turf was just emptying. Most of its daily breakfast customers were moving on to their jobs as the technician stepped in. He glanced about the large high-ceilinged room. Spotting a booth toward the rear, he nodded toward the familiar faces there. He walked directly toward the four men that were on his team, pushed his hat back on his head, and sat with them. No one was eating, but he ordered a short stack and coffee.

None of them spoke until the technician had been served his coffee. "You fellows spotted your locations?"

They nodded "yes."

"Any trouble of any kind?"

Each shook "no."

"Okay, good. Leave here two at a time in five minutes. I'll be on the street; you'll be able to see me—when I wave my hat. See you back here right after, okay?"

It was good they were not the first team, he thought; something besides the Cubans was "off." These rehearsals—and there must be other teams in other cities with other Cubans practicing, too—this far in advance made the probabilities of a leak dangerously high, and all the gobbledygook in Virginia would not excuse that kind of foul-up, as far as he was concerned.

Now, outside, standing among the pockets of people looking down the street at the approaching motorcade, the technician glanced backward to his left, then to his right, and finally across the street. The motorcade flowed into the block in which the technician and his team were stationed. Where were the S.S. agents on the back of the car? He began a mental countdown calculation. The noise and activity peaked. At about sixty feet out he reached up and spun his big hat. His height made the signal conspicuous enough over the friendly, cheering crowd for each team member to see. He counted to himself, "One, two, three." The President noticed the waving hat also and turned slightly in its direction. His eyes held the technician's for a fraction of a second;

grinning, he returned the salute as the limousine moved on down the street.

The Turf held only a few coffee-drinking customers. The technician sat in the same booth he had been in earlier, sipping coffee, watching the front door. His team entered as a group and joined him. A waitress followed them to the booth and slipped away to bring them coffee.

"How d'you think ya did?" the technician asked collectively.

While the Cubans and the younger North American nodded affirmatively, the older man replied, "I might have shaded him the first time, but the second was right in there."

"Any trouble getting out and picking everyone up?" This directed to the young North American.

"Naw, it was a breeze, hardly any traffic at all around the backs of those buildings."

"I think we did it." The technician rose to go. "Well, I've gotta hit the road, I'll be in touch in the usual way. Don't any of you get lost."

They stared after the technician. It bothered them that his heart did not seem to be in the operation. The money was fantastic; why the hell didn't he show a little more leadership?

"Listen," said the Cowboy, "there's somethin' funny goin' on here. These dry runs ain't worth shit." He spat on the floor. "You reckon these cocksuckers is fixin' to set us up?"

They looked at each other, then quickly down at their coffee. Earlier they had guessed, but for two days now they had known for sure. In the silence of the booth, as they sat there, they could hear a noise, dimly, rising.

Outside, the President paused in his set speech, then took the leap: ". . . What we hope to do is lessen the chance of a military collision between the two great nuclear powers which together have the power to kill three hundred million people in the space of a day. That is why we support the test ban treaty. Not because things are going to be easier in our lives, but because we have a chance to avoid being burned."

In the cafe, the "Executive Action" second team heard a low but rising cry of what they did not recognize as hope from the conservative far-Western throng in an adjacent square.

Highway 10 stretched 325 miles between Missoula and Billings. The technician was more than halfway to the "Garden City" of western Montana as he pulled back onto the main highway from the gas station in Butte. There was not a lot of traffic, and the highway was in fairly good shape. He had been making good time. He expected that he would arrive between six and seven. They could get dressed up a little, go to dinner at the Florence. Anne always liked it there. She'd probably get a little tipsy; she always did when they celebrated his homecoming. They'd make love, and then maybe they could talk about the future some. He lingered over the anticipated intimacy. It had been a long time since he had been with his wife. She was a real woman in his eyes. His current assignment added to the desire. If only he could tell her.

As a boy he had been caught prankishly playing with fire. The neighbors had threatened him with severe consequences, frightening him beyond reason. Running home, he had confessed his crime to his mother. Amidst the tears and fears, his mother had embraced him and allowed him to cry away his fears into her breasts. The warmth, love, and security of that moment remained with him. He doubted that he would ever cry like that again. Yet he would cling to Anne in the same way, sucking her breasts, feeling their swelling, warm reality against his face.

"Missoula 150 miles"—the road sign interrupted his visceral reverie. He checked his watch. Three thirty. Good. He would be there on schedule. He settled into his driving confronting the realities and implications, as far as his relationship with Anne was concerned, of

Missoula, Montana—September 25, 1963

The waitress presented a second bottle of wine. The technician glanced at it briefly, uncomfortably. As she went about refilling both his and Anne's glasses, she managed to spill a drop or two at every stop. When she retrieved the empty bottle, a few red drops settled and spread in that spot as the new bottle replaced the old.

Anne leaned close to him, protectively placing a hand on his leg. "I'm getting intoxicated." The words were thick, endorsing their meaning.

The waitress placed a tentative hand on the unread menus. "Will you order now, sir?" She already knew the answer but waited sullenly to be told.

"Are we going to eat or not?" Tom, too, knew the answer, but waited for the confirming words.

"I told you, you go ahead, I'm all tied up."

"Not at all?"

"No, I'm all right."

He pushed at the menus slightly. The waitress promptly picked them up and sped across the room to her station, failing to see an upraised waving hand in another corner of the room.

"You know how I feel about food."

He watched her pull steadily at her wineglass. "You want something from the drugstore?"

"It's really strange. It's three years last week, and I still get all tied up when you either come home or go out on a field trip."

They both drank from their glasses to cover the silence. She was right, it was three years. Three years ago they had come here to the Florence Hotel dining room to celebrate. They had thought at the time that it was the best place in Missoula. That night the time had been magic, but now each time they returned they drew something away of what had been deposited then. Tonight the balance was zero. Anne continued speaking but sounded less drunk than before. Looking at her, he thought, as he always used to, how beautiful and intelligent she must look to her sixth- and seventh-graders.

"I had pork roast and everything; why didn't you let me cook dinner at home? Who wants to go out after you've been away four weeks?"

"I'm sorry." He truly was. It had seemed like a good idea at the moment. He had wanted to do something nice for her, but she too had wanted to do something for him. They knew they were both being something less than honest; he had hoped to forestall any chance of the kind of episode they were building to. She had only wanted to prove her worth. Both were failing.

"I thought you liked this place. We always...."

"I don't cook when you're gone." She finished the wine in her glass and reached for the bottle, but he anticipated her, refilling both glasses. The second bottle was nearly empty now.

"Well, you can cook it tomorrow." He hoped that that expectation could be fulfilled and that he would not have to bring any more sadness to her. They regarded each other closely for a minute and then another, longer minute. It could have been a first meeting, as the melancholy loneliness each felt began to dissolve into a careful consideration. Anne reached tentative fingertips across the shadow of his beard; the lightness of her touch hit him harder than a rifle's recoil.

"You certainly have a wonderful tan. You look wonderful." Her eyes were bright. He finished the wine in his glass and emptied the bottle into it and then threw that down too. "The weather's been terrible here," she slurred.

"Desert surveying. Hotter than hell." Reaching out to flip over the check, he took a few bills out, leaving them on the table. He slid out of the booth, helping her up, protectively. They stopped at the coat area and then walked into the lobby of the hotel. Standing now in front of the elevators, he helped her on with her well-cut cloth coat with the beaver collar.

As she fluffed her hair up over the collar, she spoke back over her shoulder, a little more brightly than she really felt, "Oh, I've got that Peace Corps literature."

He had been surveying the lobby, enjoying the quiet simplicity that this place always communicated to him. It was built in a style that had been nationally popular twenty-five years earlier: rounded corners, marble floors, a glass-brick wall at one end of the desk, plenty of low overstuffed furniture, and a painting of three cowboys riding into the room from a dusky ominous horizon, hanging over the now seldom used fireplace at the far end of the lobby. It was always kept immaculately clean and neat, no matter how busy. He felt for this place and its isolated charm. But even here he knew there would be those that would hire him; even within this architectural anachronism the power game existed, "What?"

"The Peace Corps form we talked about." They passed through the revolving door out onto Higgins Avenue. She was aware of his reverie and allowed the slushing noise of the fabric strips on the door-section bottoms to drown her out. "Oh, never mind." They could talk about it later, tomorrow perhaps. Out on the street the night air reminded them that September in Montana was nothing so much as a preview of winter. She turned to him, trying to cast out any vestige of melancholy, snuggling in close to his left side, wrapping both arms about his; she turned her face up to him, completely without guile, guilt, or fear. "Well, you look good, anyway."

The early-fall chill in the air washed away the lassitude of the wine as they walked home north on Missoula's main street. In the street the usual assortment of cars cruised the drag. The university and high-school students prowling along, looking at and being looked at.

Demonstrating their emerging personalities in modifications of the cars they drove, revealing the adolescence of their more recent past in the way they drove.

After a few steps he gently extracted his arm from hers and hugged her close to him. She burrowed into him, seeking the warmth and closeness, pressing her head into his chest. "This time we've got to go to that Gulf Coast place. You'll get a suntan there . . . and it's peaceful," he said, and squeezed her more tightly into himself, tilting over so that his cheek caressed the top of her head. He inhaled her scent, her hair, felt alive. "Your hair looks nice that way."

"Oh, thanks—it's a 'Jackie cut.' " Newly fashionable hair styles were one luxury she allowed herself. It had been very difficult to do, but he was away so much, and the attention she received from the hairdresser could not have been more harmless. "Oh! I wish we could have gone before school started. The next time off I get is the end of October, the state NEA conference—"

He stopped her, resenting any other obligation or commitment: "I'll have to work it out."

"You know, the first few weeks, you just begin to get to know the kids and all, and I'd hate to . . ." The words trailed away, muffled into her collar and his chest. It was as if the resentment of the other's life had physically moved from him to her. It was too late. Both felt the unreasonableness of their attitudes slice between them. He tried to halt it.

"Take sick leave. . . . You know, you don't need to work if you—"

"What am I supposed to do all day? I'd work at night too, if I could." The damage had been done. She pulled away from his embrace, physically punctuating the emotional distance. "I'm thirty-five years old, I want—"

"I give you all the money." It was the last thing he wanted to say. Too many nights alone had dulled his sensitivity, just as they had sharpened hers. They were now merely another couple bickering about money, the mechanics of survival, as if they spent every day and night together. Their pace quickened as they stepped off the curb at Broadway to cross Higgins Avenue. It infuriated her when he opened up his long stride and she had to half-trot to keep up. Her trim but womanly body was exactly one foot shorter than his.

"I'm not talking about money, Tom! Are you talking about money? You told me you're not on a long-term contract; why don't you stay and. . . ." They stopped for the light to change that would allow them to cross Broadway and then continue on along toward the post office. The traffic signal stared back at them.

"I'm committed." She ignored the undertone of despair in his husky voice. He had no right to expect her to hear his meaning, and he knew that even if she had, he would have been unable to describe or explain it.

"Christ, why do you even come home!" The light winked a green-eyed invitation at them. "I was going to write you not to come home at all this time, but I didn't even have an address!" She had not intended to mention that, but now that it was out, she said it all as they turned eastward on Broadway. "I just feel humiliated all the time."

Her voice broke, and some wetness reflected the streets' lights from her cheeks. She shivered. It might have been the chill wind off Hellgate Canyon, but it wasn't. They slowed their pace, now only a couple of blocks from home. She brushed at the tears, wishing it hadn't happened, and sniffed vigorously, as though it were the cold weather.

They walked in silence, each sorting through a multitude of possibilities, looking for a way out. He glanced at her sideways, impressed as always at the determination in the quiet Irish-English features. She deserved more; he wanted to give her more. He wanted to give himself more.

"I won't leave you without a forwarding address again. I couldn't help it. I swear. And listen, I'm getting too old for this field work, even though they pay the earth." They turned north on Pattee Street and angled across the street in front of the post office's side door. "I'm going to find out if. . . . Or maybe I could go back to teaching."

Now he slowed their pace, caught up in his fantasy. Anne fell a step or two behind to watch him. His energy now was directed outward and years seemed to slip from his shoulders. Trotting a step or two to catch up, she offered encouragement. "You could get—"

"Sure, teach government and basketball, like after Korea." He shuffled a step or two to his right, crouching slightly and pivoting on his left foot. He followed through, turning quickly, catching her in a two-armed embrace. He lifted her up, her eyes shining into his.

"We could stay here or move wherever you say. I love you, honey, but I get so lonesome. . . . I'm all tied up."

A cloud passed over his face, and he slowly lowered her to the sidewalk. They were on the corner of Pine Street now, the apartment just across the street, its porch light burning. As her feet touched the cement just in front of his, she reached up, brushing at his hair, patting at his cheek. "You're not afraid to go home, are you?"

He held her eyes for a long moment. It was all there, and now she knew, despite her cultivated naïveté. He was containing some big hurt inside himself and couldn't tell her how or what. She had to trust and endure, but she had already done that. Three years of trusting endurance and a schoolroom full of other women's children was not what she had had in mind. But he was worth it. She knew he would be worth it.

He gathered her under his left arm and started them across the street. In the middle of the street he stopped and looked down at her, his voice, from long ago, when he was barely fourteen, asking a girl for a dance. "Take you to the Gulf Coast, honey?"

The question rattled on the chilled surface of the street. She broke into a grin. "Promise?" He broke contact and began to run to the apartment door. She chased him, "Promise!" More a demand now than before.

He leaped the four steps, threw open the door, and feinted to one side as she tumbled into the living room. He bounded in after her, flinging the door shut with a bang that bounced back at them from the large graystone Federal Building directly across the street.

Salt Lake City, Utah—September 26, 1963

Standing in the awesome Mormon Tabernacle, the President delivered a speech that certain people in Texas, if not Virginia, called "the outright Communist line."

> I urge this generation of Americans who are the fathers and mothers of 350 million Americans who will live in this country in the year 2000, and I want those Americans who live in 2000 to feel that those of us who had positions of responsibility in the sixties did our part. . . .
> If this nation is to survive and succeed in the real world of today, we must acknowledge the realities of the world; and it is those realities that I mention now.
> We must first of all recognize that we cannot remake the world simply by our own command. When we cannot even bring all of our own people into full citizenship without acts of violence, we can understand how much harder it is to control events beyond our borders. Every nation has its own traditions, its own values, its own aspirations. Our assistance from time to time can help other nations preserve their independence and advance their growth, but we cannot remake them in our own image. We cannot enact their laws, nor can we operate their governments or dictate our policies.

Second, we must recognize that every nation determines its policies in terms of its own interests. "No nation," George Washington wrote, "is to be trusted further than it is bound by its interest; and no prudent statesman or politician will depart from it." National interest is more powerful than ideology, and the recent developments within the Communist empire show this very clearly. Friendship, as Palmerston said, may rise or wane, but interests endure.

The United States has rightly determined, in the years since 1945, under three different administrations, that our interest, our national security, the interest of the United States of America, is best served by preserving and protecting a world of diversity in which no one power or no one combination of powers can threaten the security of the United States. The reason that we moved so far into the world was our fear that at the end of the war, and particularly when China became Communist, that Japan and Germany would collapse, and these two countries which had so long served as a barrier to the Soviet advance, and the Russian advance before that, would open up a wave of conquest of all Europe and all of Asia, and then the balance of power turning against us, we would finally be isolated and ultimately destroyed. That is what we have been engaged in for eighteen years, to prevent that happening, to prevent any one monolithic power having sufficient force to destroy the United States.

And third, we must recognize that foreign policy in the modern world does not lend itself to easy, simple black-and-white solution. If we were to have diplomatic relations only with those countries whose principles we approved of, we would have relations with very few countries in a very short time. If we were to withdraw our assistance from all governments who are run differently from our own, we would relinquish half the world immediately to our adversaries. If we were to treat foreign policy as merely a medium for delivering self-righteous sermons to supposedly inferior people, we would give up all thought of world influence or world leadership.

For the purpose of foreign policy is not to provide an outlet for our own sentiments of hope or indignation; it is to shape real events in a real world. We cannot adopt a policy which says that if something does not happen, or others do not do exactly what we wish, we will return to "Fortress America." That is the policy, in this changing world, of retreat, not of strength. . . .

The position of the United States, I believe, is happier and safer when history is going for us rather than when it is going against us. And we have history going for us today, but history is what men make it. The future is what men make it. . . .

Missoula, Montana—September 26, 1963

Dawn squeezed through Hellgate Canyon. Above Mount Jumbo, black lead gradually turned to gray. Anne lay in her bed, head propped up on a pillow scrunched into the headboard. Her familiar furnishings revealed themselves to her one by one. The trail of clothes, his and hers, that ended at the foot of the bed, jolted her slightly. At first it was only the uncharacteristic disarray, but gaining recognition of it, she remembered how he had grabbed her up as they came crashing home last night. She held him now with his crew-cut head against her bared breast as he slept, his arm stretched across her middle. She fussed at his hair, petted his face, traced the swell of his lips with her fingers, from one corner to the other, finally gently petting her nipple. Firm and erect, she pressed it against his lips. She tracked the nipple around his mouth from bottom lip to upper lip. He moved slightly, firming his grip around her waist. She tensed, her buttocks firm and tight, legs slightly spread, toes curled tight against the bottoms of her feet. Her eyelids lowered, remaining closed just slightly longer than a blink. It was over.

Last night, behind the slammed shut door, he had overwhelmed her, taken her to him with a determined and intense passion. Clutching each other, moving together crab-walk-wise from the living room to the bedroom, removing their own clothes one-handed so as not to have to relinquish the contact. By the time they had fallen across the bed, he was so aroused and purposeful that that alone would have been sufficient for her. But her own drives had been working, too, and she had only needed for him to hold her up at an angle, as he towered over her, and gently rub her throbbing clitoris. She had worked up the courage to ask this of him, and as she saw the knotted shaft of his phallus plunging in and out of the bushy triangle of her sex, she had called out, "Don't shoot, oh, please don't shoot yet, Tommy!" And he, the technician, had bit his lower lip and held back by picturing the President, his wife, and his children dead in their coffins.

He had fallen asleep on her breasts just an instant before she had dropped off. Her detailed reverie had started that strange build in her.

Enough! She took note of the full light inside the apartment. She had to get ready for school. She slipped from bed, substituting a pillow for herself under him. She covered him completely, kissed his cheek lightly, gazed at him for a full two minutes. Then she turned and began doing what she always did at this hour on a Thursday morning.

II / OCTOBER

Dallas, Texas—October 3, 1963

U.S. EXPECTS VIETNAM PULLOUT BY END OF '65
SECURITY COUNCIL TELLS ESTIMATE AFTER REPORT BY M'NAMARA, TAYLOR

Washington—The United States can complete the major share of its military mission in South Vietnam by the end of 1965 unless the "deeply serious" political turmoil there causes a setback.

This policy position was stated by the National Security Council with the approval of President Kennedy after Secretary of Defense Robert S. McNamara and General Maxwell D. Taylor reported to him Wednesday on their week-long survey of the Vietnamese struggle against Communism.

McNamara informed the President and the Security Council that the military situation has progressed to the point where 1,000 American troops can be withdrawn by the end of this year. It is estimated unofficially that the United States has around 15,000 military personnel in the southeast Asian nation.

CRITICAL OF DIEM

The U.S. declaration strongly criticized the government of President Ngo Dinh Diem and his brother, Defense Minister Ngo Dinh Nhu, for its repressive actions against Buddhists.

While the political crisis has not yet endangered military operations against the Communists, the Security Council said it "could do so in the future."

It did not name any government officials in its indictment of the Vietnamese political situation. But it decreed that the United States will continue to oppose "any repressive actions in South Vietnam."

LODGE CONCURS

Ambassador Henry Cabot Lodge, who has been in close contact with the President and conferred with McNamara and Taylor, concurred in the report. . . .

Billionaire R. Howard Ferguson pushed a button: a completely disguised wall safe opened, and the old man pulled out a strange-looking red telephone. He dialed Virginia. The telephone, as well as the one in the Virginia communications room, was electronically scrambled so that no one could tap the conversation.

"Foster, you read the papers? I can't hardly believe it! The son-of-a-bitch has set a date! Do you believe he means it?" He listened to Foster's answer. Foster was one of the few men in the world that Howard Ferguson would listen to.

"Christ's sake, Christ's sake! A red takeover by sixty-five? That's how I read it, too. Now, look, I'm just an old country boy, and I've seen some sights and done some things in the Trans-Jordan, but I always stopped that kind of thing at the water's edge, but this is too much for me. He's buggin' out, he's kissing their ass, I mean *he's selling us out!* He's a traitor, he oughta be shot down like a dog.

"How much money do you need, I'll get it to you through Mexico City and my number-one man—who's gonna look after my interests with you East Coast boys —his name's Allen, Arthur Allen."

Then he dialed Henry Prince, whom he had not talked with since the first Virginia meeting in Evanston, Illinois. Prince was not home. Ferguson decided to sit and wait. He sat there, drained, immobile.

Ferguson's bank had lent Henry Prince more than fifty million dollars for a plane, the G222, that would never—could never—fly. "Unless the investigation of Prince's American Synergy consortium is stopped right now," decided the old man of oil, "we are all going to jail."

So the Vietnam story was less than half his reason for making the commitment, finally.

He tried another number. As he waited, he fumbled a bottle of bourbon out of the desk and poured a shot. The white liver-spotted hands shook as he raised the tumbler. He thought, "I can't stop it anyway. It's out of my hands now." He gagged slightly on the whiskey.

Washington, D.C.—October 5, 1963

Preston skimmed the page as he reread:

> ... in order to stave off the day of reckoning and the need for decision they have put at the head of our affairs a grand magician ... this is the senile, arrogant master who will stride us: here he comes, our mumbo-jumbo. ... It is not right, my fellow countrymen, you who know very well all the crimes committed in our name. ... Eight years of silence, what degradation! And your silence is of no avail; today, the blinding sun of torture is at its zenith; it lights up the whole country. Under that merciless glare, there is not a laugh that does not ring false, not a face that is not painted to hide fear or anger, not a single action that does not betray our disgust, and our complicity ... today, we are bound hand and foot, humiliated and sick with fear, we cannot fall lower. ...

He closed the book and turned the Mozart record over. The writing, by Jean-Paul Sartre on revolution in the colonized countries, was profoundly disturbing to him. "Revolution"—anarchy and disorder, Foster called it. He sighed, these weekends of reading and music were no longer the pleasure to him they had once been. He poured himself another cup of coffee, and for reassurance surveyed the elegant and austere bachelor quarters that he had made so many sacrifices to decorate to perfection, as he understood impeccable masculine taste. His eyes caught and held on some metallic flakes near the compact wall bar. He knelt down to study them, but could see nothing else out of place. Nevertheless, he emerged a moment later from the bedroom with an electronic device that looked like a sophisticated Geiger counter. He checked slowly around the small apartment, the device held in front, keeping one eye on the sensitive needle. As he passed over his hi-fidelity stereo set, the needle jerked to one hundred percent on the scope. Preston felt his heart crash against his chest as if the needle and the electronic device were an extension of his life pulse. Then he froze. He was under electronic surveillance.

After he had dressed, he strapped on a tape recorder and a gun before donning his Spanish-made raincoat. In the corridor the maintenance man was painting a fixture. Was it a fixture? Was the Negro a real maintenance man? Ripples of paranoia streaked his unprotected back as he forced himself to walk normally to the elevator.

He drove for an hour without purpose or direction, studying his rear-view mirror so closely that twice he narrowly missed a crack-up in Georgetown intersections, but he could not detect anyone following him. Finally, in a complete state of nerves, he pulled into a pocket-sized suburban park deserted except for a little girl of about eight and an older woman whom he took to be her nurse.

It was overcast now, and Preston turned up his raincoat collar with trembling fingers. He was beginning to shake with chill but could feel his shirt soaking with perspiration under his gun. Reaching under the coat, he pushed the small tape recorder's "On" button and adjusted the sensitive speaker receptor so that by stooping slightly and speaking slowly and softly his voice could be transcribed.

"In case of my death, I request that the following information be made known to the Attorney General of the United States. . . ." His mouth worked, but he could not yet find the words he needed. The little girl and the woman were watching him now. Then, "This is all I know: on June 11, 1963, I received an urgent message from . . ."

It had gotten storm dark now, and silent. He stood stooped over, looking for the words. Suddenly, he heard voices.

It was the child talking in a stage whisper. "Look at that funny man. He's all bent over, and he's talking to himself!"

"He looks crazy. Let's get away from him."

Dallas, Texas—October 15, 1963

The Chinaman looked out of place in the workman's coveralls as he sat in the passenger seat next to R. Howard Ferguson's troubleshooter, Arthur Allen, in the telephone-company truck that the Chinaman's man at the company had allowed them to borrow for an hour's work. The Chinaman especially disliked the hard hat he was required to wear, but even in this failing lower-middle-class boardinghouse area of the city he could not run the risk of being recognized. The beautifully barbered head of a 1930's European cinema star did not fit on the body of a telephone repairman, and he had been to this house several times to pick up Oswald.

The Chinaman was well known in a way, but Allen, as he drove toward the Oak Cliff section, realized that of all the spooks he knew, this eastern European mystery man, known to intelligence services all over the world as the "Chinaman," came the closest to being unfathomable. Although Allen had worked in the oil section of the industrial intelligence network that abounded with old OSS "hands" and he considered himself much superior, a new breed to replace the old men, he was forced to admit that this Chinaman was something else.

Now they pulled over a full two blocks away from a one-story converted boardinghouse. They each studied the house through binoculars. Allen was irritated to see that his companion's glasses were German. "Fucking ham," he thought. The European took out an ivory cigarette holder. "Naturally," thought Allen, lighting a Marlboro. Who the hell was this Chinaman anyhow?

Born of White Russian petty nobility, the future spymaster grew up in the nostalgia and neurosis of the emigrés, the exiles, and the pretenders in their Parisian homes and retreats. In the 1930's, as a young man, he had taken his doctorate in economic theory at the Sorbonne and been recruited by French intelligence. He was assigned to the United States, but the prodigy whose cover was to be the oil industry penetrated in earnest into the petrochemical establishment. In those days things were simple; he was merely a double agent.

He became a troubleshooter for the great petroleum interests all over the globe, helping to organize their private diplomatic and secret services. Speaking fifteen languages and being a consummate cultural anthropologist, he was able to live, love, and kill on every continent, and did. Back in America after World War II OSS and oil intelligence work in the China theater (where he, Foster, and Foster's young aide, Van Preston, first tested each other's mettle) the Chinaman, as he was now called, began to move upward in the bedrooms and boardrooms of the new, fast-developing American "military-industrial complex." Texas was the vanguard of postwar Fortress America, and Dallas was the spearhead, ideologically, of the advance guard. The ideology was anti-Communism and the Americanization of the underdeveloped world.

So the Chinaman settled down with his fifth wife and his mistress and a young boy lover (his godson), settled down in "Big D" and organized the potent Dallas eastern European intelligence community for the petrochemical private intelligence group and the Central Intelligence Agency, all the while doubling for the French Secret Service and South African Industrial Intelligence.

But Allen didn't trust him. "Legend or no legend, he talked like a goddamned liberal." And Allen was willing to "bet a steak and a whore that the phony frog son-of-a-bitch was working for the CIA at the same time." And that the CIA had been infiltrated by reds was an article of faith in Dallas oil intelligence circles. But you had to say one thing for him, he was good—how the hell else could they have gotten a real telephone-company truck if he wasn't so slick? They had worked together once before. Under an oil engineering cover they had been sent to Algiers in 1961 to set up a piece of an executive action for JFK during his Paris visit to De Gaulle. Under the Chinaman's sure hand an OAS[1] cover had been established, a patsy set up, and then the old man, R. Howard Ferguson, had chickened out. The Chinaman never told him that, but Allen had figured it out easily enough. He was, he reassured himself, just about as slick as this creep.

The truck radio sparked static: "Target[2] is proceeding in a northerly direction. Target is now approaching Main Street. Target has made left turn on Main, now moving in a westerly direction. Will not follow; 789 has picked him up. Over and out.

"789. Repeat, 789. Target has stopped for red light one block from Houston. . . ."

Allen switched on a handi-talky. The reception was poor now, but the message was clear: "Target is in place[3] at Book Depository. Repeat, he is in place." Allen smirked slightly at the Chinaman as *his* man spoke over the radio. His man was a Dallas police officer in an unmarked vice car. Allen was already pulling

[1]OAS—French-extreme right-wing anti-De Gaulle military circle.
[2]Target—subject of intelligence operation.
[3]In place—subject under surveillance has arrived at destination.

out and speeding down to the house. He was the first out, carrying a large gray metal tool kit; the older man followed jauntily, carrying the radio. At the porch the mailbox read "O. H. Lee."[4] Allen rang even though they knew that the landlady was out. Then he slipped a tool out of his shirt front and picked the lock. Through the vestibule, down the hall, he picked another flimsy lock and they were in Oswald's room. Allen went to work, while his colleague in the hard hat smoking the long cigarettes in the ivory holder made a leisurely tour of the neat, eight-dollar-a-week room: bed, night table, wardrobe, dresser, street map of Dallas, radio, bare walls. Allen's neck was red as he worked.

First he removed the molding from a section of wall and gouged a small receptacle in the wall. He changed and used tools from the doctorlike array he had spread out on the floor. Next Allen carefully picked out a square black box about half the size of a cigarette pack, drew a thin wire out of it, placed the pack and extension in the gouge in the wall, running the wire under the molding to the telephone connecting block. "Don't pirate[5] too much current from the phone company," the cigarette holder drawled in that accent that sent Allen up the wall. Allen swiveled, to see the Chinaman counting a stack of fifty-dollar bills Oswald had secreted under the dresser. Allen raged to himself that this patsy, this piece of shit Oswald was being paid more than he was, and the poor asshole didn't even know what the hell was supposed to be going on. Allen turned back; he did not see the other quickly and expertly checking a fargo[6], a Minox and two other special cameras, two electronic listening devices, a code sender, and three new miniaturized and unique electronic constructs. Had

---

[4]"O. H. Lee"—Cover name for Lee Harvey Oswald.
[5]Pirate—electronic surveillance using pirated electricity from a telephone source, with the permission of the telephone company.
[6]Fargo—a listening device that is taped to an infiltrating agent's body.

Allen, the black-bag[7] expert, seen these, they would have shaken his belief that Oswald was simply an untutored patsy.

Allen mixed paints from five tiny containers. Finding the correct shade of aqua, he began to plaster up the wall abrogations, replaced the molding, took a battery-operated hand suction cleaner out of his kit, and cleaned up the plaster and dust. The Chinaman's radio sputters: "Landlady leaving supermarket now. Appears heading home. Walking onto North Beckley now. Leave premises immediately."

Allen was packed up and ready to go, while the other was still cleaning up cigarette ashes and tugging at his hard hat. Then, to Allen's amazement the Chinaman took a small canister out of his pocket, opened the closet door, and carefully sprayed[8] the few articles of clothing hanging there.

As they hurried out, the Chinaman was humming a waltz melody, and Allen was half-audibly cursing him out for the "egghead, frog, pinko, CIA cocksucker that he was."

Chicago, Illinois—October 21, 1963

Bolton Andrews was the only black man to rise to the rank of special agent in the history of the Secret Service. He was so good that he was treated with respect, to his face; but behind his back he was cursed as a bleeding heart, a crusader, a prude, an ass-kisser, gung-ho, and a protégé of Robert Kennedy or someone else.

He worked late on this Monday. As the night cleaning women jingled outside his door, he dictated into a tape machine a rough draft of a somewhat unusual report.

[7] Black bag—illegal electronic activity.
[8] Spray—an invisible electronic substance which acts as a directional transmitter to monitor a subject over medium distances.

After sleeping on it, or rather not sleeping very well, he had decided to go to the mat with his superior on the reliability of a white racist informant. Bolton Andrews had not been the same for over a month, not since four little black girls had been dynamited to pieces in a Birmingham church on Sunday, September 15. What was eating him up was that Bolton, through his Minute Man informant, knew who was guilty of the atrocity, and he knew that the FBI knew, too, but *would not act*. And so here was the token nigger who lay awake at night fantasizing being lynched by FBI and S.S. agents in button-down collars.

Now he dictated in the empty office. Outside, Chicago was settling down. Andrews' white contemporaries had departed—from La Salle, State, the other streets of finance—to Winnetka, Highland Park, Wilmette, the other suburbs of power.

To: PRS.[9]
From: SA[10] Bolton Andrews.
Confidential informant is a male Caucasian, thirty-nine years old. Former Miami vice-squad detective until 1955, with a subsequent prison record of counterfeiting and armed robbery. Informant claims to be an area leader in the Minute Men, which he joined in 1953 while a member of the Miami police force.

Informant states that crime syndicate, ex-CIA, anti-Castro, and extreme-right-wing elements may make revenge "assassination attempt" on JFK during November 1 Chicago trip. According to Informant, a man named Milteer has already informed Miami police of assassination attempt on JFK in that city during September visit. Milteer is important member of National States' Rights Party.

Informant states that four or more men may already

---
[9] PRS—Secret Service Protective Research Section.
[10] SA—Special Agent.

be in Chicago area for this purpose. Informant states that in his role as courier it was his job to deliver counterfeit funds to Chicago contact. Informant states that the activities described below are the work of men involved in the Bay of Pigs Cuban invasion. Informant worked with Alabama Air National Guard elements during Bay of Pigs preparation as courier and pilot trainer.

Informant denies CIA involvement, but admits involvement in gun-running and counterfeiting with Cuban who *is* CIA contract.[11] Informant claims that CRC and DRE[12] have been broken up by JFK, and munitions and counterfeiting activities will now be on a "private-enterprise" arrangement. Claims that CRC people in New Orleans and Dallas are swearing to "take care of Kennedy."

Informant states that Kelly Coffee Company, New Orleans, and Trade Mart, same city, are conduits for Caribbean intelligence activities.

Informant states that Dallas conduits for anti-Castro operations include the Church of the Old Guard and the Tolstoy Foundation. Informant states that anti-Castro smuggling is being covered by KMT[13] fronts and that funding is being combined. Informant states that anti-Castro activities are also linked to *Revanchiste*[14] elements of the NTS[15] and the CIADC.[16] Informant states that in his capacity as courier for CRC he has had occasion to deal with all of the above.

Informant further states that he has delivered money and guns to and from Ference Nagy, former Premier of Hungary. According to Informant, Nagy and others in

[11] Contract—operative hired by the job for intelligence agency.
[12] CRC and DRE—CIA-supported anti-Castro groups.
[13] KMT—Taiwan-based Nationalist China intelligence.
[14] Revanchiste—West German "revenge-seeking" former Nazis.
[15] NTS—Worldwide White Russian organization, National Toilens Alliance.
[16] CIADC—Latin-American CIA anti-Communist organization.

116 EXECUTIVE ACTION

Dallas East European community represent worldwide financial and CIA and other intelligence interests of a group called Permindex. Permindex was involved in assassination attempt on General Charles de Gaulle, according to Informant, and on U.N. Secretary General Dag Hammarskjold. Informant swears he helped deliver 5,000 submachine guns to Nagy and billionaire R. Howard Ferguson. Informant states that Permindex is letting contracts now for "hit men" for unknown project and that contacts are made through the Texas Petroleum Club and a man known as Chinaman. Informant pledges to disclose actual name of Chinaman in exchange for protection and "some money." Informant alleges that Chinaman was cut off for 1961 aborted assassination attempt on JFK in Paris.

Informant states that he was also employed by syndicate circles in New Orleans and Miami as a runner and courier. Informant states that syndicate sources in New Orleans, Miami, Dallas areas are heavily involved in the shipment of guns and other contraband to Latin America. Informant states that his lawyer and all CIA contract lawyers in New Orleans, Dallas, Miami areas are involved in syndicate representation—legal, real estate, etc. Common link is pre-Castro Cuban gambling. Loss of Cuban rackets was, according to Informant, "like the '29 crash to the mob." Informant claims he overheard this statement from Carlos Marcello of New Orleans.

Informant states that as courier for syndicate and rightist political groupings, he had occasion to deliver and pick up funds at banks in New Orleans, Dallas, Miami, Mexico City, and Chicago. That said banks employ a series of front or cover companies or firms to handle illegal flow of money and contraband. Informant has promised to deliver names of fronts. He remembers, as of last meeting: Inla & Co.; Corlis Co.; Litt & Co.; Line & Co. Informant states that Meyer Lansky's Miami National Bank is depository for Las Vegas–New Orleans skimmed funds.

Informant states that counterfeiting operation is connected to Maria Kohly, President of the United Organization for the Liberation of Cuba. Kohly and three others were arrested on October 1, this year, by our Service. $80,000.00 in counterfeit Cuban pesos were intended to be smuggled into Cuba to finance underground operations.

Informant states that he wishes to trade this and other information for protection from extreme-right-wing *ex*-CIA elements that have threatened to kill Informant for stealing funds. Informant denies these charges.

Evaluation: Informant is likely overstating his importance to anti-Castro activities, but counterfeit-peso-operation information appears legitimate. Informant's Bay of Pigs story does check out.

Informant makes no attempt to hide his racism and hatred for JFK, and "assassination plan" may well be his own idea. In opinion of this agent, informant is sincere in his fear for his life over so-called stolen-funds episode. In agent's opinion the Dallas information is confusing and irrelevant. Permindex is a known neofascist trade front but is not, to our knowledge, active inside USA. The organized-crime material also checks out but is not pertinent to this branch of the department.

In opinion of this agent, confidential informant should be contracted as infiltration operative concerning possible counterfeiting, gun, and contraband activity.

C.C. ATF[17]

That night in bed a question crossed his consciousness for just a moment: "Should I send a copy of all this mess to Bobby?"

---

[17] ATF—Department of the Treasury's Alcohol, Tobacco, and Firearms Division. The Secret Service is also an arm of the Treasury Department.

Dallas, Texas—October 20, 1963

Lee Harvey Oswald stood outside the glass cubicle looking in at the newborn infants in the Parkland Hospital Maternity Ward.

"Here she is, Mr. Oswald. Just for a second." He lifted her gently, looked at her, looked at the little beaded alphabetical bracelet on the tiny wrist: "Rachel Oswald."

Dallas, Texas—October 24, 1963

Adlai E. Stevenson was trying to lift his cultivated voice above the jeers and catcalls.

The night before, General Walker had ordered his National Indignation Committee to make their presence felt at the United Nations Day meeting featuring Ambassador Stevenson. General Walker's United States Day had also taken place at the Dallas Municipal Auditorium. At both meetings Lee Harvey Oswald had been in attendance.

The police were ready to move in as Stevenson told the crowd, "For my own part, I believe in the forgiveness of sin and the redemption of ignorance." After that they drove him out with their obscenities. In the street, in front of the auditorium, a pocket-sized mob of about 150 crowded around, impervious to police intervention. A woman crashed a National Indignation Committee sign down on Stevenson's head, and a man spat in his face. From the tightening knot of angry faces came a low, obviously rehearsed chant: "Kennedy will get his reward in Hell. Stevenson is going to die. His heart will stop, stop, stop and he will burn, burn, burn."

The Ambassador, as he was hustled toward his limousine, chanced to catch Lee Harvey Oswald's eye, and thinking he saw concern of some sort there, he mouthed the words, *"Are these human beings, or are these animals?".*

New York, New York—October 25, 1963

The Muzak, the unintelligible stream of the public-address system, the sheer swarm of the Idlewild International Airport all contributed to Preston's feeling of disorientation. It was impossible because of the crowds for him to tell if he had been followed.

He was early, so he loitered in the notions shop of the TWA concourse. The headlines keyed off jabs of anxiety in his stomach and made the fashionable, subtly checked, light topcoat feel as heavy as chain armor: "TROOPS HOME FOR XMAS" and "VIET TROOP PULLOUT—JFK."

"Dr. White, please report to the white courtesy telephone at the information desk in the lobby"—the signal he had been waiting for—had to be repeated before he came to attention and headed for the SAS international lounge as prearranged. Was he being followed or not?

Despite everything, Preston had to smile when he saw Dieter Krause, beer mug in hand, waiting for him in the lounge. He had aged in the ten years since both of them had drunk beer and argued about the meaning of Faust, in Berlin in the great days of the Cold War.

They embraced in the European manner. Preston had not been able to touch a man without shame since he had left Germany. As he held on to the big man in the rumpled suit, the deferred pressure of the last months started to seep out, and he held on too long and too tight. Almost without preamble they went to the issue, both of them speaking rapidly in German.

"Ich benoetige, dringend, ihre Hilfe."

"Ja."

Everything about Preston repeated the statement, "I

need your help." The German rose and led him into the concourse, where Preston's slight hysteria would be lost among the tableau of distraught latecomers, lovers, reunions, and separations. But despite his unflappable technique, the German agent stopped in the middle of the bustle to stare at the white-faced younger man. "Kennedy? *Sie Meinen (doch) Castro?*" Preston stared back at him with the eyes of a man who has just had his glasses slapped off his face; a nerve winced at his mouth, as he shook his head.

He meant Kennedy! Dieter Krause had lived through the terrors of Fascism and Stalinism and the CIA, but this was the limit. So this was why his old colleague had contacted him to fly to New York for a twenty-minute conference and then fly straight back to Berlin without ever leaving the air terminal. How, why—he could not get it through his head—had Preston gotten mixed up in this kind of madness? Didn't he know that a million-dollar contract had already been put out for both JFK and his brother by one of the big Florida crime families?

They stood there for a moment longer. Preston had aged terribly, the German thought as he remembered the bright sensitive American whom he had taken under his wing in the city that cannot be trusted, Berlin, when the American tanks and trucks rolled toward the border with their lights on in the middle of the day, as if there were a darkness at noon. In that World War III atmosphere the veteran agent had given the young CIA operative an ironic tour of the city (and its double—the rubble of nothingness that remained of the Third Reich) and a round of native bars and restaurants that never failed to delight the sensitive palate of the "Harvard Boy," as he called him. Though youthful and attractive, in an American aristocratic way, Preston had not indulged in any sexual adventures—that he knew of, anyway; instead he had seemed to prefer to dine and talk with "Mephisto," which was his nickname for the German.

He took Preston's arm now and steered him toward
the bar and a dark corner table, ordering double whis-
keys himself in his own harsh English. He was upset,
getting too old for this. (He and Preston had sat in a
hidden underground room during one of the US–USSR
confrontations and heard the intelligence aide to the
ranking American officer in Europe tell them, to their
face, that in six hours if the Soviets did not back down,
then they were prepared to order a first strike nuclear
attack that would take 150 million Russian casualties in
the first hour alone, were prepared to do this and "not
tell the President"! When they had gone out to get
drunk, he and Preston had agreed that they were all insane—the generals, statesmen, *all* the "schrecklichkeit[18]
patriots"—and that they were both getting out before
the real Mephisto claimed their souls and their bodies,
altogether. But they had not got out. *"Für Gält sogar de
Tüüfel."*[19] So Krause was in a state of exasperation a
decade old. *"Phantastisch! Ist er verrueckt geworden?
Oder sind sie verrueckt geworden?"* "Fantastic! Has he
gone mad? Or have you?"

The drinks arrived, Preston swallowed his, almost
throwing up, then reached to take the German's too.
Krause gripped his wrist; he had only ten minutes left.

"What are you people doing in that glue factory?
Can't you control each other at all? He was your
'wonder boy,' no? All the computers and new electronic
toys, the sweet little green 'beanies' for the Superman
Special Forces? *What is it?* Cuba? Vietnam? . . . He was
your 'boy,' and now it comes back to haunt him. Ja,
Ja."

That day, in Berlin, Krause had quoted to him some
words that came back to him now. He could not remember what famous writer had penned them.

The hardest strokes of heaven fall in history upon

---

[18]Schrecklichkeit—peace through terror.
[19]*Für Gält sogar de Tüüfel*—For gold, even the devil dances.

those who imagine they can control things in a sovereign manner, playing providence not only for themselves but for the far future . . . and gambling on a lot of risky calculations in which there must never be a single mistake.

He wondered if the old hand remembered and would speak the words again today. Instead he asked a question. "Van, you have given me a few reasons, but what are *the reasons beneath the reasons?*" He paused, "or are you doing it simply because you have the technology *to do it?*"

Time had run out, as usual. He practically dragged a slumping Preston back into the concourse. As he propelled him, he snarled a whispered mockery of *Faust* into Preston's ear, his heavy face a mask except for the slashing lips and teeth.

> So, so; This I wish to have seen, to stand on free ground with free human beings.

> So, so; When/If I ask Time, 'Stand still!' for this is the elation moment; then you may chain me, then I don't mind to be ruined.

> So, so: Before the Overman (can come) the fellowman must have come.

> I am the always negative spirit, and rightfully so, for all that comes into existence is (equally) worth to be ruined!

In the men's room he stopped for breath. Preston vomited immediately. The German ran water for him, maintained the pressure so that their words could not be overheard. "Is the contract[20] already let?"

---

[20]Contract—assassination payoff to actual killers.

Preston dried his hands, handed over a boxed reel of tape. *"Die affaire is aus."* The German ran the water harder. "Talk," he spit out, "will you, before it's too late?"

"Everything is on this tape. The affair is over. The big change came after the test ban. He's had a deal with Khrushchev since the Bay of Pigs, and he's after our heads now. He's started secret talks with Castro—I swear to you! He's put that fanatic brother of his on our trail. Don't ask me why, Dieter. It's in motion, it can't be stopped. That's why I contacted you."

"Ja. This is the party line[21]?" The German listened to the mechanical words that he knew did not belong, in any authentic way, to this "Harvard Boy" who had grown up to be a monster. He turned off the water. He didn't care now if someone did overhear him. But for a moment out of time the toilet was silent, fluorescent, privileged. "Ja, Camelot and New Frontier"—he slipped into English, "are just two more of the world's dirty little back alleys now, eh? *Ja, Ja. 'Ich bin ein Berliner.'* " There were tears in his eyes; he turned to wash his face. A man entered and looked at them. They walked out quickly, onto the escalator, the German apprehensive about time, on fire to get out of this madhouse. Now it was Preston's turn to whisper in his ear.

"What about me? What is to prevent them, finally, from burning me? They've got me stretched thin running backup people all over the country. It's getting out of hand. They're not telling me everything. I think they're having me ... watched and ..."

"Van, what is it you want me to do?"

Preston's lips continued to work as the escalator touched down and they hurried toward the boarding-pass line. The German put his arm around the bony shoulders of this younger man who had risen so much higher in "political" service than he, Krause, could ever

---

[21]Party line—slang for the intelligence agencies' point of view.

have imagined for himself even if he were not within a few beers of his mandatory retirement.

"My friend, sharing your danger with *me* does not protect you. Van? You have only made another vertical link, and two vertical links can be removed as easily as one. You are not establishing a real-horizontal-*escape*[22] line, a lateral line. You're only drawing me down into *your* compartment instead of escaping from—"

"But if you share this with your people . . . ?"

"My people! The *Bundesnachrichtendienst?* Impossible. Too big. Too big! Besides, we both know who really runs my company." He was covering his perturbation with stinging sarcasm again, but the water was coming back to his eyes. "I want to help you, Van. After all, we're not strangers. 'Old hands' have to stick together, eh? I know, I saw what can happen between 'factions' after the war." In a minute they would have to part. "I *will* help you. I will keep my eyes open for you; and if the worse comes to the worst—papers, etc., you know. But you must not come to me first. . . ." Now they were embracing again. Over Preston's shoulder he saw a black man dressed in a maintenance uniform leaning on what appeared to be a vacuum cleaner of some kind. The black man was staring at them. Krause spoke softly into Preston's ear, and his big-armed embrace changed character, driving the wind out of the slender man.

"Werden sie beschattet? Ja, haben sie mich schon 'rein—gezogen? Are you alone?"

Preston tried to turn to look. People were staring at them now. The big man was obviously terribly strong; they were frozen together at the head of the line. Preston could not answer him. The German ejected him. "Ja, you have already involved me!" He took the tape out of his ancient, shapeless overcoat, jammed it into Preston's topcoat, barged ahead toward his waiting flight.

---

[22] Horizontal-escape—when an agent breaks a vertical, "need-to-know" chain in order to protect himself by sharing information "horizontally" with a third party.

Preston staggered toward the black man. He stood there holding the tape, staring at the maintenance man.

Amherst, Massachusetts—October 26, 1963

Air Force One seemed to sail through the fabulous Indian-summer sky. President Kennedy worked on the speech that he would deliver that day to an audience at Amherst College.

> With privileges goes responsibility. Robert Frost said:
>
>> The roads diverged in a wood, and I—
>> I took the one less traveled by,
>> And that has made all the difference.
>
> In America, our heroes have customarily run to men of large accomplishments. But today this college and country honors a man whose contribution was not to our size but to our spirit, not to our political beliefs but to our insight, not to our self-esteem, but to our self-comprehension. In honoring Robert Frost, we therefore can pay honor to the deepest sources of our national strength. That strength takes many forms, and the most obvious forms are not always the most significant. The men who create power make an indispensable contribution to the nation's greatness, but the men who question power make a contribution just as indispensable, especially when that questioning is disinterested, for they determine whether we use power, or power uses us. . . . When power narrows the areas of man's concern, poetry reminds him of the richness and diversity of his existence. When power corrupts, poetry cleanses. . . .
>
> I see little of more importance to the future of our country and our civilization than full recogni-

tion of the place of the artist. If art is to nourish the roots of our culture, society must set the artist free to follow his vision wherever it takes him. We must never forget that art is not a form of propaganda; it is a form of truth. . . . Robert Frost was often skeptical about projects for human improvement, yet I do not think he would disdain this (American and world) hope.

As he wrote during the uncertain days of the Second War:

> Take human nature altogether since time began
> And it must be a little more in favor of man,
> Say a fraction of one percent at the very least...
> Our hold on the planet wouldn't have so
>   increased. ...

Washington, D.C.—October 28, 1963

On October 28, Mrs. Nellie M. Doyle wrote to Pierre Salinger, the President's press secretary.

> Although I do not consider myself an "alarmist" I do fervently hope that President Kennedy can be dissuaded from appearing in public in the city of Dallas, Texas, as much as I would appreciate and enjoy hearing and seeing him.
>
> This "hoodlum mob" here in Dallas is frenzied and infuriated because their attack upon Ambassador Adlai Stevenson on the twenty-fourth backfired on them. I have heard that some of them have said that they "have just started."
>
> No number of policemen, plainclothesmen, or militia can control the "air," Mr. Salinger. It is a dreadful thought, but all remember the fate of President McKinley. These people are crazy, or

crazed, and I am sure that we must realize that their actions in the future are unpredictable.

Salinger took the letter seriously and sent it on to Kenny O'Donnell, the President's closest aide.

III / NOVEMBER

Chicago, Illinois—November 2, 1963

The Chicago team left the South Side flophouse, walking fast and carrying duffel bags and lunch pails containing pistols, silencers, and special illegal dum-dum bullets. The Chicago technician carried an automatic weapon in a musical-instrument case. The men were dressed for a football game, with binoculars and portable radios that had been redesigned to double as walkie-talkies. It was twelve noon.

The decision had been made to substitute Spanish Astra 22 automatics for the Iver Johnsons. The Astra was unique, the Cuban had argued passionately, because it had a hammer *you can set,* it *cannot* misfire. The tiny gun, which so closely resembled a miniature 45, could be broken up into four parts, as it was now, and these, plus the silencer, each man had distributed about his body. These parts could be reassembled in less than a minute, and the gun literally could be cupped in the hand like a pack of king-size cigarettes. They knew that if they could get within ten feet, the noise from the crowd and the wind would cover them completely.

Their chances were good. They knew that they had been hand-picked by Control for a daring plan and that they were the first team. All they needed was a minuscule opening for a fraction of a second. The hollow-nosed dum-dum bullets had been soaked overnight in garlic in order to cause blood poisoning. So as they waited for their transportation to the game, they looked and acted as cocky as any championship team.

132 EXECUTIVE ACTION

On the other side of town, the backup team dressed themselves in costumes: two as cushion vendors, two as stadium ushers, two in suits and ties with "funny" Secret Service credentials and lapel identification pins. All of them had small walkie-talkies strapped under their costumes; only the Secret Service imposters carried guns. Wearing overcoats, the men fanned out from the hotel to pick up individual cabs.

On the South Side, the technician and his team crowded into their waiting car—New York license 311 ORF. The driver was a thin man in his middle twenties bearing a very strong resemblance to Lee Harvey Oswald, a man he did not yet know existed. The car sped toward Soldiers' Field.

As the New York car headed east, Bolton Andrews and two other Secret Service agents fell into a surveillance pattern a good two blocks behind. The unmarked government car was in radio contact with another car, trailing them, of Chicago plainclothes detectives. At this point it had been agreed that any arrests would be handled by the local police; Andrews had been overruled.

Vienna, Virginia—November 2, 1963

Foster and Preston sat in the half-shadow watching the television. The sound was too loud for Preston.

> Seconds to go. The center is over the ball; the shift is to the right. This will be the last play in, this, the first half.

As the clock ran out, the camera zoomed in on the official as he raised his pistol to signal the end of the first half.

> That's the half-time gun, and at half-time a surprising Air Force team led by Terry Isaacson has outplayed and outscored a much larger Army

team. At half-time: Air Force Academy 3; Army 0. We may be on the verge of one of the great upsets of 1963, played here before a crowd of 76,660 excited spectators at Soldiers' Field. The big crowd here to see the first all-service academy game played in Chicago in thirty-seven years includes many government and service dignitaries, but not President Kennedy. The President had been expected but canceled his appearance this morning due to a head cold.

Foster, using the remote-control switch, changed stations rapidly; an old movie; a loud, violent children's animated cartoon; and then the news special. The film showed political pandemonium in the terrific crush of the Saigon streets.

> The South Vietnamese government of President Ngo Dinh Diem has fallen in a swift military coup d'etat. The insurgents reported over Saigon radio this morning that Diem and his powerful brother Ngo Dinh Nhu had "accidentally" committed suicide.
> American Intelligence spokesmen denied any direct involvement in the military plot and are likely to deplore the deaths of President Diem and his brother if the deaths are confirmed.
> It is assumed, however, that the coup d'etat is welcomed.
> Washington expressed confidence that there would be greater progress in the war against the Communist guerrillas.
> The Defense Department ordered ships of the Seventh Fleet to the vicinity of South Vietnam today to protect any Americans who might be endangered by disorders accompanying the overthrow of President Ngo Dinh Diem. . . .

Foster flicked back to the game. Martial music. He

turned off the set. The curtains are drawn, the two sit in shadow. They are silent. They can hear distant sounds from outside. Far away, someone is playing a piano. Finally, Preston breaks the silence. The two men talk very quietly.

"A head cold? The same excuse he used to cancel the Midwest tour during the missile crisis. Won't people notice?"

"No. '*The* people' will not notice."

"What went wrong?"

"Chicago is a shambles; Saigon is perfect. Mr. Diem will *not* be holding any more private peace meetings with Hanoi!" Foster was in a cold fury. "The Chicago scenario has been botched: One of the technicians was a bit careless. Speeding through town for no apparent reason and then arrested for possession of an automatic weapon! That brought the Secret Service in, and . . ." He gestured with open hands.

"Where's Dan? How is he?"

"If you mean, 'Will he blow his brains out like poor Dick[1] did?' no, he's steady. He's leading the salvage operations.[2] The driver's picture has been pulled from the police files, our S.S. operative is now attempting to explain away the weapon, and the others have vanished. They will not be broken or bought. In fact, they're available for backup work immediately." Foster pressed his eyes. "Are you ready to go?"

"We're prepared—but will he go to Dallas after this?"

"He'll go. He's really quite a brave man. Not a coward, and politically he has no choice—in a Democracy the President must be able to go into the streets. Texas is a mess; *and* there are the polls! He's falling. No, he has his commitments to keep, too."

"Brave? Ambition. Style. Anyway, it's been leaked to

---

[1] Dick—Richard Wisner, one of those in charge of the Bay of Pigs.
[2] Salvage operations—destroying incriminating evidence.

the press that he's going. Will his wife go with him?"

"No, probably not. No women." His eyes were completely closed now. "Are your people really reliable?"

"Yes."

"All of them? What about the decoy?"

"The actual team is being run by the best technician, next to Pop Bender, I've ever seen; actually, you met him once, in fifty-one. The Chinaman is baby-sitting[a] the decoy. I've someone ready to go on the wife and mother, too, and their safe houses are all set. Between Minute Men, Cubans, the local syndicate people, I'm actually overcapitalized."

"How much time do they need? How soon do they need to know?"

"Right now. . . . There's something on my mind that I want to talk to you about. . . ."

Foster's eyes remained closed; he seemed altogether exhausted. "Churchill said it: 'Plot and counterplot, deceit and treachery, double-dealing and triple-dealing, real agents, fake agents, gold and steel, the bomb and the dagger.'" He opened his eyes.

Corpus Christi, Texas—November 3, 1963

". . . Army beat the Air Force Academy Saturday afternoon at Chicago's Soldiers' Field before a crowd of more than 76,000, many of whom were disappointed when President Kennedy failed to make a scheduled appearance. Presidential press aide Pierre Salinger indicated that the President had a heavy head cold, causing him to cancel his viewing of the first all-service academy game held in the Windy City in nearly four decades. Back to the pro-grid beat, next weekend we can look for . . ."

The technician snapped off the car radio. He guided

---

[a] Baby-sitting—controlling operatives or potential risks with other agents.

the rented car casually through the nearly deserted streets. Heading toward the beachfront, he located the frontage road he wanted and turned left. It followed the curve of the Gulf Coast, with large patches of water visible through spaces between the buildings. The city dropped off behind them as they entered the southeastern outskirts, grown over with eateries and motels. In the off-season most were closed, and those that hadn't been boarded shut for the winter were surely closed for the night. Among the intermittent street lights, one set of neon letters flashed their welcome. He stopped in front of the long two-story building.

The abrupt absence of car noise and motion awakened Anne. He watched her softly as she stirred into consciousness. "We're here honey. I'll be back in a minute." She nodded, smiling sleepily.

Inside the office, the owner greeted him as he stepped through the door to his living quarters. "Hope you're James King?" The technician reassured him that that was so. The fat, white-haired, mustachioed man turned the registration card around on the desk for him to fill out. He quickly improvised the names and numbers called for by the blanks on the card; the motel owner reached under the counter. The completed card was exchanged for a key and envelope. "Here's your key, an' this was brought by some kinda messenger this afternoon. . . . Surely glad you're here; didn't know what I wuz goin' ta do with it if you hadn't showed." The open curiosity flashed like his motel's neon sign.

"Thanks." He looked at the plain envelope with only the hand-printed letters "James King" on it. Whatever it contained, he couldn't do anything about it now. The message could only have come from Preston. It had to be the word telling him that his team was to be dispersed; that the plan was canceled; or that his number-two team was no longer on call. It had to be. He stuffed the envelope into his rear pocket.

"You all are number one."

"What?"

"I say, you have number one. The first cabin."

"How much till Tuesday?"

The motel man turned away from the light-switch panel. "Let's see, usually ten dollars a day, and with . . ." The technician dropped a ten- and a twenty-dollar bill on the registration card, picked up the key, and headed back to his car. "Oh, that's fine, that's jess fine. Number one's down there, on the end." He pointed. The technician half-turned in the doorway, noting the direction; the screen door bounced shut behind him.

Anne was fully awake as he slipped under the wheel. He drove the few feet to the end of the building, neatly depositing the car diagonally in front of number one. "This is it."

"I couldn't tell very much about it." She was leaning over the back of the seat, gathering together a few loose items and her overnight bag. "By the time I got my eyes working, the light went out."

"We'll take a walk as soon as we get the stuff inside." He knew he must be sounding stiff and withdrawn, hoping it wouldn't show too much. The envelope in his left-rear pocket pulled at him. She pulled at him. It was too much. He busied himself with opening the motel door, flipping on the lights, going back outside to the car trunk, opening it, remembering the cotton impact dummies and Mauser rifles that now lay silently waiting in the casket shipping case still strapped to the back of the jeep, parked in a "Ferguson Petroleum Co." yard outside Dallas.

He pulled two suitcases from the trunk, slamming the lid. Passing the car, he checked it over, quickly satisfying himself that nothing more need be done; then he joined Anne in the room. She stood on the tile-covered concrete floor at the foot of the bed. It was not as luxurious as she had hoped. Her absence of enthusiasm was obvious, and he responded to it immediately. Dropping the suitcases on the bed, he put an arm around her shoulders, taking her overnight case from her.

"I know it's not the Fontainebleau but it's quiet *and*

remote. Besides, with the lights out, you'll never know the difference." He moved to put her case in the bathroom. She turned in the direction of his voice, and had to smile slightly at his grinning face peering at her from behind the bathroom door. Her disappointment was relieved, and his preoccupation was lifted.

She viewed the room again, but now was looking for positive signs. It was hard to find them. The thin plastic curtains crisp with age, hung carelessly from their brass rods. The floor was hard and cold and slightly gritty. She opened the door opposite the one they had entered, and all that they had come here for rushed in at her. Here was the beach, only a few hundred feet away the surf, and between the buildings and the waves a line of palm trees. He stood behind her, gesturing out the open door with one hand. "Here you go. . . ."

She leaned back, looking out on the beach, "Oh, yes, this is what we came for, isn't it?"

"Not altogether." He stood loose-kneed directly behind her, placing his hands on her hips, pushing his pelvis into her firm rear.

She relaxed slightly, allowing herself to be handled momentarily. "Let's go for a walk." She broke the contact, grabbed up the sweater she had tossed on the foot of the bed, and headed out the open door, snatching at his hand, pulling him along.

The breeze off the gulf was still warm, with no trace of the chill that would be there by early morning. The surf was lapping low at the absorbent sand, less oceanlike than an inland lake. The moon slipped in and out of the quick, high-sailing clouds, washing the strolling couple with a slow-motion natural strobe light. Large horseshoe crabs clung to the sand at the high-tide mark, like flagstones bridging a shallow creek.

They finally sat in the sand looking out at the gulf. Off to their right the city lights hovered over the port. On the horizon the lights of two tankers slipped past one another, one so low in the water that it looked like a raft, the other so high that it seemed not to be in the water at all. Where were they headed? He put his arm around her shoulders, nuzzled her cheek and ear with his nose, letting one hand drop casually over her breast.

She turned her face toward his. Their kiss was long, deep, arousing. His other hand moved along her bare thigh beneath her skirt. He spread her out like a picnic blanket on the sand, both her arms reaching, circling his neck, pulling him after her.

He hesitated, self-consciously searching for an intruder. He found one. Behind one of the palm trees, some unexpected, unnatural shape alerted him. He hesitated, peering through the darkness, deeper now that the moon had chosen a large dark formation to glide behind. He withdrew from her, with one swipe smoothing her clothes protectively back into position. He rose and advanced slowly toward the unnatural tree trunk. He was only a few feet from it now; nothing had moved. His approach had been slow, careful, alerting all his senses to an impending confrontation. The whole episode was like the forty years of his life, encapsulated, each new day imposing upon him some requirement or obligation.

His mind stopped; thinking surrendered to his highly developed atavistic nervous system. His will to survive submitted itself to no logic or rational process. He tensed, prepared for whatever was going to spring up, at, or away. The moon's light erupted on his confrontation with a surfboard left carelessly leaning against the tree. Recognition of his enemy hit him in the solar plexis; his knees sagged slightly. Something touched his upper arm; he swiveled in the sand, lost his balance, dropped to one knee, completely vulnerable now to his enemies. He checked back a sob of impotent rage. His wife's hands pressed his face into her belly, her fingers stroking the back of his head. "It's nothing, baby, it's nothing. . . ." His tears penetrated her dress one by one, touching her down-covered belly with bitter drops. He breathed heavily through his mouth as his head lowered along her front. His hot breath bellowed through her thin clothes, intimately singeing her. She separated her feet, her hands pulled strongly at the back of his head.

Five minutes later they walked hand in hand silently along the water-hardened sand at the surf's edge.

He lay on his back in bed listening to the water. Water splashing against the sand on the beach outside the window, water splashing against the porcelain wash basin inside the bathroom. The sounds in the bathroom stopped. Anne stood in the doorway, the light behind shimmering through her nightgown. The tableau stirred him; his passion still had not been fulfilled. She flipped off the light. As she crossed the room to slip into bed with him, he tried to flip off his desire.

"I want to make a real Thanksgiving feast . . . if they can spare you." She snuggled into him, lying on her side, her head on his shoulder, taking his arm and wrapping it around her.

"I'll be back for Thanksgiving. . . . And that's it: after Thanksgiving, I start looking for something else. Where would you like to live?" He tried not to be aware of her softness; he tried to push down his urge. He was sure she wanted only to sleep now.

Her hand played across his chest, down across his belly, rubbing lightly across his navel. "It's so beautiful here. Could we live around here? We could! Neither of us has any family anymore. I guess we don't even have that many friends." Her massaging hand moved lower on his belly. He was sure she was merely being absentminded. "This is fun to talk, isn't it?" She kissed lightly at his chest. "Should we sing a song?" Her kisses were longer now, her tongue caressing his skin caught between her lips. Her hand lowered now to his erection, fingers outlining its base against his groin. She fastened her mouth hungrily over one of his nipples and sucked.

"I don't have any friends. I don't even know how I got involved so deeply." The interior of his mouth tingled. He continued to lie unmoving but not unmoved. "I was going to go into engineering and then . . ." He stiffened as her hand gripped him now, her kissing mouth moving slowly down his chest.

"Could we have a baby?" She now began to stroke his throbbing sex, speaking into his navel.

". . . But I'm too old for it all now," he said. His arm fell away from her. He lay motionless, tense.

She lifted her head, pushing the blankets and sheet down. "You're too old?" She gazed at him, caught in her moving hand. "You're not too old." She lowered her head to the swelling organ caught in her moving hand. "I'm too old." She crouched on her knees, all pretense gone. Very gently she put her lips, flowerlike, over his sex, salivated, and began to nod her head, taking his bursting erection as deeply as she could.

"You're just a girl." He lay rigidly, legs stiff, back arched slightly, eyes closed. "You're just a girl."

He had fallen asleep before she had been willing to leave him. She curled herself back into his armpit, pulling the covers back over them. She fell asleep, smiling to herself.

Washington, D.C.—November 3, 1963

Preston stood on the balcony of the embassy pretending to sip French champagne. From his vantage point the string quartet was just bearable to him, and the incessant chatter of the wedding guests was thankfully muted to a strident buzz.

He had to admire the distinguished figure of Foster, who was holding forth to a circle at the punch bowl. The quartet shifted to a fox-trot just as Foster swung away to greet the father of the bride. "Congratulations, Mr. Ambassador. Hello, Jim, where's my girl?" The ambassador waved to the bride and groom to come over.

Preston watched the girl's young breasts lift as she hugged Foster. "Hello, Uncle Tom."

"Hello, darling. Congratulations, young man. Take good care of this young lady, you hear me." The circle laughed good-naturedly.

Preston closed his eyes to block out the fantasy of the young people in bed kissing each other the length of their firm epicene bodies, but the image became brighter, and now they were doing forbidden things to each other in his mind's eye.

"When are you leaving?" He snapped to attention at the sound of Foster's resonant voice. "You look tired, better get a good night's sleep."

"In the morning," replied Preston as they strolled toward the periphery of the balcony.

"We can talk," said Foster. "There's no bug out here. Shall we have a last capsule review of the false sponsors —we will not be in communication with each other again for some time."

From where they stood they could see guests and notables passing, and beyond, people dancing. Foster waved to friends from time to time as they passed. There was a fixed smile on his face as he rehearsed Preston. All his old vigor seemed to have returned.

"The sponsors: Castro and his committees: circles around the Communist party, the Socialist Workers' party. . . ."

"Both?"

"Let me just finish, Van. Now, for the ultras on the right. Remember, every political faction must have a guilty conscience; none of them will dare to probe beneath the surface for fear of what they might find. Everybody is involved, so 'nobody' is responsible." He waved to a couple. "Hello, old boy, hello, Sylvia, you look positively champion, my dear." Then back on a lower tone to Preston. "Remember our scenario: a lone assassin acting in the home state of the primary beneficiary of the act. No politician—including the family—is going to dig too deeply. It would not be in their interest to tear the country apart; and, after all, the slightly soiled Cubans in use here are leftovers from his brother's own executive-action-manqué against Castro, correct?"

Preston was feeling slightly queasy again; he put his glass on the balcony railing and slipped on a pair of sunglasses.

Foster called to a high official, "Hello, hello, Larry." He would not let Preston get a word in. He was possessed; Preston knew that now.

"Behind the 'misanthropic' killer looms, our first cover: the 'Communist conspiracy.' That revetment will terrify the liberals and the toughs of the tender left —'Red Scare!'—while the moderates will, as usual, be impressed with the need for stability and continuity, and they will rely, as always, on the appropriate governmental agencies." He drained his glass with a touch of a flourish. His eyes shone as he reached out for a fresh drink from a passing Negro waiter in gleaming white linen. Fortified, he went on without let-up, Preston felt as if he were being hypnotized.

Foster's voice was buzzing in his head. "Now, why the right? you ask. For the same reasons. First come our Texas billionaires and their lunatic fringe, including local police people, and the whole sad, mad underground of radio ministers, ex-agents, and crackpot patriots—remember, they actually think they're in charge, because they want to privately claim the credit. Let them. The conservatives are neutralized; and the right —who is after him anyway, for what they see as his race 'mongrelization' policies—is thoroughly compromised. . . . Hullo, Frank! . . . Do you see? Cut down by the extreme left, in the city of the extreme right."

Foster's voice was low and his posture contained, but there was a manic intensity that threatened Preston as he broke in under cover of a phrase, "Speaking as the devil's advocate"—Foster smiled brilliantly—"what if someone should, nevertheless, be audacious enough to inquire into—"

Foster silenced him with a look. "Then he will find exactly the series of tableaux we have arranged for him:

the lone psychopath of American assassination tradition. But if our hero insists on looking further, he will be greeted by the contingent, alternate scenarios: first, the 'True Believers': Castro and the revetments of the left; next, anti-Castro and the thunder of the right. Next, if necessary, our muckrakers will discover everyone's favorite—the Mafia! They have had a million-dollar contract on him for two years; you knew that, didn't you?"

Preston tried to retain some identity under Foster's blitz, "Well, yes, we have Jack R—"

Foster's charisma was too much for him. He felt as he had during the war when on the eve of some big "black" operation. Foster, younger, more supple then, had acted out all the parts—victims and executioners, agents and double agents alike—with a dizzying virtuosity that had taken Preston's breath away. Now, twenty years later, he felt himself slipping into the same hypnologic state. "Tom," he tried to say, "the syndicate connection in Dallas is Jack—"

But Foster rode over him. "Fine. Whoever. Keep him at arm's length; let him triple-hat[*] but only on the periphery." He moved in so close that Preston could smell the sweet wine scent from Foster's mouth. *"We will go back, if we have to, step by step, and if, in the end, some 'genius' should penetrate through all the layers and discs. . . .* Behold! There will stand the man: one 'William Bobo,' alias 'O. H. Lee,' alias 'Alex James Hidell,' alias 'Lee Harvey Oswald,' agent-provocateur and employee—contract number 179—of the Federal Bureau of Investigation! A riddle, Van, wrapped in a mystery inside an enigma." He sidestepped nimbly to catch another glass of champagne from a passing tray.

In the long pause, the strains of the fox-trot reached them. There was a thin glaze of perspiration on Foster's ruddy forehead. Preston attempted lamely one last time to exist somewhere in the old master's monologue. But

---

[*]Triple-hat—several covert assignments for one man.

as he opened his mouth to speak, Foster hit him with the inexorable and, to Preston, terrifying deduction of it all.

"Remember, Van, what has been done once can, if required, be done again." The two stared at each other. "It's a mistake to look too far ahead. Every hero becomes a bore at last." Preston did not feel reassured, felt he had to say something or Foster would decipher his scrambled thoughts the way he would a code.

"But why the Communist party *and* the Socialist Workers' party for the left? How do we do that plausibly when they fight among themselves like—"

"Good afternoon, Sir Alec"—Foster lifted his glass in toast, then brought it back to eye-line and studied Preston's visage through the refracting prism of the crystal—"Photographically. Wouldn't a photograph of our man be useful if it revealed him with the 'murder weapon' in one hand and publications—the newspapers of both the Communist party *and* the Socialist Workers' party—in the other?"

Preston stared at the enlarged laughing eye as Foster rubbed the glass across his forehead in a cooling motion. He knew that from Foster's angle he must appear rat-faced and pin-headed, and as he queried the magnified eye behind the crystal, his voice had a whining quality. "Isn't that too obvious with a rifle?"

"Nothing is too obvious. It's the really big myths that work best."

"I mean, really, how would you respond if Khrushchev were . . . removed, and the lone pro-capitalist killer was shown posing with copies of the *Wall Street Journal* and the *Chicago Tribune* in his hand? I mean, you—"

The bride ran out to hug Foster good-bye and whispered in his ear; he whirled her around and sent her off with a caressing pat on her tight little rear end; then, without missing a beat, he turned back to his pale-faced companion. "How would I respond?" chuckled Foster nasally. "I would reject the entire melodrama out of hand as utter rubbish, just as I would the allegations about *our* subject. But the man in the street, in the Soviet Union, *would* accept it, *and so will they here!*"

Foster showed his teeth slightly. "Don't you know who this lone assassin is? He is the 'Pale Criminal' that Nietzsche wrote about: 'But one thing is the thought, another thing is the deed, and another thing is the *idea* of the deed. *The wheel of causality doth not roll between them.*' Van, we are the idea of the deed—the rest are merely instruments."

He added his empty glass to the row on the balustrade and looked one last time at his deputy, looked at him without vanity and without pity. His hand on Preston's arm was hot right through the jacket. "Well, safe trip. We shall be waiting patiently to hear from you. Here in the, ah, 'City of Lies.'"

Corpus Christi, Texas—November 4, 1963

The technician lay in bed on his back, smoking, watching light patterns dance across the ceiling, as the morning sun glimmered on the water outside, reflecting itself. He realized he was in the same position he last remembered being in the night before. At his side Anne had wiggled her rump into his hip, and her back was pressed tight along his side. He wondered when she had moved. It had been so long since they had dared to enjoy each other as they had last night. Now he was caught in a web of self-recriminations, doubting his right to such pleasures. He remembered the unread letter in his wallet. As he leaned out of bed to deposit his cigarette in the ashtray, he scanned the disarray in the room for his pants.

From behind the double-locked door in the room that must have opened into the next unit, he could hear the sound of voices. At first there was nothing remarkable, but quickly the tempo and intensity of both the man's and woman's voice increased. It was clear that a dispute of some kind was going on. He listened but couldn't make it out. The anger was unmistakable, but the subject remained unclear.

Next to him Anne began to stir. He dropped the idea of retrieving "James King's" message from his wallet as he watched her awaken. She rolled over on her back and stretched. Her eyelids fluttered open almost as though it were painful. He watched her. He wondered why, what he was looking for, or hoping to see. Perhaps, he comforted himself, it was only to get to know her again.

Her eyes focused on his, and she threw her arms around his neck, pulling herself into a sitting position, kissing his face all over with wet smacking little kisses. Finally she leaned back, grinning at him.

"I had the wildest dream last night." She jumped out of bed and ran into the bathroom. Once inside the bathroom, she turned to peer out at him, putting one hand up to her grinning, giggling mouth. "I'll tell you *all* about it later. Are you up? I'm starving, get right into your suit; we only have three days."

From the other side of the wall the sounds of the argument intensified. Anne heard it for the first time, cocking her head, birdlike, in its direction. She frowned slightly, stepped into the bathroom, and began singing, as well as running the water, to cover the harsh sounds coming from next door.

He rolled out of bed and began rummaging through the suitcase that stood open on one of the chairs. He located his swimsuit, turned, and picked up his pants from the floor. He sat on the bed's edge, took his wallet from his pants, and removed the envelope. Inserting one finger under the flap, he opened it. He reached in to remove the folded sheet, but from the next room the other couple's voices rose to a bitter and violent pitch. He jerked open the drawer in the bedside stand; finding the expected Bible, he put the message in it. Closing the drawer, he looked up sharply at the locked door as the sound of blows came crashing through amidst the loud and abusive language. He grabbed his bathing suit as Anne's voice penetrated the distance.

"My God, someone should call the police. Are they drunk?" She turned off the water and stepped into the main room, radiant in a new two-piece blue knit swimsuit. *"I can't stand violence."*

He sat on the bed, seemingly fixated, his bathing suit dangling from one hand. He tried to smile at her, but without awareness tears had formed in his eyes. Anne stared at him.

"Is the suit too extreme?"

He shook his head "no." All sounds from the other room had stopped now; perhaps they had heard Anne. Perhaps one of them couldn't yell and argue anymore. He stepped quickly past her into the bathroom, relieved himself, put on his suit, slipped a comb through his hair, and rejoined her in the other room. She had been picking up; he watched her for a second until she was aware of him. She gazed at him for some sign of continued disturbance. There was none, but the look of concern remained on her face. He smiled shyly at her, pulling his swimsuit up as high as it could go, until his genitals were clearly outlined through the thin material. "Is this suit too extreme?" Anne grinned at him, grabbed up her Polaroid camera, and they left hand in hand to find breakfast.

Breakfast had been an extravagant affair, with orange juice, pancakes, eggs, sausage, bacon, and lots of coffee. They both read through the local daily paper, first checking the weather reports from western Montana, delighting in the cold and snowy weather descending upon that area. Their day was filled with bright sunshine and warm soft sea breezes. It was idyllic.

By midmorning they had left the coffee shop and were walking on the beach again, returning in the direction of their motel. It was nearly a mile away.

They walked slowly, smoking an occasional cigarette, watching the other people on the beach, most of whom were locals involved in their various postseason tasks.

They reminisced about their other holidays. He stopped along the way regularly, taking pictures of Anne in her "extreme" swimsuit. They ran through the surf splashing each other. They rested in the sand, soaking up the bright, nearly hot mid-autumn sun. More pictures were taken. Although Anne wanted a few shots of him, he insisted that she was the more photogenic and that it was a waste to take his picture. His insistence was stronger than hers, and he kept close possession of the camera to ensure that no photos of him ever existed.

By early afternoon they came upon a boat-rental place about halfway between their breakfast place and the motel. Although it was not really open for business, they had persuaded the old man running the place to rent them a small craft for a few hours. Since they had no fishing gear, it was only to take a ride that they wanted the boat. Once on the water they had headed back in the direction they had just come, following the beach toward the city that shot its few tall buildings into the pale blue sky.

The low-horsepower outboard worked quietly and efficiently as they traced the water's edge and examined the playground areas in front of the city. Anne lounged drowsily in the middle of the boat trailing first one hand and then the other in the water. He took a few snapshots of her in the boat.

By the time they had reached the port channel, it was about time to head back. Anne had drifted off to sleep. He sorted through the dozen and a half photos they had taken during the day, reserving three or four for himself, putting the rest inside the camera's carrying case. When she awoke under his gaze it was as if she could read his thoughts. Alone on the water they made love under the hot sun. With her eyes shut tight against the burning rays and her head skyward, she rode up and down on his spread-eagled and tumescent flesh, like a madwoman raping a dead man. Then they both slept as the boat drifted aimlessly.

Later, he turned the small boat around and opened

up the throttle on the outboard. In comparison to their leisurely pace earlier, it felt as though they were fairly flying back to the boat dock. Anne woke up halfway through their return trip, looking for just a second disorganized and maybe a little frightened. He smiled reassurance at her as she began to orient herself. She quickly understood that their speed was only his play. Overhead a helicopter lowered itself to pass above them; perhaps it was a pilot looking for nudes or lawbreakers. It lingered momentarily, then continued. He was reminded of the unread message waiting for him in their motel room.

He almost ran past the boat dock, and seeing that, nearly capsized by turning too sharply to get into the dock. The old man from whom they had rented the boat stood staring with alarm. They laughed lightly at their own casual carelessness and his overconcern. Finally docked and on their feet again in the boathouse, they gave the old man an extra ten-dollar bill to assuage the momentary anxiety they had caused him. The gratuity prompted an invitation to come again the next day. They told him they might just do that.

They returned to the coffee shop where they had had that morning's breakfast. Dinner was followed by a slow walk on the beach back to their motel room. Behind them the sun ran redly down to the gulf and fell asleep behind the Mexican peninsula hundreds of miles away. It had been a wonderfully indolent, extravagant day, only occasionally marred by some unexpected reminder that waiting for him in the nightstand's Bible was that message. He hoped it had gone away, perhaps found and removed by the motel's morning maid, but, of course, it had not.

Later that evening, Anne was preparing for bed in the other room; he could hear her singing "September Song." He took the envelope out of the Bible, opened it, unfolded the sheet and read:

```
         NNOEO
         TGIOE
         EHITE
         VFW
```

Now he took Anne's Peace Corps form and wrote across it:

```
         EXECUTIVE
```

Then he drew a grid below it:

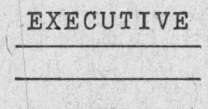

```
         EXECUTIVE
         ─────────
         ─────────
         ─────────
```

Then he assigned a number to each letter in the order that the letter appeared in the alphabet and in the word "Executive": c=1, e=2, e=3, e=4, i=5, etc.

"Tom?"

"Yes."

"Never mind."

He concentrated on the code again. He spoke the alphabet softly. He placed the appropriate numbers under the letters. The grid now looked like this:

```
         EXECUTIVE
         ─────────
         293176584
```

He now began to fill the letters into the grid. Going back to the original message to get the letters, he placed them vertically into the grid. The grid now looked like this:

```
        EXECUTIVE
        ─────────
        293176584
        ─────────
        OFONIEOEG
        ─────────
        EWTNTHEVI
        ─────────
```

He wrote "Action" on another sheet of paper. Assigning numbers to each letter there as well, he drew a grid and took the letters from a horizontal line above, and filled them in vertically again:

```
        ACTION
        ──────
        126354
        ──────
        ONEONE
        ──────
        FIVETW
        ──────
        OEIGHT
        ──────
```

The double transposition was complete. The message read: "ONEONEFIVETWOEIGHT." He placed slash marks through the letters, and the message now read: "ONE/ONE/FIVE/TWO/EIGHT."

He wrote "115,28." He opened the Bible, turned to page 115 of the New Testament, Verse 28. He read aloud softly:

> Marvel not at this; for the hour is coming, in which all that are in the graves shall hear his voice.

His worst fears were confirmed. This was the message that he had dreaded. He knew what he had to do and did not want to. Whatever had gone wrong over the weekend had "promoted" him from backup to number one. As unwelcome as that now was, what had to be done next was going to be even more difficult; he hoped it would not be impossible. He closed his eyes, sick.

Anne entered from the bathroom in the nightgown that had not been worn the night before. She stepped lightly behind him, quickly putting her hands over his eyes. Involuntarily he froze in position on the edge of the bed, leaning half-sideways over the night table, a poised killing machine.

"I caught you . . . you're writing your letter of resignation." She tried to read over his shoulder. He quickly twisted around, holding her waist in both hands, drawing her down into his lap with her back to the papers and book. He was momentarily angry. He had been trained better than that. He pushed the drawer shut, crumpling up the papers. His determined, serious demeanor creased her face with a frown. He couldn't avoid or postpone it.

"I have to go in the morning."

"Are you serious? Why?"

"I've had a message."

She tried unsuccessfully to take the ball of paper from his hand.

"You're teasing me. No one knew we were here; you said no one knew you were here. Are you kidding me?"

"I guess I must have left the address in case of . . ."

"I don't understand. I feel you're lying to me."

"You stay here another day, or . . ."

She broke away from him. Despite the gentleness of his words, his voice was edged with determination. It was couched in the familiar withdrawal that always terrified and angered her. "You're lying to me."

Her fury grew rapidly as she stomped, as best she could barefoot on the concrete floor, into the bathroom for one of its glasses.

"Where are you going?"

Ann's voice rose sharply, and beyond the wall that they shared with the other unit, the couple there heard themselves from that morning, as through a time tunnel. "Why are you always running away?"

Plowing through her suitcase, she found the pint of bourbon that had been stashed there. Half-filling the glass, she prowled the small room, throwing down several gulps of liquor. Next door their neighbors maintained their vigil, listening for more.

"Now you won't talk again."

Silence and more aimless prowling. Her nightgown swirled about her in agitated rhythm to her movements. Her voice, nasalized from the sobbing, continued upward along a scale of loudness and harshness.

"Goddamn you, talk to me. You can't talk, can you?"

Another gulp from the glass emptied it.

"You can only lie."

She retrieved her pint and refilled the glass. He was determined not to get caught up in this. Not to contribute to any irrevocable distortion of their relationship. He leaned against the head of the bed, stretching his legs out. Lighting a cigarette, he answered softly, in an unheard monotone, "Just like everybody else."

"You don't work for the government . . . or the Army, do you?"

Her rage was total now, and her accusations were clearly heard by the eavesdroppers next door. Anne seemed not to be aware of that possibility as she splashed some more of the liquor into her glass.

"You must think I'm stupid. I let you lie to me *because I was afraid you'd leave me!* You and your *goddamn* money!"

Despite the fact that she didn't feel, look, or sound intoxicated, the heavy emphasis on "goddamn" was to him a fairly accurate indication that the bourbon she was putting away was having its effect. She confronted him from the foot of the bed, standing spread-legged, punching the air between them with the nearly empty glass.

"Where do you get your money? You're no engineer . . . you're something illegal"—she drained the glass—"or *criminal,* aren't you?"

She felt her face flush; the liquor began to take its toll on her control. She turned back to the suitcase and the bottle, but the difficulty in pouring another glass of the booze was too much to overcome. She dropped her voice to a harsh, hissing whisper now, shoulders heaving, her back to him; she struggled for control not only of the situation but of herself.

"I know what it is. I should have known from the beginning."

"What?" His voice was still low, unemotional, uncommitted.

She dropped the glass and open bottle into the suitcase; the remaining whiskey bubbled into the clothes still packed in the case. She whirled, fought to retain her balance, and flung herself full length across the room at him. Landing diagonally across the bed and his middle, she pummeled his chest, shoulders, and face with ineffectual little fists, dropping tiny blows on him.

He gathered her hands in his, holding her atop him. Her pain and anguish were now being released in a drunken sobbing. Finally able to make herself understood, she spoke aloud that which even in her deepest depression she had never allowed herself to think. *"You've got some other girl!* That's why . . . you never . . . talk. . . . You brought me here to say good-bye . . . didn't you? . . . Didn't you? . . . Oh, my God . . . my God. . . . What am I going to do?"

Her tears were steady; her chest heaving for breath made him aware of the rhythmic pressure of her breasts against him. (Even now? he thought, disgusted with himself.) He gathered her into a curled sobbing figure fully on top of him now, holding her lightly, stroking her gently as though she were a colicky infant.

"Anne . . . Anne . . . baby . . . I haven't any other girl."

None of this transmitted through the wall. The other couple self-consciously withdrew from their listening post, wondering.

He petted her; the warmth from his body mingled with the liquor in hers, completely draining her energy.

"I don't care. . . . You'll never come back this time, will you? . . . You'll run away again, I know."

His answer was the simplest, most truthful statement he had made in months. It was totally involuntary. "I can't run anymore."

She raised her head, gazing fully into his eyes. He stared back, overwhelmed by what had just escaped his lips, unable to say more. He continued stroking her. Her breath washed over his face, full of the liquor. It didn't matter to him. He stroked her evenly, his eyes trying to reach some internal touchstone of sensitivity in her that would provide her with all the answers she wanted. He was literally unable to speak.

"I'm sorry. . . . You're in some kind of trouble, aren't you? . . . It's so obvious." She picked up the Bible open to the marked verse of death.

Her tears began again, but now they were for him. She laid her head gently back down on his chest, nearly whispering. "Please, what is it? . . . Can't you tell me? . . . I'll keep your secret. . . . Are you sick? . . . Are you very sick? . . . Can you talk to me? . . . I love you, Tom."

Her tears had stopped now, but he continued to stroke her.

"Are you dying?"

He only heard her voice, not her words. She lay silently now. He patted her mechanically. They slept in the same position all night.

Somewhere in Northern California—November 4, 1963

Reardon's naked body was liverish white and covered with old purple World War I scars. Preston had not seen him since the meeting in Virginia two months before, but he knew that Admiral James K. Reardon, U.S. Navy, Retired, was his baby-sitter. At the last minute, by telephone, Foster had ordered him to fly to California, then drive into the redwoods to this most exclusive of all nature clubs, there to meet Reardon and give him a roll of microfilm. Why have him make this detour instead of going straight into the Dallas target area unless they were "concerned" about him? The watchers watched, he thought, and who will watch the watchers?

This club, the Primeval Woods, was for men only. That was obvious to Preston as he looked around. Everywhere were old or older naked men; swimming in the sparkling natural pool, playing miniature golf, exercising, jogging, drinking, and talking at the outdoor bar. Some of the famous men he saw he knew slightly, like Richard Nixon, Senator Goldwater, General Wedemeyer; others he recognized from intelligence dossiers as electronic and aerospace chairmen of the boards.

Reardon, scarred and naked, approached holding two bloody marys. Behind him was spread a sumptuous buffet with varieties of fish, meats and cheeses.

Reardon looked at Preston until he undraped the towel that had separated him from the otherwise universal nudity; and now, naked too, he wrapped the towel around his already slightly sunburned neck and took the bloody mary from the approving admiral. As he sipped from the tall glass, he could not help noticing that several men talking nearby had looked over to check out his exposed body. The drink was good, the air exhilarating; he felt alive for the first time in months. Whatever Foster's motives, he was grateful for this compassionate leave. He looked beyond the tableaux of naked convivial men to the perimeter of the grounds; there, dotted against the unrivaled redwood giants, patrolled uniformed guards with German guard dogs, who appeared and disappeared in and out of the shadows of the mighty trees.

As the two men, drinks in hand, walked out toward the perimeter, Reardon expatiated about the history of the Primeval Forest and how the cardinal rule was that "No thing done nor no word said there could ever be revealed," and how the virtues of ancient Rome were recapitulated here in "God's country," where the goal was "a healthy body in a healthy mind," and there were, "Thank God, no women." The drink was a double, and Preston was feeling it; the drink, the grass under his bare feet, and the incredible air and beauty of the spot all combined to make him a bit light-headed. So much so that he compared Dallas, and his approaching assignment, unfavorably with the Primeval Woods and wished fervently that he could remain for a few days in this unspoiled retreat before going back into the world of spooks, plots, and counterplots in "Big D," as he had taken to calling Dallas derisively. Reardon had a whitish arm draped easily on Preston's shoulder, and as they walked, they might have been a living Renaissance picturization of the Platonic Academy: the old scarred soldier and the lean "boy" (with the graying sideburns and new but deep frown lines and the brown eyes that were hiding not something but everything now). Reardon knew what was wrong with this smooth-skinned lad from the eastern seaboard, he thought, and he knew what to say. They had reached the shadows of the great trees by now, and their drinks were empty. Preston was starting to lose the high feeling, and as Reardon babysat him, his depression returned worse than ever.

". . . When you think of it, what's the difference between the Congo, Laos, Indonesia, Guatemala, Bolivia, and right here at home? It comes to the same thing for the same reason."

"But there is a difference. I don't know what it is, but there is. I can't . . . Some of my best people are ready to quit. I don't feel I'm being trusted. I . . ." They could hear, dimly, another conversation from a shadowed glen. "In four years, they'll have surface-to-air missiles. It's a matter of surgery. . . ."

"So the 'department of dirty tricks' has a slight attack of the vapors? Well, goddamn it, this is war (I don't care what the goddamn eggheads or nervous nellies try to say) and a soldier—that's what you are—has to be ready to kill or be killed. That's why I thought you'd like it down here—with just the boys. Just make believe you're in Saigon with a goddamn slope behind every door and you'll see there isn't a bit of difference in the world."

As they returned out of the shadows into the clear sun, they passed men talking, drinking, and playing games. Snatches of conversation, political and profane, carried over the clear, quiet air. More men were swimming and sunbathing in the nude. Reardon headed for the buffet, ravenous.

"Hey, Barry, did you hear the one about Jackie and the nigger houseboy?"

Preston drifted away by himself. He stood with a drink, reading the posted rules of the club. A group in the background was singing a boisterous rendition of "On, Wisconsin." Preston looked haunted now. All the surrounding talk seemed nightmarishly alien.

"They need the shit scared out of them."

As he stood there naked, his fantasy was that he would be remorselessly attacked from behind; his mind was a montage of powerful and ancient bodies, their visceral and erectile tissue flaming like old war wounds. He had to get hold of himself; this was getting out of hand; *he was a professional soldier the equivalent of a full colonel* (he had to hang on to that): he would play his role.

He covered his bare and vulnerable private parts with the oversize towel and headed toward the guards and dogs there in the middle distance in the lengthening shadows of the almost supernatural trees.

Corpus Christi—Dallas, Texas—November 5, 1963

The day started as the previous ones had ended, in silence. They both awoke about the same time. Each quickly remembered how they had ended the night before, and fell into a self-conscious, embarrassed pattern of behavior. The intense discomfort hastened the packing process, and within thirty minutes they were stopped in Corpus Christi, buying doughnuts and coffee to go.

Although they were not "not speaking," conversation had been perfunctory. Minimum spoken exchanges were undertaken in the service of doing that which both wanted very much—to get out of there and away from each other. They both reflected privately about how quickly and thoroughly their long-awaited Gulf Coast trip had reversed itself. Their first year together when he had not had to be away as frequently, nor for as long at one stretch, they both remembered now as a kind of long-past and personal golden age.

Driving the long barren stretches of highway toward Dallas, immersed in the incoherent sounds from the car radio, he let his mind wander back to the preceding night. After Anne had drifted off to sleep, he lay on the bed, holding her, falling asleep fitfully, only to awaken after what seemed too brief a time. He was aware now of being quite tired, so that the drive north was punctuated with regular coffee stops.

His head seemed full of memory traces from a series of nightmares from the night before. Each stop seemed to bring into focus some detail from his half-forgotten dreams. Every hour or so a forlorn establishment would present itself, and he would stop to get coffee to go. A waitress at one was sloppy and provocative, and he was suddenly reminded of a dream that had interrupted his sleep the night before. . . .

(He stood behind Anne, his hands cupping her breasts; he saw a group of foreign-looking men rushing at them from the top of a small hill. He pointed her breasts at them, but they didn't fire, and as he whirled to locate his weapon—the weapon that would work—Anne turned, forced him down, and mounted him.)

As he returned to the car with the coffee each time, Anne seemed to withdraw even further from him. . . .

(The surfboard began to wave softly in a slow wind drifting in off the water weaving in a hypnotic pattern, luring him closer, closer; then he could see plainly that

III / NOVEMBER 161

the surfboard had a head, face, arms, and hands that reached for him; behind it were other erect surfboards moving closer on the brown water . . . his hand held the same .45 automatic that he had been armed with in Korea, but each report brought the surfboards closer, until the huge waves plunged him down into darkness.)

A group of truck drivers glanced up from their gossip in the parking area, paying him only scant attention, but it seemed as if they were like waving, weaving surfboards. By the time he headed back with his coffee, they had dispersed to their respective trucks, but he returned to the car with the jerky intermittent motions of a combat soldier advancing under fire.

Except for these coffee breaks nothing occurred to interrupt their drive, and Anne drifted off to sleep, curled tightly in the corner of the car. . . .

(He slipped his hand under her skirt . . . his hand moved higher on her leg . . . she opened up more to him, and finally, as he reached his goal, he found his hand closing around a penis and testicles. From the back seat his classmates arose laughing and jeering as his date pushed open the car door, falling out on the ground, laughing and pointing.)

He was grateful in a way that he was driving through the open nothingness of south-central Texas. There was nothing to see, to think about, but to try to grasp a measure of understanding from the relentless pressure of his own nightmares. He couldn't remember how many times he had dreamed the night before, and which were current daylight fantasies. It didn't matter much as he sped along the Texas highway toward Dallas; each episode did its damage and went its way.

Another coffee shop, and another intermission presented itself; inside he found a group of soldiers in uniform heading someplace or another. . . .

(He was loaded onto the LST in Seattle, and immediately began to search out the officer in charge . . . a mistake had been made . . . he wasn't supposed to be on this vessel . . . but, no, the orders were there . . . he had them . . . and the officer in charge had them . . . and he had all his equipment and gear. The LST pulled out of Puget Sound with all the other troops lining the railing so that he could not even look back . . . they stood motionless facing the interior of the ship, pointing at him.)

Anne had awakened while he was inside; when he opened the car door, she was looking and pointing. "Is that coffee?"

He dropped the plastic cup; it hit the edge of the door frame. "Yes, it was. . . . Why?"

"I'd like some, if you don't mind." Her voice was flat, toneless, revealing nothing except the miles between them.

He returned to the counter, shaking his pants leg, trying to dry it, looking like a big cat that has inadvertently stepped into some water, hoping that no one would notice. No one did.

Although she had seen his discomfort, Anne said nothing about it when he returned with their coffee. She sipped lightly from the cup, gazing unseeingly into the vast flat stretches of open land slipping past the car.

Then she huddled in the corner, curled into a ball as if already protecting the new life that had started inside her as they floated on the warm, brown saltwater of the gulf, as the little boat had drifted toward the sea.

He avoided any involvement with Dallas' intercourse, heading straight to Love Field. Their "luck" held, for as they walked into the Western Terminal, an announcement filled the fake marble box with a warning of first call for a 7:15 P.M. flight to Salt Lake. Anne took it. He returned the car to Hertz, then entered a phone booth, dialed a number, said no more than six words into the mouthpiece, and stepped outside to wait for the jeep. When the jeep arrived, it carried a sticker on the bumper that the technician was to see all over Dallas: *"KNOCK OUT THE KENNEDYS."*

Washington, D.C.—November 6, 1963

> (Kenney—I thought this was worth you taking note of.
> Please return, and I will answer. Do you have any thoughts?)
> RFK

TO: KO[5]

FROM: RFK

DATE: 11/6/63

Bill Kilgarlin[6] writes to me that the dinner in Houston on 11/21 is "rigged for the purpose of showing greater popularity of the Vice President than the President" (sic)!

The Coliseum holds 12,000: they plan to use only the floor, and, Kilgarlin goes on, "by persons who are more closely identified with the Vice President than the President. Tickets for the affair have been taken in large blocks by interests that have never been too friendly with the Democratic party in the past."

He warns that the 10,000 balcony seats will not be open to the rank-and-file and that ". . . those in attendance may well indicate by their applause, etc., a preference for the Vice President. . . ."

Finally, he denies that he and other liberals are spreading stories that JFK advance people are dealing exclusively with LBJ people, saying, "I suspect that its origin can be traced to sources close to the Vice President."

Foster sent his photocopy of the memo to Howard

---

[5] KO—Kenney O'Donnell, special assistant to the President.
[6] Bill Kilgarlin—Houston Democratic chairman.

Ferguson in Dallas with his comment in the margin: "Do not underrate these boys! RFK very dangerous."

Dallas, Texas—November 7, 1963

There was nothing out of the ordinary about the technician's 1962 pickup truck. All anyone would have seen was a man dressed in utility clothing as he turned onto the Elm Street extension, parked in front of a wooden fence, and got out. The area around the Texas School Book Depository was deserted on this cloudy Thursday. The technician slipped on a railroad man's jacket and cap and walked casually around behind the fence. A few minutes later he reappeared, knelt down to pry up a storm sewer inlet grating, swung into it, emerged five minutes later. An old car, driving down Main, right on Houston, and left on Elm, passed slowly.

Because the technician was unaware that the School Book Depository would figure in the plan, he barely glanced at it as he strode quickly up to the Dal-Tex Building on the Plaza across Houston Street. Twenty minutes later he looked down from the roof of the County Records Building. He made notes as he studied his pickup truck in the near distance. The old car circled slowly down Houston to Elm again.

Dallas, Texas—November 7, 1963

The communications room in the Dallas "safe house" did not compare with the one in Virginia, but it was sufficient for Preston's needs. With his customary orderliness he had rearranged the old photography studio in the failing West Dallas section of town to suit his needs and those of his aide, the ex-Army Intelligence sergeant named Valentine who looked enough like Lee Harvey Oswald to be his brother.

Valentine was screening the film of Oswald's "arrest"

in New Orleans for passing out Fair Play for Cuba leaflets. Just as the film ended, Preston entered with coffee. "Enough cream? How are you doing?"

"Fine. Just so's we can get the hell out of here before Thanksgiving."

"I know, I know. It's tight as hell. Let's try the Spanish again." Preston adjusted another reel of film onto the projector. The picture and sound were of Oswald and David Ferrie; the crucifix in the background identified the setting as Ferrie's New Orleans combination shrine/medical laboratory/arms cache/apartment. Oswald was obviously unaware that the meeting was being recorded.

"Lee, I believe it would be more authentic if the oral application were made in Spanish, don't you?" At this point both men switched from English to Spanish. Oswald talked fast, as if by rote.

"At the Cuban Embassy in Mexico City: I inform them that I am a Communist, a Fidelista. I have set up a committee for Fidel Castro in New Orleans. For this I was attacked and beaten by the *gusanos*. I was arrested and sent to jail— My wife is Russian—"

"Wait, and then you show them the newspaper clippings."

Oswald caught himself, irritated for having forgotten the clippings. "Here are the clippings of my arrest. My wife is Russian; I lived in Russia—"

Valentine turned off the projector, turned to Preston, and began an immediate imitation. "I am a Communist, a Fidelista. I have set up a committee for Fidel Castro in New Orleans. For this I was attacked and beaten by the *gusanos*. I was arrested and sent to jail. Here are the clippings of my arrest: My wife is Russian; I lived in Russia—"

Preston broke in in English. "Very good. Very credible. Let's take a break. Drink your coffee."

The look-alike lit a Camel. "Thanks. Say, what the hell does this poor bastard think he's doing?"

Preston smiled and stretched. Now he felt as if he

were in Foster's role as mentor. He enjoyed himself: "Mr. Oswald believes that he is a rather important, middle-echelon operative on his way to Cuba, there to work as a black agent,[7] setting up an anti-Castro spy ring; that sort of thing. In Cuba he will be ever so slightly, but adequately, exposed by our apparatus to the Cuban apparatus. All the while, of course, you're covering for him here."

Valentine was trying to follow. "Same as his deal in Russia?" He paused and smoked. "But who the hell does he think *you* are all this time? And what—"

Preston went right on, consciously imitating Foster now: "Whereupon the Cubans, in their turn, will intrude a rather important middle-echelon operative into the United States to shadow Oswald, in the hopes of learning something about *our* operation. Is this quite clear?" He smiled patiently. "Our man knows, all the while, of course, that we will be following the man following him." He paused. "Have I lost you?"

They smiled. Each man knew the obscure rhetoric of the clandestine pecking order; each man had to lie to the man below him and yet retain his trust. Valentine was a reassignment from the Chicago first team, and Preston was damned glad to have him. The two had hit it off at once, and this partially made up for the strain and alienation that had developed with Tom, the technician. If he could, he would have put Valentine in as Handler.

The look-alike sipped his coffee, not knowing how, exactly, to react. Suddenly he began again in Spanish. "My wife is Russian. I lived in Russia. . . ."

Preston laughed and rose, signaling that the coffee break was over. The two men sat down at a desk. "This calendar refers to the agenda that you will set up this week:

1) Used car
    address and details

[7] Black agent—Illegal operative.

2) Gun shop
3) Rifle range

"All right. Now you're going to have to 'ham' this up. I mean, it's all got to be crude as hell. Lay it on thick!" He snapped on the film of Oswald talking in Spanish.

Vienna, Virginia—November 7, 1963

Foster sipped the one after-dinner Scotch that he permitted himself. When it was over, at Thanksgiving, he would break training, he promised himself, savoring the prospect of the holidays. He tinkled the ice cubes. He was concerned about Reardon's latest report on the Dallas police, but then stilled his anxiety by recalling Napoleon: "The art of the police consists of not seeing what there is no use seeing."

He rose, turned on a reading lamp, sliced open an envelope with his jeweled daggerlike opener, and smoothed out several sheets of long, yellow legal paper. The sheets were from the pad of one of the President's speech writers. Stolen from a White House wastebasket that day, they obviously represented a rough draft of an upcoming executive statement. Without glasses, he scanned the stuff:

> The Family of Man is more than three billion strong. It lives in more than 100 nations. Most of its members are not white. Most of them are not Christians. Most of them know nothing about free enterprise or due process of law or the Australian ballot. If our society is to promote the Family of Man, let us realize the magnitude of our task. This is a sobering assignment. For the Family of Man in the world of today is not faring very well. . . .
>
> Even little wars are dangerous in this nuclear world. . . . The Korean conflict alone, forgetting for a moment the thousands of Americans who

lost their lives, cost four times as much as our total worldwide aid budget for the current year. . . .

I do not want it said of us what T. S. Eliot said of others some years ago: "These were a decent people. Their only monuments: the asphalt road and a thousand lost golf balls. . . ."

The struggle is by no means over. It is essential that we not only maintain our effort, but that we persevere; that we not only endure, in Mr. Faulkner's words, but also prevail. It is essential, in short, that the word go forth from the United States to all who are concerned about the future of the Family of Man that we are not weary in well-doing. And we shall, I am confident, if we maintain the pace, we shall in due reason reap the kind of world we deserve, and deserve the kind of world we still have.

He decided that he would allow himself another highball. "I'm getting old," he thought.

Irving, Texas—November 7, 1963

Valentine drove his blue-and-white Ford slowly through the Dallas suburb. Passing a furniture store with a sign in the window, *"GUNS SOLD AND REPAIRED HERE,"* he pulled over to park. Before entering, he quickly removed a false moustache, his own glasses, and a baseball cap. He reached over and took a rifle from the back seat.

"This is a furniture store; we don't repair guns." The salesman told him that the sign in the window was long out of date and recommended that he drive to the Irving Sports Shop on Irving Boulevard just a few miles away.

At the sports shop he was waited on by a man in his thirties who asked, "What seems to be the trouble?"

"The plunger, the firing pin is broke."

The salesman nodded in agreement as he looked into the breech.

"How soon can you fix it?" Valentine-"Oswald" asked. "I'll need it right away—pretty soon, anyway."

"Be ready in a couple of days. Cost about two and a half dollars." He took out a tag. "What's the name?"

"Oswald. Lee Harvey Oswald."

Dallas, Texas—November 7, 1963

The technician sat in the drafty and all but empty Texas Theater staring without seeing at a John Wayne movie. Ten rows behind, staring at him, sat Bolton Andrews of the U.S. Treasury Department who was supposed to be on vacation, visiting his "auntie" in Brownsville, Texas. Both men were immune to the mindless morality being acted out on the screen and the flat and hollow dialogue that almost echoed through the empty theater. Both were half-lost in the memories of other holiday seasons when they had been among the living with people that loved them and they could love.

When he couldn't stand any more, he rose and half-staggered on his long legs up the aisle and out into the deserted lobby. He never noticed the black man leaning on his hand as if he were asleep.

Washington, D.C.—November 8, 1963

Pierre Salinger was in the midst of dictating a reply to a Mrs. Nellie M. Doyle of Dallas, Texas. He puffed on his big cigar as he talked: "I most appreciate your letter of October 28. I think it would be a most unhappy thing if there were a city in the United States that the President could not visit. The President certainly hopes that he will be able to get to Dallas, if not on this current trip, sometime in the future."

170   EXECUTIVE ACTION

The next day, November 9, Foster played the tape of that dictation to Admiral Reardon. Salinger's office had been electronically surveilled from his first day.

The listening post for all White House surveillance was a suite in Washington's famous old Mayflower Hotel. Two adjoining suites were rented by the year by the lobbyist for a real-estate and development corporation with its home office in Miami. The board of directors—a combination of industry, intelligence, and the crime syndicate—used the second suite which was not equipped with electronic equipment for their parties and business when they were in the nation's capital.

Dallas, Texas—November 8, 1963

The technician sat drinking beer, listening to the six o'clock news. For the third night in a row he would sit in the unlit hotel room, drink two beers, go to bed, masturbate thinking about Anne, and go to sleep without eating. In his mind he was seeing Anne cupping her breasts in her hands, for him to kiss, the nipples erect and hard as rubber. It was too early; he needed another beer or he would never sleep afterwards, and he had to sleep, because he was in the countdown pattern by days now, and his team had to be worked out every day. He forced himself to listen to the news:

> The President drew chuckles when asked about Senator Goldwater's charge that "manipulation of news by this administration has become a pretty big project."
>
> I am confident he will be making many charges even more serious than this one in the coming months and, in addition, he himself has had a busy week selling TVA. . . .
>
> [*Laughter*]
>
> and suggesting that military commanders overseas

be permitted to use nuclear weapons, attacking the President of Bolivia while he was here in the U.S.,
[*Laughter*]
involving himself in the Greek elections...."
[*Laughter*]

Dallas, Texas—November 9, 1963

Valentine, his hair combed like Oswald's, walked through Dealey Plaza and into the Downtown Lincoln-Mercury agency. Paul Bogard, the salesman, greeted him Texas style and jotted the name "Oswald" down on the back of a card so he wouldn't forget his prospective customer's name.

"I like that red convertible job out there."

"Can't blame you for that. She's a honey. A lot of horsepower under that hood. You come at a real good time, too. We're cutting prices—clearing out for the sixty-fours. Let's take a look at it."

The impostor and Bogard circled the red Mercury convertible in the American ritual, the rite of passage for the used car.

"How does it ride?"

"Smooth. Real smooth. Why don't you give it a try?"

Valentine did not know that Lee Harvey Oswald did not drive, did not know how to drive an automobile. Either Preston did not know either or had made an inexplicable slip; or had David Ferrie or the Chinaman not known or not included the information? So Valentine now played his part to the hilt as he had been instructed: he zoomed down side streets, slammed on the brakes, and as he later told Preston, "scared the living shit out of that salesman."

"You sure have a style," Bogard told him when they screeched back into the lot.

"I like it. If the price is okay, I'll take it," the impostor said loudly as he slammed his door. They clumped into the office, where two other salesmen were drinking Cokes and envying Bogard his sale.

"Yes sir, she's a real bargain—only $1995—and she comes with your radio, your heater, and your whitewalls all included."

"Okay. I'll take it. I want credit—and I want it now. I want to drive this buggy off the lot."

"Alrighty. You just come in and meet Mr. Simmons, he's our credit manager. You working right now, right?"

"No. No job."

"You got some income, though, huh?"

"Welfare check."

"You got a bank account?"

"No. That's why I need credit."

They were all used to the Texas style, but this young man was just too mean-sounding. "Well, I know," said Bogard, "but we'll need some kind of—"

"Look mister—forget the whole damn deal. Maybe I'm going to have to go back to Russia to buy me a car."

"Russia?"

Valentine needed more distance to retain his credibility. He almost burst out laughing at the look on the three salesmen's faces. God keep him from ever having to put up with the shit that these pitiful goddamned salesmen had to put up with. He turned and poured it on about fifteen yards out from the office. Bogard was standing forlornly in the door.

"Yes, Russia! I'll have some cash coming in just two weeks. Maybe I'll be back then. You just hold that red buggy for old *Lee Oswald*. You hear?"

He had thought up the last part of the act, about coming back, because old Bogard had looked so damned pitiful standing in the door with the untouched Coke in his hand.

At that moment the real Lee Harvey Oswald was sitting at his typewriter composing a cover letter to the So-

viet Embassy in Washington, D.C., on orders received
the night before from the Chinaman:

> FROM: LEE H. OSWALD, P.O. BOX 6225,
> DALLAS, TEXAS
> MARINA NICHILAYEVA OSWALD,
> SOVIET CITIZEN
>
> TO: CONSULAR DIVISION
> EMBASSY U.S.S.R.
> WASHINGTON, D.C.
> NOV. 9, 1963

Dear sirs;
 This is to inform you of recent events
since my meetings with comrade Kostin in the
Embassy Of the Soviet Union, Mexico City,
Mexico.
 I was unable to remain in Mexico indefi-
nily because of my mexican visa restrictions
which was for 15 days only. I could not take a
chance on requesting a new visa unless I used my
real name, so I returned to the United States.
 I had not planned to contact the Soviet
embassy in Mexico so they were unprepared, had I
been able to reach the Soviet Embassy in Havana
as planned, the embassy there would have had time
to complete our business.
 Of corse the Soviet embassy was not at
fault, they were, as I say unprepared, the Cuban
consulate was guilty of a gross breach of regulations, I am glad he has since been replced.
 The Federal Bureu of Investigation is not
now interested in my activities in the progres-
sive organization "Fair Play For Cuba Committee", of which I was secretary in New Orleans
(state Louisiana) since I no longer reside in
that state. However, the F.B.I. has visited us

here in Dallas, Texas, on November 1st. Agent James P. Hasty warned me that if I engaged in F.P.C.C. activities in Texas the F.B.I. will again take an "interrest" in me.

This agent also "suggested" to Marina Nichilayeva that she could remain in the United States under F.B.I. "protection", that is, she could defect from the Soviet Union, of couse, I and my wife strongly protested these tactics by the notorious F.B.I.

Please inform us of the arrival of our Soviet entrance visa's as soon as they come.

Also, this is to inform you of the birth, on October 20, 1963 of a DAUGHTER, AUDREY MARINA OSWALD in DALLAS, TEXAS, to my wife.

        Respecfully,

Dallas, Texas—November 11, 1963

The technician crossed to the telephone booth in the station next to the hotel. There were a number of booths in the vicinity of where he was staying, and he used them with no pattern so that he could be sure that there were no taps on them.

"This is Mr. Bryan. I'd like you to run something in the Personals again. The message is the same: 'Dear Vivian, I am still waiting. Signed Norman.' How much would that be for a week this time? You need that today? I'll be right in."

Either Preston was going to stay in touch with the now number-one team, or he, the technician, was going to reject any responsibility. This silence was unlike the Preston he had worked with overseas. From the beginning the operation, the communication, the backup had been erratic. The technician thought all this as he strode down Main Street at high noon on this bright Dallas day.

Dallas, Texas—November 11, 1963

The plain tan four-door Chevrolet moved along Dallas' main street. At the first intersection after passing the Ferguson Diversified of Dallas, it turned right and pulled into the first available curbside parking space. Preston, in his customary dark-toned Brooks Brothers suit, got out of the car and locked it, putting the keys with their large plastic "Hertz Rent-A-Car" tag into a jacket pocket. He deposited enough change into the parking meter to obtain the maximum time and began walking back in the direction he had just driven.

He entered the lobby of the high-rise building and began to scan the names listed on the directory. Apparently unable to find the desired name, he turned abruptly to the receptionist located in the circular information booth in the center of the lobby.

The middle-aged woman, looking more like a small-town elementary schoolteacher than the receptionist of a large modern metropolitan office-building complex, had noted his entrance and momentary search. She anticipated his approach. "May I help you, sir?"

Preston took a paperback novel from his coat pocket. "Perhaps. I'm looking for the building's executive offices." She recognized the signal.

"They're on the top three floors. Oh, is that the new Fleming spy novel? It looks very interesting. What's the title?"

"*On Her Majesty's Secret Service.* Are you a mystery fan?"

"Oh, yes sir. I love a good mystery. I guess my favorite is *The Third Man.*"

"Yes, that's a good one. I enjoyed it very much; you've reminded me that I've intended to reread it for some time now."

"If you'll just go through that door there, to the right of the main elevators."

"Thank you very much." Preston turned and walked toward the door indicated, marked "Private." As he reached for the knob, the receptionist pressed a button beneath her desk, and he heard the nearly inaudible click as the electronic lock was released. He pushed the door open only enough to allow himself to slip through. He was now standing in a vestibule where a small open elevator stood waiting. There were no buttons or signs. He entered the elevator, the door immediately sliding closed behind him. The whir of the elevator machinery was his only indication that the device was operating. Within a few seconds the elevator opened again, and Preston stepped out into an alcove that was an exact replica of the one he had just entered on the ground floor.

Another door stood facing him, but this one had a button on its right side which when pushed apparently caused the bright light to come from the round opaque circle immediately above it at eye level. A second or two later an electric buzzing sound indicated that the door lock was released. Preston turned the knob, pulled the door, and entered into the room on the other side.

The first thing he noted was that the two walls of the story-and-a-half-high room were one-way glass. His eye skimmed over the top of Dallas and fell on the horizon miles beyond the city's edge. In the middle of the air-conditioned room was a large-scale model of the downtown area of Dallas placed in the center of a mahogany table so that a natural wood border completely surrounded the waist-high model. This expensive frame was punctuated with notepads and pencils placed every few feet. The only other natural object in the room was a tropical tree of some indistinct variety, perhaps banana, growing from a large off-white porcelain planter in the corner formed by the two glass walls. As Preston turned slowly to survey the remainder of the conference room, he studied a huge full-length aerial photograph of Dallas that was mounted on the wall that contained the door through which he had just entered.

III / NOVEMBER

The remaining wall was bare save for a metal panel containing some two dozen buttons in neat rows of four each. Alongside this panel was the only other door in the room. Several naugahyde-upholstered business chairs were placed about the mahogany table-model arrangement facing generally toward the aerial photo. Piped-in music blandly filled the remaining vacant volume of the room.

The 101 Strings' version of "Stranger in Paradise" was abruptly halted by a twanging voice. "I'll be right in." The music returned. The door Preston had not used opened and two men entered the room. The door shut. R. Howard Ferguson walked with short steps across the room, extending his hand to Preston. "Preston, it's great to see you. This is Arthur Allen."

Arthur Allen was in his late thirties. He had a crew-cut and wore military-cut, starched khaki work clothes. His rhythm of sharp, direct, and exact behavior and speech filled out the absoluteness of his militant body image. He was clearly submitting himself to inspection by a superior officer. Howard Ferguson had himself been raised and enriched by the same traditions and rituals, and Preston felt something warm and protective between the old man and this subordinate. "Yes, I know. It's a pleasure to meet you."

Allen stepped toward Preston, extending his hand. In another setting the entire encounter could easily have been mistaken for military ritual. A salute perhaps. "Well, how do you do? I've heard a lot about you."

"Nothing distasteful, hopefully." Preston had accepted the offered hand and only now began to disengage from the contact. These gung-ho 007 types worried him.

The billionaire, after having made the introduction, retreated from the other two, the panel of buttons his destination. Glancing over his shoulder to verify that he had their attention, he pushed some combination on the panel. The wall on which the panel was mounted began to rotate. Two equal sections jutted suddenly halfway out into the room and then slowly began to recede into their former positions. Simultaneously a kitchen entered the room from the just-opened space, set up with an instant oven, a wet bar, and an array of small drawers.

The instantaneous rearrangement of that corner of the room occurred nearly noiselessly, as Howard Ferguson's plain Texas tones informed them that, "Sandwiches hot off the barbecue—on the roof—and beer, cold as 'n Eskimo's ass. Here you go, gentlemen."

It was becoming increasingly difficult for Howard Ferguson to resist partying these days, regardless of place or circumstance. It wasn't that he had really abandoned to any degree the dedication of his youth; it was just that he was doing a little catching up, taking and making his pleasure at any opportunity. There had been precious little of it during his younger years and middle age. Now, while he continued his contributions, he was going to have a good time too. The younger men distrusted him.

This new dedication to making life somewhat less grim now found him serving his juniors (in age as well as position), and in a multi-million-dollar office building that bore his name. He was now involved in bringing the sandwiches, milk, and beer from the serving area of his mobile kitchen to the conference table.

On his third round trip he settled into the one chair that had its back directly to the planter in the corner where glass met glass. Preston gently separated one of his sandwich halves into yet two more halves and nibbled lightly at the nondescript inoffensive center. He replaced the sandwich on the serving dish and drank down half of his glass of milk.

Arthur Allen, on the other hand, had already completely devoured half of his sandwich and was sipping, nearly sucking, at the top of his beer can. Howard Ferguson rolled his head back, opened his throat, and let half of his beer can's contents cascade down his throat. He tilted forward and placed the beer on the table in front of him. "Okay, Art, shoot."

Arthur Allen sprang to life. This was the anticipated moment, and Ferguson had raised the curtain. "You want to show him that aerial of the plaza, Howard?"

The aging tycoon, whose mouth was now full of sandwich, quickly washed down all the debris with another quarter of his beer; the foam on his chin was neither clearly his own old man's spittle nor suds from the brew. "Sure thing."

Allen, who had been neither in nor out of his chair, hopped across the room toward the panel of buttons. When he pushed the correct one, another aerial photograph slid out of the ceiling. This shot was of Dealey Plaza only. Before the photo had completed its descent, he stood beside it, explaining, "Now we got a man with access to the photo labs, just in case. We figure the only possible problem will be motion pictures. But the angle of the sun is completely blocked by the tree configuration here between noon and one P.M." He moved to the sliding kitchen and retrieved a three-inch, three-ring black binder and thrust it at Preston as though it were a rifle being offered by a recruit to the officer of the day. The plastic-encased eight-by-ten glossies inside were of Dealey Plaza's grassy knoll from many angles. The locus of each photo was the shaded areas under the trees.

Preston was genuinely impressed and uncustomarily made no effort to conceal it. "This is excellent. Are you certain there are enough men?"

Despite his taut, tense demeanor, Arthur Allen was now speaking in precise measured tones, nearly patronizingly. His added emphasis and vocal punctuations might have irritated anyone who was as exhibitionistic as he. But his audience was not. Each, for his own reasons, welcomed Allen's condescending vocal presentation. It did not allow for reflection or hesitancy. Listening to him made the anticipated and uncertain future seem to be an inescapable fact, as irrefutable as history.

"I figured it and figured it till my brains fell out, and I know we got the right amount. Too many's gonna get too obvious. The freeze'll be on them witnesses so bad they'll be standing there for twenty minutes 'fore they go anywhere with their films. Man, everybody's going to be scared shitless. Our men'll be on 'em in seconds. We can cover the entire area with eight good men and a load of cash promises."

It was difficult to know when Allen had finished speaking, but the breathy pause at the end gave Preston his opportunity. "Fine. Now, disembarkation?"

Allen continued to buzz about the huge aerial photo of Dealey Plaza, touching first one location and then another. "Beee-u-ti-ful. Haven't had anything this tight in years." Arthur Allen had at least one other disconcerting habit. He could shift from one colloquial accent to an entirely different one within a single sentence; starting a statement with his own version of a midwestern twang, using his authentic Texas for a burst of adjectives, and finishing the sentence with the caricature of a very strong New York or New Jersey sound. He was, literally, the All-American Boy, talking in tongues, and if he were not energetically, though aimlessly, moving while he spoke, he would have sounded phony.

Howard Ferguson continued in his role of host, paying particular attention to his principal guest. "You gentlemen want some more beer . . . uh, milk, Preston? Another sandwich? I'm gonna have one."

He pushed himself slowly to a standing position, moving the chair he had been sitting in slightly backward.

"I'll take another beer if you got one," Allen said.

Preston declined the offer with a shake of his head at Ferguson, who had by now moved to the serving center and was looking back at Preston for his answer. Then, in nearly the same gesture, but now with a completely different direction, Preston nodded at Arthur Allen to continue.

"Now. The getaway—short and sweet. You got two teams of two men workin' and we got three, right?" Allen spoke "right" as nothing more than a peremptory challenge. Preston was now becoming critically aware of yet another "bad actor" and filled in the silences with random fantasies of what would happen to Arthur Allen if he, Preston, were to reply, "Wrong."

"Now, your team number one is behind the fence." He waved his hand across the area on the huge aerial photograph while Preston studied the eight-by-ten glossies in the binder. "The weapons and the brass[8] go in the trunk of the car. That's the backup's job. Same with the Cubans in the Dal-Tex Building and the Records Building. The Cubans are dressed up like tramps, right?"

Preston moved into a somewhat more alert posture; it was clear this next phase to be discussed concerned him. "How? You have two flight plans?"

Ferguson had moved from the kitchenette with sandwiches and beer, handing Arthur Allen his in passing. Ferguson settled into the same chair he had been occupying and scooted it up to its former position, more or less. He did manage a little better angle, so that his gaze could drift out of the one-way plate glass.

Arthur Allen began sucking at the top of his new beer can. "We got 'em, all right. Teams one and two are on the train. Team one by zero plus ten,[9] and two by plus twenty; train pulls out of position at plus twenty-eight seconds. The visual angles are jest beee-u-ti-ful; let me show you."

Preston was not interested in being shown right then, and pressed on, "What about team three?"

"Cubans go out as 'witnesses' dressed like bums—in our black-and-white[10] at plus a hundred and twenty seconds." Allen moved from the border of the Dealey Plaza aerial to the control panel. "I'll have some movies going in a few minutes that will show how tight this visual angle is on the trains."

One quickly pushed button initiated the descent of a

---
[8]Brass—cartridge casings.
[9]Zero plus ten—last shot fired, plus ten seconds.
[10]Black-and-white—police car.

movie screen from the ceiling. Another push and a projector lowered into position opposite the screen. Allen touched the knob that dimmed the lights and strode to a position to the left rear of the projector and its mountings.

The projector whirred into motion at Allen's cue. On the screen Dealey Plaza sprang to life once again, photographed from the center of the triangle of grass bordered by the Elm Street extension, Main, and Houston streets. Through the pillars of the pergola on the grassy knoll a train could be seen, resting immobile.

Allen raised his voice, too much, over the noise of the projector. "You see that train, there, behind the monument?"

Preston did not raise his voice at all. "Yes, I do."

Allen did not hear him; in fact, he did not really stop talking. "Well, now. You just keep watchin'." As the film continued, the train began to move. Reflections from the train windows made a curious thing evident; just as the last car of the train passed out of view, the viewers found themselves looking at another train; the optical illusion is complete—it is as if the first had never moved.

"That's extraordinary." Preston was truly impressed.

"Wasn't that just as pretty as a baby girl?" Allen's excitement was shared by both Preston and Ferguson. Now he threw his voice over the projector even more. "Now, look here. We got it from another angle." He trailed away to a sotto-voce muttering well below the noise level. "Is this . . . Yes, it is." Again too loud, "This shows a couple of our boys gettin' on it just before it goes."

Some spliced leader ran its image through the projector's lenses. This time farther away, the point of view was from the Houston Street edge of the grassy triangle midway between Elm and Main streets.

The wide-angle lens had caught two men getting out of a car parked behind the fence. They strolled at their ease to the first train car on the spur of the track nearest the fence. As the train slowly moved out, the camera panned to show another train on a spur farther away from the fence but at exactly the same angle.

"There, now." Allen's pride was not only becoming somewhat more of a nuisance, but was driving him to stylistic excesses that he would never have attempted otherwise. "You see, any son-of-a-bitchin' camera bug will never see the train move out with that one right in there behind it. *Never!*"

Preston, still seated as he had been from the beginning, rolled his head backward to the right. "It works. Now, Mr. Allen—"

"Call me 'Art'." His tone missed its mark, spoiling Allen's momentary illusion of having ordered a superior to call him by his first name. Both the request and its odd sound were ignored.

"Now, what about the varying density of the sky as the windows of the first train pass in front of those of the train in the rear?"

"Airbrushing."[11] Allen walked nearly sideways back to the control panel and punched. The screen and projector returned to their respective ceiling hiding places. Allen returned to the conference table and stood close by it.

Preston concentrated on a new looseleaf binder of test shots. "Yes, yes. . . . Perfect." These stills were virtually the same angles and views that had been seen earlier in the movie. A set of "before-and-after" shots had been constructed by airbrushing. Peering over Preston's shoulder, Arthur Allen was again unable to distinguish between the two sets of photos.

"Now, just before the parade, we'll block off Houston Street, which will give the train clear passage out of the area. Both teams'll be clean out by one-minute-thirty."

Preston continued to push on; he wanted to end it quickly. "Good. Now, the decoy?"[12]

---

[11] Airbrushing—method of altering photograph, using artwork.
[12] Decoy—Lee Harvey Oswald

"Oswald should get the hit right in the building."

"Contingencies." Preston eyed both men closely.

Allen answered him. "All right. Now, look at this mock-up." He scurried to the model, grasping a pointer that had leaned against the far end. Preston stood and walked to the Dealey Plaza end of the table model. Allen began his explanatory declamation.

"We'll have a man on communications at plus twenty. He'll also call Oswald's movements. First man goes in, hits Mr. Oswald, and lays the evidence. If anything screws it up, we'll call him out of the building. Now. if we have to, we set Mr. Oswald up as a cop-killer. Mr. Oswald goes up the street and uses public transporation to his rooming house on Beckley; takes as much time as he wants; gives us a chance to get the cop in position. The cop gets his radio instruction to remain at large in the area. Our people are in position on Patton."

Using the pointer with foillike grace and thrusts, Allen pointed to various locations in the model as he referred to them, or traced the routes to be used by the individuals or groups. "He's got to go down Patton once every three or more minutes. Then Mr. Oswald goes to his house and waits for our signal. Our people hit the cop. That'll bring police to the area, Mr. Oswald continues on to the Texas theater, here, as ordered. The minute Mr. Oswald moves, he's arrowed." The pointer's tip hit toward the Texas Theater building—touché!

The pointer-foil was withdrawn, its tip coming to rest on the floor immediately beside a black leather right big toe. Allen's two hands folded themselves across each other at the other end of the pointer, pushing the tool into position as if at parade rest. His eyes ignited the space between himself and Preston, while the self-congratulatory grin that arced from ear to ear contradicted his posture; but for this one second, he couldn't help that. "Now, is that tight, or is that tight?"

Preston glanced up at him and quickly away again. "Looks very good. Just one question."

"What would that be?" Allen resigned all of his straining parts to a less tense participation.

Preston leaned in and over the model, looked down at the theater building, examining closely all of its approaches and retreats. "What if you miss at the theater?"

Allen broke from the encounter and moved to retrieve his beer, dropping words in his wake. "You got to be kidding. With half the department answering a hotshot call for suspect in the area where a policeman's guts are layin' all over the ground? Shit. It couldn't happen." He dropped into a chair in front of his beer can and wrapped his long-fingered, strong hand around it.

Preston picked his way across the room, weaving in and out of Allen's verbal leavings, regaining his chair also. "What if it does?"

Howard Ferguson stretched himself onto his feet like a sun-dazed old tom cat atop a fence. "Well, you'll have him in the damn police station."

Preston turned carefully to the old Texan. "You think it's wise to make a hit there?"

Allen sat on the back of his head, studying his legs and feet stretched out under the table; the tone of his voice and steady concentration on the space in front of his eyes told all three of them that his words would be done if they needed to be done. "Hell, he's the dummy, the pigeon, the one sure thing in this. His picture'll be all over; he'll be a 'kill-on-sight.' Listen, if we lose him in the Depository and let him slip by in the damn theater, I'll hit him myself."

Preston studied him carefully for a minute and privately acknowledged this spontaneous "backup"; then his words torpedoed through space and hit Allen amidships so that the younger Texan's ears twitched slightly. The hair along the skin cover at his cervical vertebrae raised up and then rested again in a shuddering ripple upward. Allen noted the style and delivery and filed it away for future practice. "Just make sure you have the

Depository *open*—not *sealed*—for at least twenty minutes, just in case."

That concluded the day's business. Howard Ferguson fussed, picking up singly each item of debris produced by the meeting and returning it to the kitchen. He beamed proudly at his suddenly subdued protégé, reminded himself of what he had gotten up to do, started fussing again. When all was on the serving counter, he stepped to the button panel and returned the kitchenette into its wall. Preston's thoughts blacked out the old man's busy-work. Finally he leaned forward out of his chair slightly. "By the way. How is he?"

Arthur Allen pulled himself into an erect seating posture but did not shift his eyes from the cavernous space into which they stared. "The dumbell? . . . He's okay. . . . The Chinaman's watching him." His laugh was tonelessly flat and unamused. His stare continued without let-up, like a late-fall rain on the Texas-Louisiana border, where he had been born.

Preston stood, arranged his costume. He walked slowly in back of Allen's chair and touched the crisply starched left shoulder briefly, at the same time nodding his good-bye to Ferguson. Moving to the door through which he had entered this room, he left with them both the certainty of his control and command: "I'd like to run tests on the shade under the trees at least twice more." The door clicked shut immediately behind him, and his last word seemed finally to free Arthur Allen, whose eyes focused on the doorway where Preston had stood. Howard Ferguson was dreaming out the window again, or he would have been concerned by the emotion that etched Allen's face.

Dallas, Texas—November 13, 1963

On Wednesday the Secret Service sent Lawson, the advance man, to meet with Chief Curry and to investigate the layout for the fast-approaching presidential visit.

Chief Curry had suggested that the luncheon be held in the Trade Mart. After inspecting the classic Texan monolith, Lawson sent a favorable report to Washington, and Curry's choice of setting for the banquet was confirmed.

That afternoon the chief began what turned out to be a two-day meeting with his deputies; the S.S. agents, Lawson and Sorrels; and the local host committee. The numerous special problems created by the President's visit to Dallas were anticipated and discussed. The S.S. agents were concerned with the security in and surrounding the Trade Mart.

"We'll put all our extra forces in that area," promised the chief.

On the map of the city which hung on one wall in the small police conference room, Curry traced the proposed motorcade route through the center of Dallas to Dealey Plaza. "This route—from Love Field to the Trade Mart—takes forty-five minutes. I recommend that this section—here, along the Central Expressway—be eliminated. It's too risky."

Curry continued to trace the route on the map. "Down Main Street, past the railroad overpass, and then there's only freeway. We'll take you guys over the route if you like."

"Yeah, we'd better check it out once for ourselves."

But when another member of the force took Lawson and Sorrels over the route, he turned left in front of the Old Court House onto Houston Street. Neither agent noticed the discrepancy between the route they were now on and the one Curry had proposed in the conference room. Also, they did not notice the old dusty car with its two occupants following them along the proposed presidential route.

"We'll have to arrange it so that the motorcade turns right onto Houston. That ninety-degree turn followed seventy yards later by a one-hundred-and-twenty-degree turn to the left into Elm Street is contrary to Secret Service regulations," Preston said to Valentine.

188   EXECUTIVE ACTION

"Hey, look!" said Valentine, his false teeth clicking slightly. "They're not going to check it out any more!"

"Just where the inspection should have begun, and they're calling it a day. We're in luck."

Washington, D.C.—November 13, 1963

The President speed-read the speech he was to deliver to the AFL-CIO in New York on Friday and penciled in on the margin "Senator Goldwater has just asked for labor's support—before 2,000 cheering Illinois businessmen." Then he noted on a yellow pad a reminder to himself to check the details of next week's two birthday parties: John Jr.'s third on Monday the 25th and Caroline's sixth two days later on the 27th.

Dallas, Texas—November 14, 1963

Preston swung up the poorly lit stairs, under the blinking *"CAROUSEL CLUB"* sign. The strip music that greeted him as he climbed set his teeth on edge. At the top, he paid his dollar admission and walked in to a "nite-club" that should have had but did not have sawdust on the floor. He barely glanced at the stage with the runway that penetrated out into the audience; one of the stripper's made-up ass cheeks was just disappearing into the stage-right wings. Two men applauded. He looked around trying to find the owner, Jack Ruby.

Just to Preston's left a table full of police officers, all but one in uniform, were drinking and talking loudly. Here and there people were drinking beer. The cheaply costumed waitresses brought glasses full of whiskey, calling out the brand names as they set them down, as one did now to the police table.

"J and B; Old Grand Dad; you ready yet, Lou?"

"Sure am. Give me some Cutty, honey."

He sat down at an empty table in the back and

ordered a beer; then he picked Jack Ruby out of the low-hanging blue smoke. Ruby sat at a table in fervent conversation with a uniformed policeman and an older civilian. He was leaning over talking out of the side of his mouth, thus strengthening the impression that he was a creature sent out from central casting to play an attendant hood in the B-movie world of the Warner Brothers in the 1930's. The shiny suit, the white-on-white shirt open at the neck, the slick hair and liquid eyes, the run-on "gift" of gab: a fatal nonentity, mused Preston, in the vanguard of the *Lumpenproletariat*; why did he always have to meet, deal, and double-deal with these police characters and criminal rabble, in the no-man's-land of the intelligence world.

"This man is to Meyer Lansky what I am to Thomas Langston Foster." The concept jolted Preston. "He is a creature of the underworld, while I . . ." No, he could not say that he inhabited the "overworld." He was an amphibian, scuttling like a crab from Virginia to New Orleans to Washington to Dallas. "Perhaps Jack Ruby is more authentic in his role—as a gangster, a gun runner, a courier for Evil, a CIA contract devil—more authentic than I am," mused Preston. "What in God's name is a 'conflict manager,' an 'operative,' a—what had Foster called him?—an 'arrow of longing'?"

Preston stared at the greasy life force that was Jack Ruby, and seriously contemplated suicide for the first time in his life. (In World War II they had depended on the clans of the real Mafia for the Sicilian invasion, and they were still paying for it. J. Edgar Hoover had made his deal during the war's crisis, and to this day, Preston speculated as he drank the beer, the bureau could barely lift a finger against the syndicate. The same thing could happen to his people, Preston thought, but what choice had he? Now the Cubans were moving into the rackets, and the only decent people left were the right-wingers, and they were fanatics.)

He lifted his hand, trying to catch the eye of everybody's friend Jack Ruby, who was at that moment scribbling furiously on a napkin. So he finally sent the waitress over.

"You put this in," confided Ruby, "and I'll get the dough to print one hundred thousand. You put this here in about 'Wanted for Treason!' Here." He pushed the napkin toward General Walker's self-styled volunteer public-relations man. Out of the side of his mouth he sprayed the police officer. "Johnny, you handle the pickup and delivery, okay? We need about twenty-five guys to pass 'em out. Let me know how much you need." The waitress arrived to point out the well-dressed man sitting across the room waiting. Ruby swung around to wave and yell, "Hey, buddy!" Then he told the waitress to, "Bring these boys what they want." As he left, the policeman tried to read the napkin written in Ruby's gutter shorthand while the rightist (who was actually a fascist and anti-Semitic German Jew) read over his handiwork on the leaflet again.

"Hey. How you doing, buddy? What ya drinking?"

"I just ordered a beer, thank you."

"What, beer? In my place, for you, it's the best. What'll you have?"

"Beer is fine, Jack." The waitress arrived with Preston's obligatory beer, and Ruby snarled at her, "Get a glass for the man, for Christ's sake." As she left he said out of the side of his mouth, "You like her? Want her? I'll fix you up, okay?"

"Perhaps some other time, Jack. There are a few details I want to go over with you before—"

"She's great, buddy. Give you a great blow-job. I've had everyone who works here. Every dame in the joint." He must know, Preston decided, that he was speaking pure Warner Brothers dialogue. The lights dimmed suddenly, a record blared out, and another stripper trudged on. The police table kept talking loudly, and Ruby tried to wave to them to "drink up." At the same time, he was commenting on customers that were coming and going, hissing orders to the waitresses, and side-mouthing something to Preston about ". . . the

Below the despicable advertisement attacking President Kennedy which appeared in the Dallas **Morning News** the day of the assassination. It was inserted by a certain Bernard Weissman who served in Germany under General Edwin Walker. Walker was relieved of his command for propagandizing for the John Birch Society in the army. The ad cost nearly $1500.00 and according to the German magazine Der Stern, was financed by the right-wing oil millionaire H. L. Hunt.

WHY did you host, salute and entertain Tito — Moscow's Trojan Horse — just a short time after our sworn enemy, Khrushchev, embraced the Yugoslav dictator as a great hero and leader of Communism?

WHY have you urged greater aid, comfort, recognition, and understanding for Yugoslavia, Poland, Hungary, and other Communist countries, while turning your back on the pleas of Hungarian, East German, Cuban and other anti-Communist freedom fighters?

WHY did Cambodia kick the U.S. out of its country after we poured nearly 400 Million Dollars of aid into its ultra-leftist government?

WHY has Gus Hall, head of the U.S. Communist Party praised almost every one of your policies and announced that the party will endorse and support your re-election in 1964?

WHY have you banned the showing at U.S. military bases of the film "Operation Abolition"—the movie by the House Committee on Un-American Activities exposing Communism in America?

WHY have you ordered or permitted your brother Bobby, the Attorney General, to go soft on Communists, fellow-travelers, and ultra-leftists in America, while permitting him to persecute loyal Americans who criticize you, your administration, and your leadership?

WHY are you in favor of the U.S. continuing to give economic aid to Argentina, in spite of the fact that Argentina has just seized almost 400 Million Dollars of American private property?

WHY has the Foreign Policy of the United States degenerated to the point that the C.I.A. is arranging coups and having staunch Anti-Communist Allies of the U.S. bloodily exterminated.

WHY have you scrapped the Monroe Doctrine in favor of the "Spirit of Moscow"?

MR. KENNEDY, as citizens of these United States of America, we DEMAND answers to these questions, and we want them NOW.

THE AMERICAN FACT-FINDING COMMITTEE
"An unaffiliated and non-partisan group of citizens who wish truth"

BERNARD WEISSMAN, Chairman

best in town." He almost had to shout over the music's crescendo, "You want her!" pointing like a sports referee at the stripper bumping to her finale. There was scattered applause this time.

"Jack, you're too generous, but just now we really should talk."

"We could bang her together after the show. She's great."

There was a slight edge in Preston's voice. "About the envelope for the Colonel?" Ruby knew he had gone a little too far; he could tell. (These New England *goyem* were cold propositions. The guy was probably a faggot, for Christ's sake.) "Look, if I was outa line...."

"No, Jack, the suggestion was charming; it's just that I'm operating under a bit of a deadline. I have to leave town shortly." The blond Harvard conflict manager and the swarthy Jewish hood looked at each other for a moment from behind their respective masks. Each had personal contempt for the other, and each knew that the other knew, and knew that he knew. But each knew that the other was capable, both technically and morally, of anything, so professionally they could talk the same language.

"Yeah. Okay, I'm listening," said Ruby out of the front of his mouth.

Preston wound it up quickly. "The Colonel meets with his people Thursday, that's the twenty-first. A week tonight."

"Same place?"

"Yes, off the oval. They have rocket launchers. You bring the cash for the seagoing stuff for Cuba. Here's half the money; you're getting the balance from your people, correct?" Ruby nodded. "Eight-thirty, please be prompt. The understanding is that all deals are off unless *everything* is in place for the paramilitary people by Thursday, November 21, correct?" Ruby nodded again (this guy came on like a fucking college professor; he would give odds that this joker was as queer as a three-

III / NOVEMBER 193

dollar bill). "Oh, one other thing—contact Oswald and tell him you want to see him this Saturday morning. And have him help you with moving the material and introduce him to some of your people." He made the reason for his coming to Ruby's in the first place sound like an afterthought. The little mobster from Chicago was a street-wise hood, but he was out of his league with the spooks from the Ivy League. He bit a fingernail and moped to himself. ("Look what this fucking RFK was doing: they had Joe Valachi in Washington spilling his guts about Mickey Cohen, Frankie Carbo, Kid Cann —Jack Ruby? Something had to be done, the fix with the feds had to be put back in!")

He sucked the bitten cuticle and raged to himself as the music blared up again. "Me—Yankee Rubenstein, Jack Ruby—the Trafficante family picked *me* to go back into Havana with them as a front man. These fucking government fags supposed to move into the Bay of Pigs, and us waiting every fucking day in Nassau with more fucking gold than Fort Knox to go back in to open up the fucking casinos again, and these fed phonies bugged out on us, on the Trafficante family, for Christ's sake!" When they received the news that the invasion had failed, Ruby and Big Tony Antanolfi had gotten blind drunk and beat up a queer. "Suck my joint!" he had kept yelling as he slapped the bald head bobbing up and down below him. Now he fumed to himself and felt like beating up this Preston, this swish spook. The music smashed into his eardrums as the new waitress swung past. Now the cheap movie in his head turned carnal. He made a mental note to get her later on his office cot and cut her in the ass. He could see her on all fours, dog style, as he crouched behind rubbing KY jelly into her hole. Then he saw himself smoothing jelly on his *schmuck* and ramming it into her *tuckus,* while he pulled her back and forth by the hair. He'd "get even" yet, he vowed, for losing his big chance with a top mob family. Suddenly he had a vision of the swollen, milk-white hemispheres of his sister's *gluteous maximus*, and he snapped off the image the way you would a motion-picture projector.

They stared at each other. Like two aides-de-camp, was Preston's compulsive thought. Something was wrong when he equated himself with this . . . man. Foster would have known something was wrong. "Torpedo, trigger man, hustler, pimp, soldier, flotsam, kike . . ." He tried to separate himself from the little man, but he could not do it.

Ruby stared flatly at the elegant figure slouched in the chair across from him. "Homo, cocksucker, closet queen, nance, pansy . . ." Preston's return stare brought him back to the issue, temporarily.

"Where should I meet Oswald, in Irving?"

"No. He's spending this weekend in Dallas. Now, do not, *do not,* mention me or that I even exist."

"Hey, what gives with this guy?"

"Why?"

"He's weird, you know what I mean? Never says nothing to nobody. This guy could be an informer, you know what I mean? What's so important about him to you guys?"

"Oh, he's all right, I think."

"Okay. It's your dough. Is that everything, pal?"

"Yes, I think that concludes our—"

"Now, let me fix you up with a piece of ass. On me! Okay?"

Dallas, Texas—November 16, 1963

If Foster had complete faith in him, he would not have sent Reardon on to Dallas for a checkout, and Reardon could only have been given permission by Foster to bring the Chinaman along for the briefing. Even if Foster had not forbidden him any contact with Virginia, Preston had so many questions now that he would hardly have known where to begin. He had to face the truth:

compartmentalization had broken down or been discarded. But what about afterward? Who had bugged his telephone? Were they going to cut him off at the knees? It was past lunchtime, and Preston, who had been working in his shirt sleeves since dawn, was hungry as they conferred in the artificial light of the windowless electronic room. Preston felt as if he were on trial as the two impeccably dressed older men settled back to debrief him.

Preston talked around the subject. Why should he trust them, either? Korea, Vietnam: he was no stranger to the black art of interrogation. At least, he thought, they were not likely to attach electric shockers to his testicles. He looked at the low ceiling as he talked.

"He has problems, but he's doing fine. Made a speech against General Walker. Joined the ACLU. But at home, things are different. They fight, his wife's just had another baby, so she lives in Irving with our babysitter, he lives in a rooming house on North Beckley and sees his wife only on weekends—but, as I say, he couldn't possibly be better for our purposes."

"And where is it you've got him working?" questioned Reardon.

"Texas School Book Depository Building." The Chinaman stood up importantly, taking over.

"Let me show you the pros and cons of that motorcade." He stepped to a large map stand that Preston had previously set up, flipped to a scale map of Dallas. He used a pointer to designate the various routes like a Viennese Herr Professor.

"The most direct route from Love Field, where the President will come in, and the Trade Mart, where the lunch will be, is either by Stemmons Freeway—here— or Harry Hines Boulevard, which is here. To get the biggest crowds, however, the best route would be straight down Main Street through Dealey Plaza—right here—and then a right turn, after the Triple Underpass, onto Industrial Boulevard."

"And where is it you've placed your man?" Reardon

addressed the Chinaman, but Preston reasserted himself. "Texas School Book Depository, corner of Elm and Houston." Preston excused himself, as if going to urinate. He could sense their eyes like bullets across his back.

In the toilet, which was as dilapidated as the rest of the house, he slumped down on the closed commode. The door did not lock, and he had a vision of Reardon and the Chinaman bursting in to do him some outrage. He was still having nightmares about the night Reardon had tried to do just that at Preston's cottage at the Primeval Woods in northern California. He stared now at the rust in the bathtub and smelled the fetid odor of the rubber shower curtain; then he closed his aching eyes, and the Primeval Woods took root in his remembering.

Preston had retired before midnight from the increasingly drunken and aggressive scene around the barbecue fire. He was scheduled to leave California for Dallas the next day and had used this as an excuse. The nature of the jokes and general conversation had sobered him. He had not expected senators, former high government officials, retired military men, and executives from industry to speak about women and Negroes so obsessively or with such viciousness and humorless sadism. To Preston the jokes and banter were a kind of gutter libretto to some mutually fantasized highly colored inner comic book whose pulpy theme was a concatenation of black male sexual organs as big and hard as baseball bats and liberal "nigger-loving" nymphomaniacs begging on hands and knees for "all of it." One midwestern insurance magnate kept repeating, "Yes, sir, the coon cut Jackie in the brown, cut her in the brown!" The obligatory image, for all of them it seemed, was the President's wife being penetrated in her every orifice at once by big black boys, apes, coons, and their big black "meat." Always black meat and white meat, bags of meat, thought Preston, as he stared at the twisting figures in the flames.

He felt as if he were an anthropologist watching half-naked high-ranking males from some protohuman species displaying themselves around the primal flames. But what he saw, he knew sickeningly, was peculiarly human. As he walked away into the darkness, Richard Nixon and General Wedemeyer were leading the group singing: "Away, away—away down south in Dixie."

The night was chill majesty. He could not see the patrolling guards or hear the police dogs; the guest cottages were all dark, and as he walked, the sound of the night insects slowly came to dominate the singing and shouting back at the hotspot of fire in the universal and star-filled darkness. Preston felt as if—wished—he were on another planet. What he had just seen and heard had bruised him, had made him feel more lonely than at any time since his divorce. He walked, unable to look up at the studded sky, until he reached his cabin.

He had been asleep for about two hours when he heard someone swing open and slam his door, making noise with an almost sadistic suddenness. Preston, open-eyed, did not reach for his gun or move; the intruder was obviously a fellow guest.

A heavy weight creaked the mattress of the double bed. Next to his head he could make out someone's too highly polished cordovan loafers, but the man's head was out of view at the bottom of the bed. The man, whoever it was, was humming the Notre Dame fight song to himself. After a minute he flung his left arm up Preston's leg from the knee to the thigh, the spreading splayed hand and fingers dropping into Preston's crotch —half caress, half locker-room horseplay.

Preston rolled out and up in one move. The lights! There was Reardon shaking with silent laughter, swinging up to sit heavily on the bed's edge.

"Hey, boy! You missed all the fun. I'm telling you."

Preston tied his terry-cloth robe securely. "I'm sure. What times does my car—"

"What's your story, old Van? You know what I mean? What's your story? You know, everybody's got a story." He sat there in silk sport shirt and slacks, spotted with barbecue sauce, the expensive cloth hiking up and clinging around the paunch and congested genitals. His skin was red with sun and alcohol. He was lighting up a nonfilter of some brand with his World War II Zippo and grinning at Preston as if he were preparing to punch him in the mouth. Preston sat down as if he *had* been jabbed lightly.

"Which end of the stick are you hitting from, Van boy? Ha-ha-ha. Ha!" The ashes dropped on the floor. "You don't know what I'm even talking about, do you? Do you? Right. Let's get it all out on the table. You don't fool me. I've been watching you. Close." He stamped out the cigarette on the floor, knowing that would rub Preston raw, too, and brushed vaguely at the sparks on his bulging lap. Preston just sat there.

"Don't you know that most of us trust that Virginia fruit salad you work for about as far as we could throw it? Crawling with pinkos and fellow travelers since the beginning—say *what?*"

"Nothing." Preston relaxed a bit, already blocking out the terror of the groping in the dark and settling himself to listen to still another drunken, red-faced anti-Communist harangue. So he was thrown off balance when Reardon lit a new cigarette, snapped the lid of the Zippo loudly, and challenged him directly.

"So which way do you jump when the crunch comes? You know what I'm saying? No. Listen boy, all this talk about a surgical operation? 'Surgical operation'—that stuff makes the grass grow green, Van. We are going to have to terminate a lot more people than just the one we're talking about removing 'surgically.' We're talking about race war, civil war, and choosing sides, 'old boy.' "

Preston stood up. His breathing was light, and he hoped Reardon would shut up before he had to threaten to expose him to Foster. Reardon ground out the butt and stood swaying, facing the pale younger man.

"Now you're awake, huh? Times have changed.

We're faced with a new monster. You can't just 'surgically,' uh, decapitate this new monster—you've got to cut his . . . appendages off."

Preston made his move. "Does Foster know that—"

The big red face opposite was split by a yellow-toothed grin and a bark part cigarette cough and attacking laugh.

"Hey, 'dear boy?' Who's reporting on who to who around here? Remember?" So Reardon knew that he knew that Foster had sent him to baby-sit Preston. It was cold now; Preston started to tremble. Reardon wasn't drunk at all.

"We're recruiting right now for 'Operation Martin Luther Coon.' Ha-ha! And you know this mad dog Malcolm X is in a nigger-versus-nigger—"

"Get out!"

After a staring pause, Reardon commenced to sway again, then staggered over and threw that same left arm out and around Preston's shoulder. "Damn, I'm drunk, Van. What'd I do—fall into the wrong cabin? Christ's sake. Where the hell am I? Cold as hell! Point me in the right direction, old boy. You know what Bob Hope told us, 'Watch out for bad ice cubes.' Ha-ha! I got ahold of some bad ice cubes tonight, old boy. That's it, just point me out. I probably won't see you in the morning, car'll pick you up around seven. Good sailing, boy." He rattled off into the dark, humming the Notre Dame song again. Preston was afraid to call Foster from any telephone in the Primeval Woods. He just sat there shivering again, his hands tucked between his legs cupping his cold package of sex.

Preston opened his eyes to the peeling paint and cracked tile of the Dallas safe-house toilet. He had been a fool to think that he would never see Reardon again. As soon as this was over, he intended to have the whole thing out with Foster in person.

There was a Texas water bug scuttling around the bathtub bottom that froze instinctively when Preston turned his sad eyes to gaze at the black life on the dead-white-and-rust tile. His tense mouth relaxed slightly at the corners. He stood up, still staring at the black bug.

The flushing of the unused toilet drowned out the little laugh he gave when he changed his mind and decided, on the instant, not to squash the bug into the gritty tub tile. He washed his already spotless hands and returned to the conference.

They were looking at a map of Dealey Plaza. The Chinaman continued, "Here's the Depository. In order for the motorcade to pass it, they'd have to make a jog right on Houston Street and left on Elm—here—and then through the underpass to Stemmons Freeway."

"That's a long way around to nowhere, isn't it?" Reardon interpolated.

Preston rose and took the pointer somewhat brusquely. "It's the perfect place for triangulated gunfire. Man here in the Records Building, one next door at Dal-Tex, decoy here in the Depository, and your backup men over here on the grassy knoll, where they've got excellent cover." He traced the route with the pointer. "They'll have to slow down to ten or twelve miles an hour to make the turnoff, and once they've passed this point, they've walked right into the trap, there's no way they can get out."

Preston leaned over him with a diagram. "The solid line follows the route that's going to be published in the papers. The broken line is the double-detour (Regal off Main to Houston, sharp left off Houston into the hairpin on Elm). This is what we need. Otherwise we'll have to place the decoy at Love Field or possibly another building along the route. So we have a potentially serious problem. Everything's been geared for Dealey Plaza. I just have to be positive on this point."

Reardon's next statement left no doubt in Preston's mind that the admiral had been given authority for the final decision by Foster himself. The Chinaman smiled as Preston received his orders. "If that's where you want the parade to go, that's where it'll go. I can think of a dozen arguments right now and a dozen people who'll listen to them. Let me handle it."

"Where will you start? Washington?" Preston's tone was already differential.

"These things are *always* settled on the local level. The President's there to please people, isn't he? To get their votes. So he does what they want him to do. Every time. Merchants, businessmen, bankers—*they* do the deciding on where he goes. And when it comes to those fellows, I know where the bear sits in the buckwheat. Dealey Plaza. I guarantee it."

"Very well."

Preston fingered another dossier stamped "TOP SECRET":

Name	*Code Name*
President John F. Kennedy	Lancer
Mrs. John F. Kennedy	Lace
Vice President Lyndon B. Johnson	Volunteer
Mrs. Lyndon B. Johnson	Victoria
White House	Castle
Air Force One	Angel
Presidential Limousine	SS-100-X
Presidential S.S. Car	SS-679-X
S.S. Chief James Rowley	Domino
Pentagon	Calico
FBI	Cork
L.B.J. Ranch	Volcano

Then he changed his mind and closed the cover. They were both looking at him again.

The Chinaman fingered an envelope out of his pocket, walked over to the desk, and slipped it impertinently into the dossier folder. Then he and the old man marched out without looking back.

Preston flipped open the folder. The checkmarks beside the names of several departments of the Dallas

Police indicated their infiltration by oil intelligence and right-wing agents. Texas was taking control, he thought, over Virginia.

Dallas, Texas—November 17, 1963

"Hey, buddy, you're firing at my target," a middle-aged man in a well-cut Western sports outfit was complaining to the impostor, Valentine. "That's my target." He pointed again. Valentine squeezed off two more perfect shots at the target, refusing even to acknowledge the man.

"Mister, that's my target. Would you mind very much just firing at your own?"

"Why don't you just go and fuck yourself." Valentine smiled nastily, then picked up all the shells that had been expended from his rifle, put them in his pocket, tugged at his crotch, spat, and concluded, "That's a little advice from Lee Oswald. O-S-W-A-L-D," he spelled it out.

Dallas, Texas—November 17, 1963

The final meeting, in the Dallas safe-house electronic room, included Van Preston, Howard Ferguson, Valentine, and the Chinaman. Preston had to make the hard decision to meet with the Texas people—he knew that Foster would have frowned on the idea—because there were just too many loose ends yet to be tied down, and Ferguson had insisted on a face-to-face discussion. He was able to offer them brandy, but the dinginess of the equipment-full room on the chilly Sunday night was depressing, and the men did not waste time. Ferguson, especially, seemed ill at ease without his man Allen. Preston had drawn the line at bringing Allen; they were already straining compartmentalized security with a confab like this. It was only Ferguson's case of last-minute nerves that had forced Preston to bring in the Chinaman to give him ammunition in quelling doubts.

Foster could contact him, but he could not respond. He, Preston, had all the responsibility but no real power except to go forward—like a car downhill, with no brakes. All of these irregularities in communication with Virginia were purposeful, he knew. As far as Virginia was concerned, it was obvious that they considered the operation already in motion. The car was hurtling down the incline with him in it, and the brakes and steering mechanism were in Virginia. He was merely the computer that someone had punched.

Before launching into hard intelligence, Preston had won an agreement from the billionaire that he would leave Dallas on the twenty-second, and take the Chinaman with him, for a ten-day vacation out of the country. He had made that a condition of the conference. Now Preston spread out his notes on the desk.

"On November 22, the only important officials remaining in Washington, D.C., will be Secretary of Defense McNamara and Attorney General Robert Kennedy. The secretaries of State, Treasury, Interior, Commerce, and Labor will be in the air en route to Tokyo. The President and the Vice President will be in Dallas. To confuse matters and give our men as much time as possible, a code book will be removed from the Tokyo-bound cabinet plane, and the Washington, D.C., telephone system will suffer a temporary blackout."

"That'll help," mumbled Ferguson.

The tycoon was really unsure of himself, Preston concluded ironically. Everything was so much simpler, so much more elegant in a foreign country. Texas tycoons, fanatics, gangsters, degenerates; it came to him suddenly: the reason that the operation seemed out of sync and for his pervasive sense of disorientation was that what they were doing—this *coup?—they were doing at home, in "our own country."* His thoughts raced as he talked softly to pacify this old man who insisted, maddeningly, on sticking his nose into what he would have left to professionals in Kuwait or Trans-Jordan or anywhere but *here*—*home*—in his far-flung oil empire.

"The Secret Service detail is under regular orders to stay with the President no matter what happens. Once they've got him to a hospital, they'll probably filter back, but for the first half-hour you should be entirely free of them.

"I'll have six men on the scene with Secret Service credentials. Their insignia for this trip, incidentally, will be double white bars on red.

"I forgot to mention that the chief of the White House detail is so pleased with matters that he's decided to stay in Washington." He threw the Chinaman a look, and he took the ball, talking in his confidential, seductive manner to the old man.

"Going through Oswald's address book, I found the name and telephone number of a man named Fred Hastings. Hastings, we discover, is an FBI agent working out of the Dallas office.

"He's visited Oswald's wife once and her landlady twice since the first of the month. He knows Oswald works at the Book Depository, and we have to assume that he *also* knows the President's motorcade will *pass* the Depository. Neither the local nor Washington office of the FBI has passed that information on to the Secret Service."

The irascible oil man was obviously not totally reassured by the smooth-accented European. "Yeah, yeah, but what about the other damned intelligence outfits?" The voice now was a drawling whine.

Preston took over again, trying to sound patient, and thinking: These bloody billionaire amateurs—this entire situation is turning into some kind of circus for Caligula. "The Office of Naval Intelligence is watching Oswald. The CIA regularly monitors his mail. They know, for example, that ten days ago he wrote the Soviet Embassy about returning to Russia. They have not informed the Secret Service of that fact. Neither has the State Department informed the Secret Service that they've issued him a passport good for travel in Russia. In fact, the Secret Service"—he looked up from his notes—"doesn't even know that Lee Harvey Oswald exists. His name appears nowhere in their files."

The old man took a pill out of his pocket and bumped around looking for water. He would not look at Valentine once his lookalike, Oswald, had been mentioned, and even the unflappable Chinaman swirled his brandy snifter a trifle too stagily to be believable. Ferguson worried as he poured the water.

"Doesn't *anybody* give a damn whether he lives or dies?" In the silence, he answered his own question. "I don't know. I *do* know that something's wrong, something's *terribly* wrong. Hell, Dallas has one of the highest murder rates in the country." The old voice vibrated with something like passion. "Yet they're sending this young man into hostile territory with less protection than you or I would give to a favorite dog." They all stared at him. Somewhere amidst all that oil and megalomania, the old Texan loved some innocent long-dead image of his country, like an old man remembering a mother forever young and loving and timeless. He shuffled and turned to face them, his eyes narrowed. "No search of the buildings in Dealy Plaza? No Secret Service agent stationed in Dealey Plaza? Not one? God almighty."

It was going from bad to worse. Ferguson sat now with his head hanging. Preston signaled the Chinaman that the meeting was at an end. "Don't worry," the Chinaman's eyes answered expressively, "I can take care of the old fool." Preston wound it up and opened the door for the exit. "The lead car will carry the chief of police, the county sheriff, and the two top-ranking Secret Service agents. It will be a sedan. They won't be able to see a thing." Then for all their sakes he said, "Don't worry."

Washington, D.C.—November 18, 1963

The FBI teletypist dispatched a TWX message to all regional offices:

"ATTENTION ALL SECTIONS: INFORMANT, SOUTHWEST AREA, REPORTS POSSIBLE ATTEMPT ON PRESIDENT'S LIFE. PROBABLE DATE, DALLAS TRIP—22, NOVEMBER."

Dallas, Texas—November 19, 1963

The reddish glow from the special sodium vapor lamp turned the cubicle nightmarishly bloody.

The only noise in the darkroom was Valentine's soft humming and the slight sound of the solution, in the photographic developing tray, lapping lightly over the blank photographic paper.

Valentine's hands were deft and quick as he turned the paper and rippled the solution above it. Through the waving liquid, the face of Lee Harvey Oswald came, by stages, into a red focus. Next he placed the wet paper into the big chrome dryer. The motor driving the cylinder hummed along with Valentine.

Now Valentine began the delicate task—matching Oswald's head to another picture of his, Valentine's, own body. In the second photograph Valentine's hands held a rifle and two left-wing newspapers; a pistol was tucked obviously into his belt. The head had to be matched to the other body and then rephotographed and processed.

From the first photo he lined up Oswald's head over his, Valentine's, chin plus the rest of Valentine's body. Red-handed, he held up the wet paper and admired his craft: Lee Harvey Oswald, holding a rifle and two newspapers, stood lounging in the glistening photograph.

Dallas, Texas—November 20, 1963

Mary Sue Arnett turned her 1958 Chevrolet down the ramp into the police garage and parked. She felt blue; it was her period. In the rear-view mirror her police woman's haircut struck her as particularly unfeminine today, making her look in her forties. She walked to the elevator and waited; Jack Ruby, whom she knew only slightly, appeared on foot from around a corner. They nodded. The little fat man was humming "You're the Cream in My Coffee" under his breath; it got on her nerves. I had better curb my nerves, Mary Arnett thought to herself, as she felt a hot flash.

All the familiar noises of her section—the Radio-Patrol Division (RPD), seemed exaggerated: telephones, teletypes, typewriters, radio dispatching. She went to the water cooler to take another aspirin. The other RTD secretary greeted her without looking up from the dispatch in her typewriter, "Hi, Mary, boy what a night. Six liquor stores and a murder in Oak Cliff."

Mary sipped her water. "It's gonna be a scorcher. You better get home and get some sun."

"I'm gonna sleep. This city has me beat to hell." Mary moved in, taking the headphones and the typewriter from the night-shift woman, with no break in continuity. At once Mary Arnett noticed an expensive, beautifully tinted envelope standing on the old desk among the grimy paraphernalia between the In and Out boxes.

Mary Sue picked up the envelope. "What's this?"

'I don't know. It was there for you when I came on last night; looks like some wedding announcement or something." Mary Sue caressed the expensive paper as she slowly opened the surprise. She was enjoying every moment; the night girl stood there impatiently watching. Mary Sue needed a beautiful surprise like this; she needed it today. When she saw what was inside, she

208 EXECUTIVE ACTION

gave a kind of breathy caricature of a sigh of rapture.

"Oh God! Well, I . . . I . . . I been invited to President Kennedy's luncheon."

"No. You're kidding!" exclaimed the night girl, her voice charged with ambivalence. "Why, people all over town can't get tickets to that luncheon." She looked closely at the invitation. "You can't go; you're on duty."

"Listen child, I'm going to be there—you better believe me. What am I gonna wear?"

All this time a crew-cut, uniformed police officer had been reading calls into his microphone; now he swiveled around toward the two excited women.

"Hey, will you two cut the chatter? We got a whole police department out there waiting for us to tell 'em what to do!"

Washington, D.C.—November 20, 1963

At the working breakfast with the legislative leaders of the Congress, the President was by turns appealing and adamant. "Gentlemen, I don't care if you have to stay in session all year if necessary. It's my judgment that the hour is at hand in the fields of education, civil rights, mental health, and tax reform. And, gentlemen, I need your help against the misguided attempts to shoot down the bill that will allow us to sell wheat to the Soviet Union. Wheat in large amounts." The lifted eyebrow and pragmatic hint were not lost on some of them. "I would also like your answer on the emergency assistance program for the totally destitute areas of eastern Kentucky. . . ."

After breakfast, JFK discussed Vietnam with his two closest aides, in preparation for a luncheon conference on that disturbing subject scheduled for Sunday, November 24, with Ambassador Henry Cabot Lodge. He wanted, he repeated, to be ready to explode Lodge's usual hawkish arguments and optimistic predictions of victory and "light at the end of the tunnel." "We cannot turn back now," he told them, "no matter what Lodge reports; *we have set the date for withdrawal.*" Then they talked about politics and Texas and politics.

The President saw the alarm in their eyes when he smilingly but seriously mentioned his decision to debate the Republican candidate for President in 1964 on television, whether he be Rockefeller or Goldwater. "Well, let's pray it's Barry." And that made them smile, too.

Before going back to their offices, they played their favorite game of speculating about a second term: trips to Italy, Japan, India, Pakistan, Indonesia, the Philippines, and most important, a tour of the Soviet Union. Because of his initiative on the nuclear test ban "Everything is possible!" his aides assured him.

Chicago, Illinois—November 20, 1963

Bolton Andrews brooded over whether he should waste his time any further. He rubbed his eyes, sipped coffee. Since the Chicago arrests he had been unable to secure even minimal cooperation with the Cook County state's attorney, and his superiors refused to press the matter. But through his cousin in the secretarial pool at police headquarters he found out that (1) the men arrested for illegal possession of weapons were no longer in custody; (2) the names under which they had been booked were aliases except for one, "Vallee" or "Valentine"; and (3) his arrest pictures were missing. This stunk so bad to Andrews that he knew he either had to drop it or risk even more departmental displeasure over a case that had never even been officially opened, that he, in his unofficial trip to Texas, had been unable to open. Texas was bad news; he never wanted to go back to Texas. He swallowed the last of the bitter coffee.

Now his redneck informant had called him at three A.M., hysterical. "Fuck it!" Andrews depressed the "Record" button.

To: PRS.
From: SA Bolton Andrews.
Re: Chicago counterfeiting and possible JFK assassination attempt.

In early morning of 10-18-63, confidential informant stated to this agent that his life was now definitely in jeopardy, that "he was next."

Informant states, and this agent has verified, that on November 9th, 1963, a former colleague of Informant, of the Miami P.D., conducted the following interview with an unidentified informant of extreme right-wing organization:

> A plan to kill the President is in the works. He will be shot with a high-powered rifle from an office building. The gun will be disassembled, taken into the building, assembled and then used for murder. They will pick up somebody within hours afterwards, just to throw the public off.

This tape is now in custody of PRS.

Confidential informant states that he was a courier for Chicago—New Orleans—Miami syndicate. In this work informant worked with a Miami—Dallas courier Rose Cheramie. Rose Cheramie, according to informant, was involved in both syndicate and CIA Cuban contraband through Jack Ruby of Dallas.

Confidential informant states that Rose Cheramie was set up for an automobile accident near Eunice, Louisiana, on 11-18-63. Informant states that his fellow ultra-right-wing members were involved and that these are the people looking for him in connection with stolen funds and counterfeit plates.

This agent has verified that a Rose Cheramie is in the Emergency Care Ward of the East Louisiana Hospital in Jackson, Louisiana.

III / NOVEMBER   211

The doctor in charge told this agent that as Cheramie came out of coma she stated in his presence, and presence of nurse and orderly that President JFK was to be assassinated in three days.

The doctor's opinion is that she was hysterical, as she told him that someone was out to get her.

Informant states that if this department will not protect him, then he will go to Canada and from there to Rhodesia or South Africa.

He pushed "Off." He had never given an informer money out of his own pocket before, so he was nervous, but, by the same token, his department head had never asked him for the names of a "confidential informant" before, either. That had been their only response. And the Protective Research Section had given Texas the green light, and the President had ordered the two agents off the bumper of his car in Tampa on November 18, and Protective Research was buying that for Texas, too. Andrews checked his book; there were only twenty-eight S.S. agents in Texas. There were 115 files open on potential threats in Texas. Andrews felt sick; he knew that on November 8, PRS had spent ten minutes inspecting potential threats in the Dallas area.

The secretary dropped a mimeo on his desk. Bolton Andrews was to accompany the presidential party to Texas, it said.

Dallas, Texas—November 21, 1963

The technician walked slowly away from Dealey Plaza. The streets were quiet. For ten o'clock it seemed to him that there wasn't much happening in a city this size. He found a restaurant that seemed inviting and entered, to find the main room nearly full. People in twos, threes, and fours occupied nearly every table. He found an empty table along the back wall near the kitchen door. He was dressed in a suit, shirt, and tie. Background music filled the room; as he glanced around, he noticed the liquor bottles on nearly every table, but failed to consider it remarkable.

A blonde in her late thirties, not yet so hard that her basic good looks had been completely obscured, approached his table. She was outfitted in a nondescript, dirty drip-dry white uniform that identified her as an employee.

"Can I help you, sir?"

"Vodka martini over, please."

"It's against the law."

"What is?"

"To serve drinks here in Dallas."

The waitress had worked in enough of these places for most of her life that she recognized all the signs. She had nothing going on tonight, and this seemed like just the right kind of lonely man. Probably an out-of-town salesman or some such, she thought to herself as she continued to explain the "rules" to him.

She waved back at the others in the room, leaning over the table in a gesture of helpful intimacy. Revealing a little cleavage, she became his ally. "You see, you can bring in your own bottle. That's not against the law. You can buy liquor next door at the drugstore if you like." Just a hint colored her voice now, "and I'll provide the . . . setup."

He smiled at her, at her cleavage, at her invitation, and at himself. It was just the thing to occupy his mind and time for these last few hours, to make them move. "Oh, I see . . . you're not against drinking." His eyes moved from her face to the cleavage. "Just moderation."

"Huh?" She hadn't heard him. It wasn't that she didn't understand, she simply had been preoccupied with what his eyes were doing.

"Why don't you bring a glass and some ice. I'll be right back." He rose quickly, winked at her, and walked out. She stood, watching him walk away, looking him up and down. Despite the suit, she knew he was no businessman, no salesman, an athlete or an outdoor type for sure. She hurried off to bring his glass and ice; this dull Thursday evening in November was turning out much better than she had expected. He drank vodka, and she had just bought two quarts of orange juice that morning. She stopped off in the "Ladies."

He stepped out on the street and discovered a liquor-drugstore next door to the restaurant. He entered quickly, reaching for his wallet. Near the entrance, the liquor-cigarette counter was busy. A middle-aged woman buying a half-pint of blended bourbon forced a hysterical laugh at some mundane comment of the college-age boy behind the counter. He occupied his time by glancing through postcards arranged on a revolving rack. One in particular caught his attention. It was a colorful view of the Corpus Christi beachfront. From the back of the store a jukebox played Johnny Mathis' version of "It's Not for Me to Say." The combination made his eyes squint.

"Yes, sir, what'll it be."

"Huh? . . . Oh, yeah . . . huh . . . Got a phone?"

The clerk pointed back toward the three booths snuggled into a far-rear corner, dismissing him curtly by moving on to the next waiting customer. Trade was brisk.

He put a dime in the slot, dialed "O" and told the operator the Montana number he wanted to speak to collect.

What the technician forgot in his anxiety was that this was Dallas, "Big D." That not only the pay telephones in the liquor store a half-block from his hotel were tapped, but that a total of fifteen others, besides his room instrument, were plugged into the electronic and surveillance room of Preston's safe house in the West Dallas section. The technician, for all his experience, had simply underestimated the outreach of the oil intelligence complex into the police, the utilities companies, the hotel where he was staying, every public telephone that fell within normal walking distance from the hotel.

The ringing sound alerted the thin man sitting in the bowels of the West Dallas house, filled to overflowing with electronic equipment. A tape recorder started automatically to record, energized by the tiny impulses emitted from the telephone's ringing. Preston entered the room from some other corner of this basement command post, energized by the same sound. Valentine, on duty, adjusted his headset as Preston fitted his to one ear. Illumination in the room seemed to come only from the dials of the various instruments. Preston listened a moment, then reached out to unplug his subordinate's headset, while he continued to listen. As the slim man slipped out of the room, Preston also switched off the recorder but continued eavesdropping.

"Hello."
"Hello, Anne? Tom."
"Hello."
"How are you doing?"
"All right."
"I've been thinking.... Can you talk a minute?"
"Sure."
"Still planning Thanksgiving?"
"I don't know. Are you going to be free?"
"Anne, I have to see you. It's important."
"Anytime."
"Thanks, thanks, Anne.... I'll stay in touch now."
"Good-bye, Tom."

Dallas, Texas—Night, November 21, 1963

Stretched out on the bed in a motel room, he realized he was in the same posture he had been in that last night with Anne. He wished now that he had bought a bottle while he was in the store. But the phone conversation with Anne had left him even more aimless than he had been before he entered the restaurant earlier. He recalled the waitress and felt no regrets at having not returned for what had been promised. The excitement of such a casual encounter was quickly dissipated into loneliness and the empty aching absence of identity that he had experienced his whole life.

From the motel parking lot, voices drifted in to him, reminding that other people seemed to belong to yet other people, and their lives revolved about living activities. The irony did not escape him. His life revolved about dying activities. Someone rattled the ice machine close by his open window. He got up, looked out, seeing a shirtless young man filling a cardboard bucket with ice; from the balcony above his own, a female voice stage-whispered down that the shirtless fellow shouldn't forget to bring a couple of Cokes. In his mind the girl above looked like Anne in the pale blue shortie nightgown she had worn their last night together.

He pulled the curtains, snapped on the small bulb that illuminated the head of the bed. He rummaged through his suitcase briefly, finding those four snapshots of Anne wrapped up in his swimsuit. He was sweating lightly. He had to sleep tonight—without dreaming.

He climbed back on the bed, searching out every detail contained in each picture. The image of his wife in that "extreme" blue knit two-piece suit dominated each picture. He cursed himself lightly for not having kept more of them, all of them.

His reverie began to diminish as he found himself looking at his wife's pictures more and more as though they were a *Playboy* layout. He opened his pants, and his erection freed itself. Concentrating now on the one photo of Anne leaning into the camera's lens, revealing nearly all of her full breasts, he began to masturbate in earnest.

Ejaculation drained away his dread and energy. Holding the snapshots against his chest with one hand while the other still clutched his pulsating sex, he twitched off to sleep.

Lying there in the little death, he looked dead.

Dallas, Texas—November 22, 1963

Preston cleaned up the electronic room one last time. He was eager to get out and hear the seven A.M. news. Valentine had stripped the place the night before prior to leaving. Both of them had gone over every inch, wiping clean for fingerprints, wearing thin rubber gloves. Now Valentine, wearing the uniform of a Dallas police officer over his work clothes, was killing time driving an old Dallas police car through the suburbs. In his pockets he carried shells that he had fired when impersonating Oswald. He would lay the 6.5 shells and the other "evidence" at the school book depository while all hell was breaking loose and then he would kill Mr. Lee Harvey Oswald, who had had the misfortune to be a dead ringer for Arthur Valentine. In the trunk of the official-looking vehicle were two rifles: one was a clean, powerful 7.65 Mauser, the other a defective, old 6.5 mm. Mannlicher Carcano.

He checked the empty desk again. On the desk top were two sheets of paper. The technician's decoded classified ad—still unanswered—and a coded message from David Ferrie flown in and delivered by hand by another Civil Air Patrol contract agent just an hour before. Everything completed, Preston sat down to decode. Ferrie would soon be in Galveston counting down, ready to fly out to the Caribbean.

> The Secret Service broke every rule in the book last night in Fort Worth. Nine went to the Fort Worth Press Club for drinks. Two returned to their rooms, seven remained for periods of from thirty minutes to two in the morning. Seven went to the Cellar Coffee House. One stayed from two

to five A.M. All three night guards left the hotel and went to the Cellar House. Four of the nine who violated rules last night have key responsibilities in the Dallas motorcade.

Dallas, Texas—November 22, 1963

"Boyd?"
"Here."
"High?"
"Here."
"Walker?"
"Here."
"Tippit?"
"Here."

No one was missing from the police watch that morning.

"All right, you men, let me have your attention. It is now 0800 hours. Your police radio network Channel One is being used today exclusively for the motorcade. Got that? So you men stay with Channel Two.

"The entire motorcycle complement will be detoured to Love Field. No unidentified planes will be permitted in or around Gate 24; all entrances and exits to the field will be sealed; all passenger areas will be patrolled.

"During the route the Secret Service will deal with any breaching of police lines, and only if *they* indicate will police officers join them in crowd control. Get that clear now. I don't want to hear any static later on from any of those smart-ass Yankees."

Dallas, Texas—November 22, 1963

The technician and his team all ordered steak, eggs, and potatoes except for Gonzales who was a practicing Catholic and ordered cereal and a Dixie beer.

Behind the counter the fresh coffee was sputtering, and the morning news started.

> ... and on the eve of the Texas trip JFK joined Jackie in greeting seven hundred guests at the annual White House reception for the justices of the Supreme Court.
> It was Jackie's first appearance as hostess at an official White House function since the death of her infant son.
> The President has announced the withdrawal of one thousand advisers from Vietnam today. During the last two months two thousand advisers to the South Vietnamese government stationed in Vietnam have been brought home. The President reiterated his statement of last week that all American advisers would be out of Vietnam by the end of next year. He said that we have no long-standing commitment..."

The plain little diner was in the Oak Cliff section of Dallas, but even here a man entered, as they ate their wordless meal, passing out the circulars with a profile and full face of the President and the headline, on the simulated wanted poster, *"WANTED FOR TREASON."* They read the handbills with their second cup of coffee. Then the technician leaned forward, and they scraped their chairs toward the table.

"Go on back to your rooms now. At nine thirty exactly you'll be visited by *your* S.S. contact and your backup man. He'll just knock on your door three times." The technician tapped on the table lightly twice, and then once with the butt of his knife. He looked at the Cubans; they nodded that they understood and did not require Spanish translations. Oh, the bastards, he cursed mentally, remembering the look they had given him when told that they would have to dress like tramps for the escape scenario.

"They will be your escort from the scene in case of

any problems. Remember now, don't make contact with your man after the firing unless it's an emergency. He'll be watching *you*. Rely on *his* judgment to approach *you* if necessary. Only if you're sure that you know something that he doesn't know *and* you're in serious trouble—then signal him on your walkie-talkie. When you two get into the police car, give them your guns and radios and the rest," he said in Spanish.

"Jesus," said Cowboy.

"Jesus," said the southerner, "just how in the hell many backup people are there in this thing?" The special news coverage of the President's trip to Dallas was continuing; the owner turned up the volume for the regulars starting to fill up the place. Outside, there was a very light drizzle.

". . . now for the local news. The President's breakfast this morning was sponsored by the Fort Worth Chamber of Commerce. At 8:45 this morning, President Kennedy emerged from his hotel in Fort Worth and strode across the street to greet a crowd waiting for him in a parking lot.

"Then the party hurried to the airport for a short flight to Dallas. The President is to address a luncheon at the Trade Mart here following a motorcade tour through downtown Dallas.

"The temperature is perfect—sixty-eight degrees—warm and refreshing to greet the President of the United States."

"Here, keep one of these. The S.S. guys will be using these today." He handed out Secret Service lapel pins.

"These guys are all-important. Don't compromise them unless your life is at stake. Now, when we meet to debrief, you've got to give me a line on *any* firm witnesses. Don't rush. Take it easy. And one more time: do not handle any ammunition without your gloves; they have a new method for testing even fragments for prints.

"Any problems?"

"Negative."

"Questions?" He stared hard at the Cubans.

Hickham Field, Hawaii—November 22, 1963

Two Secret Service men exited the presidential Air Force jet that would carry the cabinet members to Tokyo. The early-morning island sky blessed the peaceful airport scene in quiet colors. Another agent, toting a square briefcase and, like the others, wearing dark glasses, approached them on the runway. The three of them stood there in the morning breeze under the profound oceanic sky. Each wore an ear plug and almost invisible cord connected to a concealed walkie-talkie; each wore the coded double white bars on a red background lapel button for identification. The man with the briefcase introduced himself as "Osheim from Chicago." They all wore the same blue suits and striped ties.

The first man told the third man with the briefcase, "It checks out clean. They're due in about 0600. Pilot's waiting for the codebook. Today's color is blue for transfer." The other man patted his briefcase, indicating that the code book was inside. The two told the new man about the "partying" they had enjoyed on the big island the night before, then left him alone on the strip.

Inside the plane, he opened his briefcase and waved a *"TOP SECRET/EYES ONLY"* envelope as a greeting to the pilot. "Hi, code book."

"Right. Safe's open."

As the pilot turned away, the agent dropped the envelope back into his briefcase, closed the safe, and left quickly. Across the strip and back in his car, he took the glasses off to rub his eyes before half-undressing and changing into a loud tropical shirt and cap.

It was the surveyor.

Dallas, Texas—November 22, 1963

S.S. agents Hickey and Kinney tested the private switchboard that linked the Dallas Sheraton Hotel and Washington, ate breakfast, left the hotel, arrived at Love Field by nine A.M.

With the White House Communications office they began their checkout of 100-x (the President's limousine, code name "Lancer") and 679-x (the Secret Service follow-up car, code name "Half-back"). They examined the engine, trunk, and chassis; checking the oil, water and batteries; and removed the seats to search for detonating devices.

Vienna, Virginia—November 22, 1963

As part of a busy morning of preparation for travel and his weekly seminar at Georgetown University, and before the arrival of Reardon and the others, Foster composed a coded message to a penetration agent in the Chicago office of the state's attorney for Cook County, Illinois.

That man, together with an operative on the Chicago "Red Squad," initiated the scenario that day that would, on the strength of perjured informant testimony, send Bolton Andrews to the Federal penitentiary for conspiracy in a case involving counterfeit money. Then they would kill Thomas (Tom-Tom) L. Hooks, his informant, the man who had feared so for his life.

Then Foster called his daughter, who adored him, and told her that he insisted on bringing a very special wine for the family Thanksgiving dinner in Boston.

Fort Worth, Texas—November 22, 1963

The First Lady was disgusted at the sounds reaching up through the drizzle to the window. "Come on, Jackie, come on, Jackie." The growing crowd of some four thousand were actually hog-calling her name by a quarter after eight in the morning. The early morning downtown crowd of unskilled workers and unemployed were getting on her nerves, and she relieved a sense of guilt or anxiety by picking a quarrel with her secretary over what outfit she should wear that morning for the political breakfast, still an hour away. Since she had lost her baby just a few months before, she could not make herself feel clean or beautiful. Though the street mob loved and revered her in their way, she felt dried out and constantly uneasy. Now she peered out the window, down at her husband below.

In front of the red brick Texas Hotel, flanked by the governor of Texas and the Vice President, the five thousand now in the parking lot could see the lithe, familiar form of JFK as he waved his arm in greeting to them. For his part, the President could spot the police snipers and others with riot guns stationed on the roof of the bus terminal and the adjoining building.

He faced them erectly. The crowd took in the superbly tailored figure: blue-gray two-button suit, gray-striped shirt, dark blue tie.

"Mr. Vice President"—the President chopped out the words in that accent so fascinating to these southwestern sensibilities—"Jim Wright, Governor Connally, Senator Yarborough, Mr. Buck, ladies, and gentlemen: There are no faint hearts in Fort Worth . . ." They roared as he punctuated the greeting with the short arc of his arm and pointing finger.

"Where's Jackie?"

"Mrs. Kennedy is organizing herself," he jested. "It takes longer, but of course, she looks better than we do when she does it." They whooped now and slapped their thighs, and even the troopers and their horses that flanked the temporary speaker's platform seemed to break into a little equine jig.

As JFK and LBJ made their exit, after the short remarks in the rain, they could hear the cheers and rebel yells fade behind them. The S.S. on their walkie-talkies passed the code word that they were on their way back into the hotel. But JFK pulled LBJ into a corner when they had regained the eighth floor presidential quarters. The S.S. stood respectfully apart, watching the tense, half whispered exchange covertly.

"Did you refuse to ride with Senator Yarborough yesterday?"

"Shit. Who told you that? Ralph don't want to ride with me or with John."

"What do you think we ought to do about it, Lyndon?"

"Let the stuck-up super-liberal son-of-a-bitch ride by himself if—"

"Lyndon, if for any reason—political, personal, or philosophical—you find yourself unable to ride in the same limousine with Ralph Yarborough, then you have my permission *to walk!* Now, let's grow up, shall we?"

The President left the big Texan standing in the corridor like a perfect fool with the S.S. laughing, to themselves, at him.

Dallas, Texas—November 22, 1963

Lee Harvey Oswald huddled over the pay telephone at the Texas School Book Depository, and talking low, made a collect long-distance call. The Hertz Rent-A-Car sign on top of the building read 9:02.

"I can't go to the bureau, I told you, because they want me to stay with it, to keep the whole thing under control. This is what they're telling me." He listened impatiently to the voice on the other end.

"It's political; what else could it be? They just want to scare the shit out of the public so they'll . . . What? Yes, that's the point—he's supposed to be in on it himself . . . What? No, I'm just supposed to set up a distraction . . . What?" He listened again to the man in Washington, D.C. Someone on coffee break turned on a portable radio.

"Looking forward to next year's vacations, the White House announced that the First Family has leased Annandale Farm on Narragansett Bay at Newport, R.I., for the months of August and September. Annandale, the same estate that a group of Rhode Islanders wanted to buy and present to Kennedy as a permanent Summer White House in 1962, will replace the First Family's summer home at Squaw Island in Hyannisport. It adjoins the estate of Jacqueline Kennedy's mother and stepfather, Mr. and Mrs. Hugh D. Auchincloss, where Jackie played when she was a teenager.

"His wife, Jacqueline—making her first campaign journey with him since the 1960 primaries—was wowing the crowds at every stop; San Antonio, Houston, Fort Worth, and now Dallas.

"The President was wowing them too. He

"I'm calling you because I want to cover myself, just in case. I mean, there's a lot of funny shit going on, and I can't get a straight story from anyone. I'm not getting hardly anything out of this, but I'll play along, but I'm no patsy. I'm not taking a set up for . . . What?

"Listen, I'm not calling G2.[13] You call G2 if you want, but I'm on record with you, right? I never thought they'd take it this far, but I don't give a fuck as long as I'm covered. Huh? No, I got security. They got a guy here on the Dallas police force that's supposed to have me covered in case this thing gets out of hand. Huh? No, I don't know his name, but he's supposed to contact me during the day."

[13] G2—Army Intelligence.

started the day in Fort Worth. Talking to a crowd of rank-and-file Democrats in his hotel parking lot, then to a Chamber of Commerce breakfast inside. The Chamber gave him a broad-brimmed hat; the President, smiling, promised to try it on back home at the White House. He put in a Happy 95th Birthday call to former . . ."

Dallas, Texas—November 22, 1963

"On September 25, President Kennedy announced the withdrawal of 1,000 American advisers from Vietnam, leaving a total of 16,500 military advisers remaining there.

"The President said that a further announcement regarding the withdrawal of additional advisers could be expected within the next six weeks.

"On September 25, President Juan Bosch of the Dominican Republic was overthrown by a civilian junta. Today the State Department . . .

"A few weeks ago, there was a lot of talk regarding a coup in Saigon. Chatter died down, perhaps indicating it was actually in the making.

Captain P. W. Lawrence instructed his aides that:

A. Chief Lumpkin would be in a white Ford, with the Secret Service personnel, about eight or ten blocks ahead of the motorcade.

B. Next would come the advance motorcycle escort.

C. Next, Chief Curry's vehicle would be number one in the escort.

D. Next a press vehicle and then another motorcycle escort, and then the President's car.

That was the sequence, the plan as Captain Lawrence understood it at 9:30 A.M. He did not have the faintest idea that those orders had already been countermanded in the field by Minute Men below him

"During the same period, the U.S. stepped up its economic pressure against the Diem regime, suspending a ten-million-dollar-a-month commercial import program, reducing sales of U.S. surplus commodities that ran up to $2,000,000 a month, cutting off part of the CIA's $350,000 in monthly payments to the Vietnamese Special Forces, and stopping funds used to finance Ngo Dinh Nhu's secret police."

in rank, and oil intelligence agents far above him.

Dallas, Texas—November 22, 1963

"The President and Mrs. Kennedy are seated in the back seat of the limousine, with Governor and Mrs. Connally taking the jump seats just in front of them.

"A Secret Service agent, trained to react to any emergency, is driving the car, and a whole carload of Secret Service men are in the vehicle just behind the President.

"A spokesman said that this would be the greatest security ever to protect an American President—but it is clear that it won't be needed today. Few protesters, the atmosphere here is friendly."

"Early this morning, handbills had been

The walkie-talkie on the dresser in the southerner's room alternated police calls and news continuity of the motorcade.

He checked out his ammunition; a clip in his suitcase of frangible, hollow nosed slugs specially cast from a silver and lead alloy with no jacket, so as to disintegrate on impact, and treated in garlic so as to cause lead poisoning. Then he checked the identity kit in the imitation-black-leather cardcase that had been delivered to him, and tried on the skin-tight surgical gloves.

He put on his poplin, rain-resistant jacket. Then he took it off again and circulated bearing a picture of the President with the caption, 'Wanted for Treason.'

"There has also been a full-page ad in the *Dallas Morning News* today sponsored by the American Fact-Finding Committee, demanding to know why the President had 'Ordered the Attorney General to go soft on Communism.'

But these are only passing clouds, hardly noticeable, in the happy mood of Dallas today.

headed for the toilet to relieve his insistent bowels.

The technician was in his count down when the knock came. His back up men stood in the hall: one dressed as a tramp, complete with cracked, weather-beaten face and hands; the other was an S.S. carbon copy: crew-cut, blue suit, striped tie, double-bar insignia, walkie-talkie ear plug in plain sight, and shined shoes. Softly, in the door jamb, he again mentioned to them the sewer outlet on Main Street that they were to stake out, where he would surface at approximately 1:30 P.M. Then he slumped into a chair, after locking the door behind them. He had never seen them before, and he wondered if he ever would again.

He leafed through the plastic enclosed pages of a looseleaf notebook of maps, diagrams, and photographs. There was the overlay of Dealey Plaza, the sewer system, the getaway-car positions—the inventory that had taken him not quite three months to collect. The maps and blueprints were merely the abstraction of an action now.

At the back of the oversized book were the

pictures of Anne taken at Corpus Christi on their last holiday. He studied the montage of life reflected in the happy and serious poses of this girl. This woman who could have saved him; he knew that now.

The old saying that the men of the clandestine paramilitary life were the only true men, the "men of their word" was, he knew now, just another lie. The only "true-man" moments of his life had been with Anne, when he wasn't too paranoid to get it up. That's the truth, he thought.

He stroked the face on the film lightly. The blue bathing suit; the shy and tolerant eyes; the high shoulders and the image, in the blue knit, of the breasts. God.

The technician was a failed Catholic, and he debated now whether he should get down on his knees and pray.

"Pray for what?" he demanded out loud as he searched the cloudless sky for a sign of rain.

Dallas, Texas—November 22, 1963

Julia Ann Mercer was parked at the corner of Elm and Houston as she checked her watch against the Hertz

Rent-A-Car sign atop the Texas School Book Depository—9:57, and the weather was clearing up fast.

As the twenty-three-year-old Dallas resident steered the car west on Elm Street toward the triple underpass just ahead, she saw a truck parked on the curb just at the base of a grassy knoll. On the plateau above the slope there was a fence that connected the railroad overpass with a pergola made of concrete. Around the fence were bushes and half a dozen trees. The pergola was about halfway between the Book Depository to the east and the overpass to the west.

In a short time that little area would command the attention of the world. Now there was just a truck illegally parked half up on the curb. There were two men with the truck. It protruded into the street, blocking traffic, and Miss Mercer was obliged to stop her car and wait for a moment until the lane to her left was clear and she was able to pull out. The truck was a green Ford pickup with a Texas license plate. On the driver's side, in black, were the words "Air-Conditioning." Along the back of the truck were what appeared to be tool boxes.

The illegally parked truck did not seem to bother three policemen who were standing and talking near a motorcycle on the bridge. They paid no attention to the badly disguised rifles that the southerner and the cowboy had hauled out of the truck and carried up and behind a grassy knoll.

Dallas, Texas—November 22, 1963

Jack Ruby hung over the teletype machine at the *Dallas Morning News*. His hat was tipped back slightly. No one paid attention to the familiar figure who had just placed his usual weekly nightclub advertisement.

Rockefeller to Avoid Pennsylvania Drive for

230 EXECUTIVE ACTION

Delegates Now. Governor Rockefeller agreed yesterday that the need for Republican party unity in Pennsylvania took precedence now over his quest for the delegate votes at the party's presidential nominating convention next year. At the news conference, he stressed repeatedly that party unity was vital if the Republicans were to win state and local offices in Pennsylvania and place votes in the Republican column.

Lost Soybean Oil Puzzles Wall Street. Exporter charges that tons of commodity are missing. Stock prices plunge. Prices on the New York Stock Exchange dropped sharply yesterday, triggered apparently by investors' reaction to the brokerage-house suspensions . . .

Ruby was sweating. He ankled to the pay phone and tried again to call David Ferrie in Galveston. No answer. He was alone now. He settled into a swivel chair, gazing out the window, across Houston Street toward the Texas School Book Depository.

Dallas, Texas—November 22, 1963

The hit man from New Orleans stood five-foot-six and weighed 220 pounds. Draped over his arm was a camel's-hair coat. He rocked back and forth on his heels in front of the statue of a Texas ranger on a raised pedestal in the Love Field passenger lobby. The inscription on the pedestal was *"ONE RIOT, ONE RANGER."* From where he stood he could keep an eye on his target at the Braniff ticket counter. Portables carried by passengers told of the presence of the President in Dallas.

"Bustling officials have just steered the President to his limousine so that the motorcade can begin. It is

"Does your Flight 86 guarantee a connection with Lufthansa Flight 7 from New York this afternoon?"

to follow an eleven-mile route through downtown Dallas.

"The big black limousine has been flown down from Washington just for the occasion. Because of the pleasant weather, its plastic bubble-top has been removed and those bullet-proof side windows have been rolled down."

Preston's voice was tense.

"We do. Eighty-six is on time. Boarding right now, sir, at Gate fifty-eight. Up the escalator to your right." The ticket agent stamped Preston's boarding pass. As he did the first Christmas carols of the season began to play on the Muzak.

Preston abruptly half turned away and averted his eyes in order to avoid making eye contact with a former Vice President of the United States, Richard M. Nixon, who was hurrying toward the boarding gate to catch American Airlines Flight 82 bound for New York's Idlewild Airport.

Seconds later, on the escalator, Preston stared over at the heavy set underworld type across from him on the down escalator. He thought of Jack Ruby.

Walking down the corridor, Preston glanced into a mirrored panel on his left. In the reflection, fifteen paces behind him, was the heavy set man carrying a camel's-hair overcoat. As if struck, Preston swung his eyes away to the garishly decorated murals on the right wall: the nation's Capitol, and by its side a violent bull-fight tableau. Like a scene in a nightmare, he saw himself and his pursuer in a figure-ground relationship to the painted Capitol building and the bloody bull-fight. He veered into one of the small empty waiting rooms, hoping against hope. The lyric on the Muzak, as he sat half-crouching, panting, was . . . "He's making a list and checking it twice . . ."

The killer turned in and sat opposite, staring at him as if he were a bug. The little waiting alcove was completely curtained by fake planters. Then, as if inside his head, he heard his flight number being called.

Still as in a dream, he moved out heavy-legged toward the boarding gate. He and the killer entered the last corridor together. ". . . Rudolph the red nosed reindeer had a . . ."

Preston never looked back. "My God," he thought quite lucidly to himself, "they're going to kill us all."

Dallas, Texas—November 22, 1963

Outside the Market Hall on the lighted electric sign was the greeting *"WELCOME PRESIDENT AND MRS. KENNEDY."* Police with folded arms formed a cordon around the entrance to the big building.

The organist sat practicing "The Eyes of Texas" in the cavernous indoor bowl of the Trade Mart that had finally been chosen for the presidential luncheon. The elongated speaker's table, the fresh flowers, the gleaming silverware, yellow and green parakeets nervously positioning themselves on the crosswalks above the red-and-blue-tinted fountain: the organ music resounded and bounced off the huge empty space that more than anything resembled a vacant movie sound stage in the hiatus just before the day's shooting.

Moving through the spaces, while the organ echoed out, were waiters and Secret Service agents with the double white bars on their lapels and the radio plug, with thin electronic cord descending into their jackets, from their ears, as if they were early arrivals at a convention of deaf people.

Dallas, Texas—November 22, 1963

The big green Marine Helicopter circled over Dallas' Love Field. The sun was glinting brightly through the clouds now, and the crowd of more than five thousand was starting to gather. Banks of television sets were turned on in appliance and furniture stores making a honeycomb of imagery in color and black and white; roofs, porches, and windows were starting to fill up with onlookers. Uniformed officers armed with ropes for crowd control appeared at Love Field; adjoining streets were blocked off; every window and roof was under surveillance by police and sharpshooters. There were four hundred police officers at the airport. Two hundred at the Trade Mart, the President's destination.

The row of cars was lined up along the airport fence; each bore a sticker on the window that read *"PRESIDENTIAL MOTORCADE"* and a number.

A tall, gray-haired man with the Secret Service lapel insignia of double white bars on a red field approached the line, walking casually. In the background the scarlet-nosed *Air Force One* was zooming into view. A voice on the field intercom repeated, "D.V. arriving. D.V. arriving. Attention, Distinguished Visitor arriving."

Maintenance was just finishing dismantling the presidential limousine's heavy four-piece plastic bubble-top, now no longer needed because of the quick weather change.

The gray-haired man with sunglasses stepped quickly over to the line of the various color and make automobiles. He studied number seven for a moment: presidential limousine, a long, black, open Lincoln with jump seats and flags on flagpoles on the fenders. The car in front, number six, was a 1962 red Buick convertible full of camera equipment. A cameraman was just focusing a 16-mm camera on the presidential limousine. He aimed at the spot where John Kennedy would be seated. Then the cameraman began to run to catch up with the rest of the press corps already waiting to cover the President's arrival.

The roar of *Air Force One* drowned out everything else now. The gray-haired man bent over the temporary maintenance driver of the presidential limousine, yelling in his ear. He flashed a wallet and a letter-sized directive of some kind and gestured repeatedly to maintenance to move the limousine. The driver nodded, and as the gray-haired man half-trotted away, pulled number seven, the President's vehicle, in front of number eight, the Secret Service car. Vehicles six, five, and four were pulled out. The maintenance man gestured them to the rear of the line, following the instructions of the directive which the gray-haired man had left with him. The President's limousine was now third in line, while the press car was far back, out of sequence, and out of sight of where the President would sit.

The eight-million-dollar *Air Force One* had flown a total of 75,682 miles when it honed in on Love Field. The FAA monitors had had the world's most elaborate flying machine in their radar scopes as it lifted away from Fort Worth. *Air Force Two,* carrying the Vice President's party, and a back-up plane completed a caravan of three giant jets making the thirty-three-mile hop from Fort Worth to Dallas. In a padded cockpit, the five Air Force officers adjusted for the nasty crosswind. The wheels hit with a puff of smoke, bounced and finally settled, splashing through the reflecting puddles that dotted the strip.

There were thirty-six aboard the President's jet. Some of the S.S. men aboard tried to put together Alka-Seltzers for their hangovers. Jacqueline Kennedy, who had helped decorate the plane's interior, sat staring grimly out the window. Her pink suit was too heavy for Dallas' fast-changing, brightening weather, and she had not slept well. She had had another of her nightmares.

Air Force One had stopped. The dignitaries waited below. The plane door opened. Behind the fence, the waiting crowd surged and cheered. From the plane door the first Secret Service agents, in their big wrap-around sunglasses, appeared. And then, to the crowd's delight, Mrs. Kennedy in the pink suit. A band strikes up "The Yellow Rose of Texas." Mrs. Kennedy is presented with a big bouquet of *red* roses. (The black S.S. agent, Bolton Andrews is in the crowd working on his own time. He watches. "Now, why in the world do they give her red roses here in Texas?")

Mrs. Kennedy stiffened. They were pushing a wheelchair toward her and someone was shouting. "This is Mrs. Anne S. Dunbarr 85 years old. She's a loyal Democrat."

The President ignores the Secret Service restraint and plunges forward to shake hands, following his wife along the length of the friendly fence. Beyond the warm, larger-than expected crowd were signs that he did not see—*"YOU'RE A TRAITOR"* and *"IN 1964, GOLDWATER AND FREEDOM"*—and they were not lettered crudely by hand.

Pilots, airport personnel, and stewardesses stood next to Lancer, smiling in the sun as the President's motorcade inched away from the field. Some snapped on shoulder-strap portable radios while they could still see the fabled heads of John and Jackie Kennedy.

"Mrs. Kennedy is dressed in a strawberry-pink suit with a nubby weave and a purplish blue collar.

"A matching pink pillbox hat is perched atop the dark, familiar hairdo which has changed the coiffures of a nation.

"After breakfast President Kennedy called Uvalde, Texas, wishing happy birthday to John Nance Garner, Vice President in the first two terms of Franklin Roosevelt. Mr. Garner is ninety-five years old today.

"Today is a busy day for the President and his First Lady.

The pigeons kept taking off from the roof of the School Book Depository as soon as they would land. The pigeons were not used to the crowds and the loud overlapping sounds from all the portable radios.

The crowds were definitely much larger than expected. The full autumn sun played down on the secretaries and office workers coming out to eat their lunch and watch along the President's route.

Higher than the Hertz sign, which now reads 12:15, was the county jail, which commanded the approach of both Houston

"They began with a breakfast in Fort Worth, a short flight here to Dallas, and the motorcade is now winding its way through Dallas. Then they go on to the Trade Market, where the President will address a lunch meeting, then a $100-a-plate dinner this evening in Austin. The Kennedys will spend the night at Vice President Johnson's ranch in Stonewall, ninety miles from Austin."

and Elm Streets. In the area room the prisoners—black, brown, and poor white—pressed to the barred window to spy the sunshine, the pretty girls, the reporters, the President, whom some of them loved and some of the white men hated. The pigeons flanked out past the jail windows and the shadowed faces peering hopefully through the interstices of the bars.

Jesús Gonzalez was feeling the brandy that he had been drinking on an empty stomach. Fernández, as he made for the records building, felt for his old comrade Gonzalez. He knew why Gonzalez did not care whether he lived or died. It was almost three years ago to the day that Manuel Barker had come to them in Miami with the fabulous story that a "great company" was outfitting and arming a guerrilla army for the invasion and liberation of the beloved Cuban homeland.

Proudly they had joined the 2506 Brigade and trained like dogs in the Canal Zone; their hopes high, their trust in the American advisers almost absolute even when in-fighting among the Cuban factions, packed together in the base camp, became ferocious. Still they believed in the "great company" and the American technicians.

Then after the utter defeat and bungling of the invasion, after the betrayal of the "great company," the USA, this man, this JFK who was now on his way, had told them in Miami Orange Bowl, ". . . The Brigade is the point of the spear, the arrow's head." Forty thousand of them had stood, then, and wept, shouted, cursed.

Now it was all over. The arrow's head was unleased. Fernández knew exactly how his fellow *Brigadista* felt, why he was drunk, why he did not care whether he lived or died.

Fernández had his back turned to Gonzalez, pissing on the roof of the Dal-Tex Building. Gonzalez was bending his ear about all the horse shit they had put up with for more than three months now. But what really bugged his ass, he said, was that he and Fernández had to dress up like bums and be hauled away in a police car afterwards like criminals. Why? Because they were Cubans! These stinking anglos had left them high and dry *twice* before, and Gonzalez told Fernández that he was ready to forget the whole thing.

"We got to go man," Fernández reassured him. "C'mon, man, you got to go, go to the second floor on the fire escape. C'mon, man, let's clean up all these cigarettes and shit here and get going."

Jesús Gonzalez stood swaying in the wind and drained his flask. Fernández finished policing the area, picked up his duffel bag with the rifle in it, and turned to make his way to the County Records Building without another word or look at Gonzalez.

The southerner and the cowboy lounged back on the trunk, which contained the guns, of the dirty car behind the grassy knoll. The older man smoked and the younger fiddled with the walkie-talkie, looking for police calls. They could see, from where they stood, some railroad men on the bridge at Elm and the Freeway. The cowboy chain-smoked and squinted up at the railroad men and decided against saying anything about it to the kid.

Police Information Network

"11:30. *Air Force One* has just gone into its final landing approach.

Receiving the radio message, Sergeant Whatley of the Dallas police force

"Weather fine and clear. Temperature seems to be remaining about the same. A considerable crowd all along Mockingbird and Lemmon avenues.

"We're moving out slowly.

"Just turned out of the field onto Cedar Springs."

"12:01. We're at Lemmon and Inwood."

"12:05. Railroad underpass on Lemmon. Kennedy's halted the motorcade to visit with a group of schoolchildren."

"12:10. We're at Lemmon and Oak Lawn."

"12:14. Turtle Creek Boulevard."

"12:20. Harwood and Ross. We're almost downtown."

"12:24. We're turning west onto Main Street at the Court and Police building."

immediately contacted two squad cars to be sure that the two main streets circling the airport were blocked off.

Still at the radio receiver, Whatley remarked to one of his men, "With this weather, they'll probably use the open cars for the parade. Already a lot more people out than we'd anticipated. Sure am glad we've got so many men on today."

The Police Radio Network sent out a stream of continuing information. Big D was rising to the occasion. Whatley recorded the motorcade's location on his map. At Main Street he could hear the crowd's cheers and shouts coming in over the radio.

At 12:29 Whatley relaxed enough to wish he had some more coffee. While leaning back in his chair and taking a long drag off his cigarette, he thought, "Not too much longer to go. In a little while I should be able to get away for lunch to go with that cup of coffee."

A moment later he received a call for an ambulance at Harwood and Ross to pick up a woman who had fainted in the crowd.

> "Well, sure hope that's the biggest and best excitement we have today," he remarked to his assistant, Vernon.

A quarter of a million people. Crowds beyond any expectation jammed the Presidential route.

Behind the President's Lincoln, "Lancer," was the S.S.car, "Half back," filled with agents, automatic weapons, and a double-barreled shotgun. Next came the Vice President, followed by "Varsity," his Secret Service vehicle. Next, the mayor's Mercury (the mayor's brother, General Charles Cabell, Deputy Director of the CIA, had been fired after the Bay of Pigs.) Next was the small press car (the larger press bus, number eighteen, was still farther back). The motorcade spread over half a mile. The major wire-service reporters were more than six hundred feet behind "Lancer"; the President's doctor was far back, in the sixteenth car.

The temperature read sixty-eight degrees on the School Book Depository sign; it was now warm and beautiful.

At Lemmon and Atwell streets the throngs were massive; Governor Connally sat up in his seat, staring unbelievingly at the masses of people.

At Craddock Park some children held up a sagging banner: *"MR. PRESIDENT, PLEASE STOP AND SHAKE OUR HANDS."* He did.

The black agent, Andrews, had his service revolver drawn. He had become frantic when three other Treasury men—all of them extremely hungover from the last night's binge in Fort Worth—had brushed off his news of a tip that there would be an assassination attempt. They thought that Andrews was getting paranoid over what he had now taken to calling the "Chicago White Wash." When he couldn't tell them "Who the hell in 'Big D' is feeding you this horseshit?" they brushed him off. Crazy nigger.

The S.S. had *orders* not to be in Dealey Plaza. So, revolver drawn, he looked up at the Hertz clock—12:26—and climbed for the roof of the county jail. In the area room just under the roof, the poor prisoners clung to the bars, already seeing the cops in the near distance and imagining the glory of the moving motorcade moving toward them and their angle of refraction high up in the crackling November Texas air.

"Jackee!" screamed one section of the crowd as the motorcade crossed Live Oak nearing Main Street. Field Street was a roaring canyon. At Live Oak they were packed, standing ten and twelve deep. The motorcade had to brake, as people surged over the curbs, from twenty miles an hour to fifteen to ten to seven.

As they turned into Main, the scene struck the President as a twelve-block tunnel of curb-to-curb crowd, signs, confetti, waving office workers, bright warm sunshine. "Thank you, thank you," like a litany the President never stopped nodding his thanks to the people.

Children and nuns pressed forward at Main and Ervay; the S.S. men descended and trotted alongside the limousines. From the seventh floor of the Mercantile Building billionaire H. L. Hunt looked down at the mob.

Past Field and Poydras and Market and Houston. Senator Ralph Yarborough stared incredulously at Vice President Johnson as the motorcade turned right on Houston. "What is this? Why are we going over this way? They've made the wrong turn!" The Vice President's driver, Hurchel Jacks, overheard and muttered to no one in particular, "Practically a goddamned U-turn."

And, finally, Elm. The motorcade was now snaked over three streets: its tail still on Main, its belly on Houston, its head fishhooking into the trap on Elm. In the front seat of SS-100-x, the President's S.S. communications officer radioed the Trade Mart, " 'Halfback' to 'Base'. Five minutes to destination."

They slowed to 11.2 miles per hour. In the complete

and humid darkness of the drainage system under Elm Street, the technician opened his eyes and blindly felt for the grate that opened onto the street.

His sunglassed face poked out from the storm sewer inlet on the west side of Elm, to the right of the grassy knoll. From where he stood, he could make out the figures of the southerner and the cowboy through the hedge some forty yards away. He could not see Gonzalez sitting in the shadow of the Dal-Tex fire escape pretending to listen to a portable radio. As he stared out across the green toward the Records Building and the approaching motorcade, he knew, suddenly, that Fernández was too far away. The technician made the on-the-spot decision to go underground again and come up in the drain opening on the east side of Elm, nearest where the executive limousine was slated to pass.

In the excitement no one heard the technician's voice coming out of the concealed transmitter in the umbrella man's umbrella. "Umbrella will signal go-no-go. Adjust for fifteen miles an hour. Check rubber gloves, check ammo, check clean-up, check credentials, check. . . ." Neither did anyone wonder at this man with the open umbrella in the bright sunshine, standing between the oak tree and the freeway sign facing into the mouth of Elm and Houston. All eyes were watching for JFK.

The crowd was dramatically thinner as the vanguard of what would in seconds be a funeral cortege swung the 90° on to Houston, moving now at twenty-two feet a second and veering toward Elm and the 120° hairpin turn into the death-trap. Pigeons wheeled wildly against the blue sky at 12:29.

As the procession entered the sixty-foot-long killing zone, the umbrella man raised his instrument toward the cloudless sky. Back-up Man II dropped and rolled on the sidewalk, underfoot, simulating his pre-planned "epileptic fit." The noise level, driven upwards by the motorcycle sirens, now was reaching the intolerable. The pigeons banked madly over the impending slaughter.

242 EXECUTIVE ACTION

The prisoners' faces at the jail bars hungrily watched the big black limousine turn down Elm.

The staccato noise of the motorcycle escorts, the helicopters, the portable radios, the shouting crowd, all made a bowl of sound that was split by the first crack of Gonzalez' Mauser. The pigeons seemed to explode.

McLean, Virginia—November 22, 1963

Robert Kennedy and two of his appointees in the U.S. attorney's office sat in the late afternoon around the Kennedy pool, at his Hickory Hill mansion. They awaited their Friday lunch of New England clam chowder. They had driven past Thomas Langston Foster's estate on their way to lunch.

Beech and maple trees, like a November life force, fingered their colors into the smoky Virginia sky. They sat resting, talking quietly about their plans for the Thanksgiving holiday the following week. RFK planned to go out to the cape, he said. They breathed in the autumn grace. The telephone broke the peace and symmetry of the trees and the water.

It was J. Edgar Hoover calling on the official line.

Dallas, Texas—November 22, 1963, 12:30:01 p.m.

"You certainly can't say that the people of Dallas haven't given you a nice welcome," said Mrs. Connally at the first shot. Then they all heard it. The governor shouted, "It's a mistake! My God, they are going to kill us all!"

The pigeons spun; "Tiger," Gonzalez, missed. Concrete chips sprayed upward from the Elm Street curb to the right rear of "Lancer." At one second the southerner's bullet missed the head and nicked into the President's neck.

"That's all she wrote," said the cowboy slowly and

softly as he leaned into his Mauser. The limousine was looming toward him, filling up his gunsight.

The man with the umbrella switched to the police channel as he turned to escape.

"12:30 P.M., KKB three-six-four. Go to Parkland Hospital, and move all available men into the railroad yard and determine what happened in there." He started to snake through the crowd; he had not counted on their getting the location of the shots *that* soon.

Over the Pacific—November 22, 1963

    UPI—207
    HANNOVER, GERMANY. NOV. WW (UPI)—
THE STATE PROSECUTOR
BUST
    BUST
QMVVV
UPI—207
    BULLET NSSS
PRECEDE KENNEDY
X DALLAS. NTEXAS, NOV. 22(.708 LAS THREE
SHOTS WERE FIRED AT PRESIXENT KENNEDY'S
MOTORCADE TODAY IN DOWNTOWN DALLAS
        HSQETPEST
VVU PLF208
    HANNOVER, GERMANY NOV WWKVUPI)—
THE STATE PROSECUTOR TODAY DEMANDEJ
AM QIAMONTH PRISON TERM FOR WEST
GERMANYSJS ZSTZRILIZATION DOCTOR."
X.X.X.X. X, XNXLKDN, VOGEL TOLD THE
THREEJU THAT HANDSOME DR. ALEL DOHRN.
%% WAS N IDEALIST BUT BROKE THE LAW IN
AT LEAST IP OF THE QNEPP STERILIZATION
OPERATIONS HE HAS PERFORME ON LOCAL
WOMEN
       MORE
          HS137PEST

244 EXECUTIVE ACTION

RV
SSSSSSS
FLASH
    KENNEDY SERIOSTY WOUNDED
PESTSSSSSSSSS
                                        HS 138/
SSSSSSSSSSSSSSSSSS
MAKE THAT PERHAPS PERHAPS SERIOUSLY WOUNDED
                                  HSQEOPEST
SSSSSSSSSSSSSSSSSSSSSS
    GJ   OWHL   W WOUNDED BY
        HQ139PESTXXXXXXXXXXXXXXXX
KENNEDY WOUNDED PERHAPS FATALLY BY VASSASSINS BULLET
        HS139PESTSSSSSSSSSSSSSSSSSSSSSSSSSSS

The entire cabinet crowded around the teletype machine that had brought them the same message that was ringing alarm bells in every newsroom in the world.

The government of the United States was in a plane flying ahead of the sun toward Honolulu and the emergency Vietnam conferences.

"Verify it, sergeant," snapped Secretary of State Dean Rusk.

The sergeant took out his key and went for the code book. The code book was not there.

"Break code and get me the White House." Dean Rusk's soft southern voice rose.

"I *can't* break it, sir! My orders are . . ."

"By authority of the Secretary of State I order you to break code and get me the White House! The only code name I remember is my own. Bypath!"

"8672 to White House. Bypath calling. 8672 to . . ."

"Come in Bypath. Situation Room here."

"Situation, this is Bypath. We've just had it from the ticker that the President has been shot. Is he alive?"

"Bypath, stand by on this line. We are trying to verify

... Situation to Bypath. We are still verifying. Stand by ... Situation to Bypath ... Stand by ..."

Slowly the southern wing of the plane dipped in a sharp 180-degree turn.

"Situation to Bypath ... Stand by."

Dallas, Texas—November 22, 1963, 12:30:02 p.m.

Fernández, the "fox," shot the President in the back at two seconds. With his second shot, Gonzalez, on the Dal-Tex fire-escape, hit Governor Connally from behind at 3.5 seconds.

A siren kicked on. The S.S. agents riding behind "Lancer" in "Halfback" were paralyzed, as immobile as funeral statues. Only their eyes searched the crowd in desperation. Inexplicably the President's limousine had slowed to almost a complete stop.

Washington, D.C.—November 22, 1963

"I'm sorry, sir, our lines are temporarily out of order. . . . I'm sorry, sir, our lines are temporarily out of order. . . ."

Senator Edward Kennedy ran from door to door trying to find a working telephone. But the phones in the greater Washington area were all dead.

Jefferson, Wisconsin—November 22, 1963

Rosemary Kennedy, the President's retarded sister, sat watching television in the day room of St. Collet's School. Over her shoulder two nuns stared at the screen as it appeared to the "child" to crack open while a voice called the name "John."

"She understands. Mother of God," choked Sister

Mary Elizabeth, shoving her wrist against her mouth to keep from upsetting Rosemary. But it was too late.

Dallas, Texas—November 22, 1963, 12:30:05 p.m.

Time was up. Cursing, the southerner slammed his gun into the car trunk, started to pull off the skin-tight gloves, then instead of picking up the cowboy's litter of cigarettes on the ground, he scooped up his spent cartridge case and waited for the cowboy to use his so he could scoop it up too.

In "Halfback," S.S. agent Hickey leveled his AR-15 at the crowd; the conflicting cracks of the assassination team's rifles kept him turning from side to side—impotent. In the two seconds it takes him to prepare his weapon a bullet can travel one mile.

Channel One of the Police Information Network went dead. On the Dal-Tex and Records buildings, behind the stockade fence on the grassy knoll, in the sewer, the team could hear the running umbrella man panting into their walkie-talkies: *"Shoot—shoot—shoot!"*

The technician, standing in the sewer at the opening, his face at street level, drew his deadly silencer-fitted .45 and prepared for the final contingency. The limousine was close enough now for him to shoot almost point-blank. Something must have happened to the cowboy. The roar in his face from the motorcycle escort was shredding his eardrums, blinding him, choking him.

Time was up, and the target was not even seriously wounded yet. The technician brought his head and gloved gun hand up out of the storm-sewer inlet.

7.5 seconds had elapsed: according to all probabilities and plans they had failed.

Vienna, Virginia—November 22, 1963

Foster looked at his Swiss watch—12:30—that he had had on Texas time for the last twenty-four hours, all during the countdown.

"All right, it's over," he hypothesized, sipping air as he talked. "Now, the cabinet is over the Pacific with no code book, their news will be delayed. The area code and most of Washington's phones are out. The hospital in Dallas has been penetrated. The 'lone' assassin has been executed on the spot, or at the worst his description has been broadcast. Panic! Remember, we're talking about a local crime—only a conspiracy could make it a federal charge." He paused to breathe. "Carry on, please, Gene."

A tall, aristocratic-looking man of about forty—a senior editor of a leading weekly news magazine—stated in a cultivated southern accent: "Commercial media: confused and disorganized. Complete panic! Our people taking the lead in Dallas, Los Angeles, New York, and Washington. 'President Killed by Sniper' and so forth. We can expect this neutralization to hold for at least thirty-six hours. After that the press has a stake in its *own* credibility. But at the same time, our *structure* is only as good as the *content*."

Foster was pacing now, and so were some of the others, fitfully, like caged animals. Foster interrupted, "Meaning evidence. Set aside, for now, the timing of each revelation, the false sponsors, etc.; the limousine, which will be sent back here and sanitized, as will the clothing; the autopsy, which will be military." Like so many subalterns, these men of life-long action, intrigue, and power reported to Foster as if they were not just as senior.

Smythe (the link to the Pentagon and the aerospace money): "Evidence. Still photos, tape recordings, film.

248   EXECUTIVE ACTION

Anything critical is purchased through the usual journalistic channels and sequestered."

Foster paced. "Let's go right on please." He held his watch in his hand now.

They talked in bursts now, clear, but very fast.

Daniels (the New York banker and financial conduit for the East Coast money):

"Witnesses: first, there will be no trial or immediate hearings; then the demands of the public for 'the truth' will be answered by the appointment, at the highest level, of an unimpeachable commission of national figures. All this—now and in the future—under the blanket of 'national security.' That and a sanitized report."

"And yet there *will* be those inevitable witnesses," half-shouted Foster rhetorically, before answering himself. "They will be discouraged where necessary and possible; and they will be thoroughly blended in with literally thousands of *non*critical 'eyewitnesses.' In a word, gentlemen, the witnesses will be homogenized." They all nodded at each other. "And then the archives." Foster stopped pacing and repeated himself quietly, trying to control his breathing. "And then the archives. Very neat, a very nice Phase I. A really comprehensive document—a service that answers at one stroke the public's need to know, and the media's right to tell them *what* they need to know."

He rang for drinks after starting the faked composite photograph of Oswald, gun in hand, around the room. When the "evidence" reached the magazine editor, he frowned. The line at the chin where Oswald's head had been attached to Valentine's body was very obvious.

The editor turned and spoke quietly to Daniels, the "pay master." "Connie, let's don't count our chickens. We better have our people have a heart-to-heart talk with, um, the President. They had better make it crystal clear to him that any talk of conspiracy, from any quarter, will plunge this nation into such turmoil that the Soviets will feel forced to move and that, make him understand, means an A-war. A nuclear holocaust!

III / NOVEMBER 249

Those are the stakes. Sixty million dead in the first hour—if he talks conspiracy. And, Connie, don't worry Tom with this, just get on it." He handed him the faked Oswald photo. "Very convincing," he smiled to Foster.

"They will find it in his room," said the old man.

Foster turned then and picked up some sheets of paper from an exquisitely elegant eighteenth-century writing desk. "Have you seen this yet? This was to have been his last speech." Some of the men were talking softly to each other. This provided a background sound that was barely intelligible. Over it, Foster read:

> "We in this country, in this generation, are—by destiny rather than choice—the watchmen on the walls of world freedom. We ask therefore that we . . .

At this point a very stoic Foster impatiently but lightly knocked his pipe on the table. The men looked up at once, and then fell silent. They, too, listened to the speech, but it was impossible to tell if they were actually interested or merely silent due to fear of or respect for Foster.

Foster slowly resumed. Reardon stared. Foster's New England accent sounded uncannily familiar. His voice was that of a man who is deeply, authentically moved. The words were the President's, but the ideas were his, Foster's, and had been all his life long!

> "We ask therefore that we may be worthy of our power and responsibility that we may exercise our strength with wisdom and restraint . . ."

Dallas, Texas—November 22, 1963, 12:30:07.5 p.m.

"We in this country in this generation, are by destiny rather than choice	Behind the grassy knoll, the southerner scrambled into the trunk of their car.

the watchmen on the walls of freedom."

"We ask therefore that we may be worthy of our power and responsibility that we may exercise our strength with wisdom and restraint."

"As was written long ago: 'Except the lord keep the city, the watchmen waketh in vain!'"

The cowboy's twentieth Camel of the morning dangled off his thin brown lip, the smoke circling up around his squinting eye.

The cowboy squeezed off the last shot of the day. The pigeons seemed to be suspended in frozen array. The cowboy's poisoned dum-dum blew the President's head off.

The technician felt a spray of blood wash across his face. He stumbled back and down into the sewer. In the pitch-black darkness he could feel the President's blood running down his cheeks and into his opened mouth. He went down on his knees, feeling for his gun.

Mrs. Kennedy crawled madly up on the limousine's trunk and screamed out into the terrific sound of the sirens.

"They have shot his head off! I have his brains on my hand," she sobbed to no one. And then, "I love you, Jack."

The skull, the hair, the brain, the face, the eyes, the tongue, the bone, the blood of John Fitzgerald Kennedy: exploded into a pulp.

And when they saw him afar off, even before he came near unto them, they conspired against him to slay him.

And they said one to another, Behold this dreamer cometh.

Come now therefore, and let us slay him, and cast him into the pit and we will say, some evil beast hath devoured him: and we shall see what will become of his dreams.

Genesis

Over 4 months on the nation's bestseller lists!

THE SUPERLAWYERS

by JOSEPH C. GOULDEN

The most powerful and least publicized of all the lawyers in America today are those who reside and do business in Washington, D.C. Their fees are frequently enormous. Their daily labors ultimately affect every citizen in the country. Not surprisingly, Washington's lawyers have long preferred the privacy of paneled offices and government cloakrooms to scrutiny by the press and the public.

In one of the most knowledgeable books of recent years, Joseph C. Goulden takes the reader on an eye-opening tour of the most eminent lawyers and the influential law firms that practice along the Potomac. His narrative is a blend of investigative reporting and interviews with topflight Washington lawyers. Some speak with rare on-the-record candor. Others tell startling corporate and governmental tales, both sacred and profane.

A DELL BOOK $1.75

If you cannot obtain copies of this title at your local bookseller, just send the price (plus 15c per copy for handling and postage) to Dell Books. Post Office Box 1000, Pinebrook, N. J. 07058.

A sensational novel
about a fading cowboy star
who becomes the governor
of a great state!

THE KINGMAKER
by HENRY DENKER

Every time you watch a movie. Or follow a political campaign. Every time you see the image of a ruggedly handsome movie actor turned governor. Or remember a beautiful and tormented love goddess. Or hear the latest about a scandal-prone singer and super-swinger. For this sensational novel is about the man who made them and so many others like them, and could break them at will or by whim. The man who graduated from the Mafia to carve out a ruthless empire stretching from Hollywood to New York to Washington, D.C. The man whose power may frighten you long after you finish this tremendously engrossing novel.

A DELL BOOK $1.50

If you cannot obtain copies of this title at your local bookseller, just send this price (plus 15c per copy for handling and postage) to Dell Books, Post Office Box 1000, Pinebrook, N. J. 07058.

If you enjoyed *The Forsyte Saga* this is your kind of book!

THE ATHELSONS

by JOCELYN KETTLE

The Athelsons had ruled their vast estate in Lancaster, England, for a thousand years. As the novel opens they are fighting a desperate battle against the changes brought by the dawning of the twentieth century. To the isolated manor house comes Justine, the beautiful young daughter of a black sheep of the Athelsons. Now her father is dead, and Justine is invited to take her place as a member of the family. She falls in love with the Athelsons and the land they rule and care for—and she falls in love, too, with her handsome cousin, Athel. But her grandfather, as head of the family, forbids a marriage between the two cousins. Here is a novel that brings to life a vanished time, a vanished breed of human beings, a vanished code of conduct and honor. "Passion and nostalgia . . . close to Delderfield."

—*Kirkus Service*

A DELL BOOK $1.50

If you cannot obtain copies of these titles at your local bookseller, just send the price (plus 15c per copy for handling and postage) to Dell Books, Post Office Box 1000, Pinebrook, N. J. 07058.

If you enjoyed *The Anderson Tapes*
this is your kind of book!

11 HARROWHOUSE

by GERALD A. BROWNE

Here is a novel in the Hitchcock tradition of high adventure, romance, and suspense, a story combining an ingenious *Rififi*-like theft with an ensuing chase that moves across many of the exotic faces of Europe. The place is 11 Harrowhouse, a dignified structure in London's posh Mayfair district. The target is deep within its subterranean vault—some thirteen billion dollars' worth of diamonds. J. Clyde Massey, a man whose personal wealth runs into billions, commissions the heist not for love of money but for the pleasure of revenge. For his operatives he selects a most unlikely crew: Chesser, a diamond merchant, and his sensuously beautiful mistress, Maren.

A DELL BOOK $1.50

If you cannot obtain copies of this title at your local bookseller, just send the price (plus 15c per copy for handling and postage) to Dell Books, Post Office Box 1000, Pinebrook, N. J. 07058.

How many of these Dell bestsellers have you read?

FICTION

1.	**THE NEW CENTURIONS** by Joseph Wambaugh	$1.50
2.	**THE SCARLATTI INHERITANCE** by Robert Ludlum	$1.50
3.	**THE TENTH MONTH** by Laura Z. Hobson	$1.25
4.	**BLUE DREAMS** by William Hanley	$1.25
5.	**SUMMER OF '42** by Herman Raucher	$1.25
6.	**SHE'LL NEVER GET OFF THE GROUND** by Robert J. Serling	$1.25
7.	**THE PLEASURES OF HELEN** by Lawrence Sanders	$1.25
8.	**THE MERRY MONTH OF MAY** by James Jones	$1.25
9.	**THE DEVIL'S LIEUTENANT** by M. Fagyas	$1.25
10.	**SLAUGHTERHOUSE-FIVE** by Kurt Vonnegut, Jr.	95c

NON-FICTION

1.	**THE SENSUOUS MAN** by "M"	$1.50
2.	**THE GRANDEES** by Stephen Birmingham	$1.50
3.	**NICHOLAS AND ALEXANDRA** by Robert K. Massie	$1.25
4.	**THE SENSUOUS WOMAN** by "J"	$1.25
5.	**I'M GLAD YOU DIDN'T TAKE IT PERSONALLY** by Jim Bouton	$1.25
6.	**THE HAPPY HOOKER** by Xaviera Hollander	$1.25
7.	**THE DOCTOR'S QUICK WEIGHT LOSS DIET** by Irwin Maxwell Stillman, M.D. and Samm Sinclair Baker	$1.25
8.	**NEVER CRY WOLF** by Farley Mowat	75c
9.	**THE DOCTOR'S QUICK INCHES-OFF DIET** by Stillman & Baker	$1.25
10.	**SURROGATE WIFE** by Valerie X. Scott as told to Herbert d'H. Lee	$1.25

If you cannot obtain copies of these titles from your local bookseller, just send the price (plus 15c per copy for handling and postage) to Dell Books, Post Office Box 1000, Pinebrook, N. J. 07058. No postage or handling charge is required on any order of five or more books.